A WOMAN POSSESSED

May is crazy in love with Dan Ferrel. So in love that she risks her life and freedom to spring him from the work gang. But Dan's only thoughts are for Vera. He just wants to feel his hands around her pretty throat. Just once. Because Dan's a lifer. Accused of shooting a man in cold blood, only Dan knows that the killer was hired by Vera to settle the score between them. Now he's traveling the backroads with May, trying to avoid the cops, on his way to find another woman. But while Dan searches for Vera, a work gang guard named Hawkins is searching for him—with a loaded gun he is just itching to use.

PRIME SUCKER

Hank Ireland is sitting at George's poker table when he starts to become aware of the man's wife. Amy sparks something in him. Later in the kitchen he drunkenly crushes her to him, and is surprised when she responds to his impulsive kiss. The next day Hank still can't stop thinking about her. His own wife, after ten years of marriage, treats him rather coolly, so a passionate kiss is all that it takes. Hank starts questioning his life. And what he decides is that he has to see Amy again—and soon! Which is just fine as far as George is concerned, because he has plans of his own for a sex-starved sucker like Hank.

A WOMAN POSSESSED

PRIME SUCKER

Harry Whittington

Introduction by Cullen Gallagher

Stark House Press • Eureka California

Tickets to Hell:
The Infernal Journeys of Harry Whittington's *A Woman Possessed* and *Prime Sucker*

by Cullen Gallagher

Sometimes, the title of a novel can convey the entirety of its author's body of work. *Wake Up To Murder* could aptly describe any of Day Keene's novels, in which countless people awaken next to a corpse and find their whole life turned upside down. *The Nothing Man* epitomizes the dark, abysmal heart of Jim Thompson's universe. *Little Men, Big World* sums up the insatiable egos and existential ambition of W.R. Burnett's protagonists, gangsters and politicians who will stop at nothing to have everything and invariably lose it all along the way (alternately, *Nobody Lives Forever* would be just as apt, suggesting the futility of their enterprises). *Flight to Darkness* could chart the downward trajectory of any of Gil Brewer's works. And the essence of David Goodis's melancholia can be found in almost any of his titles, from his first (*Retreat from Oblivion*) to his last (*Somebody's Done For*, thankfully reprinted by Stark House Press after languishing out of print for far too long).

When it comes to Harry Whittington, the title which best captures his work and worldview, in my opinion, is *A Ticket to Hell* (originally published by Gold Medal in 1959, and republished by Stark House Press in 2022). It's fitting for a number of reasons. First, it's hard to go a few pages in one of Harry's novels without coming across the word "hell." I'm sure part of its recurring usage had to do with the fact that it was about as bad a swear word as he could publish in the pages of paperbacks at the time. It's also a versatile word, and Harry used it with the agility of an Olympic grammarian. "What the hell…" "The hell with…" "Go to hell…" "Sure as hell…" "The hell of it…" "The hell with it…" "One hell of a…" "Hell to pay…" "For hell's sake…" "Like hell…" "Why in hell…" "How in hell…" "Sure as hell…" Or, sometimes, just plain "Hell."

More to the point, *A Ticket to Hell* charts the infernal path of so many of his protagonists. Whittington's characters aren't naive saps or innocent victims of circumstance. Sure, they might run into some bad luck, or be in the wrong place at the wrong time, but they were just where they wanted to be, and they usually knew all too well just where they were headed—they walked—ran, rushed—willingly into the proverbial flames. Here are just a few examples of his characters describing their personal hellscapes:

"He shook out his raincoat, picked up the packages and pushed open the door. And Blake took his first step into hell."—*Mourn the Hangman*

"Why this town, why this burg, why this particular hell? Did I think this hell preferable to any other? The answer was simple. It was the end of the line for me. I never consciously admitted this, or seldom admitted it, but down deep I knew it was true."—*The Devil Wears Wings*

"Abbey knew her way well. The ruts were crooked, cut by garbage trucks, but she followed them expertly. Here was a girl who'd know her way straight down to hell."—*You'll Die Next*

"For a long time after you first step into Hell you won't feel anything; the sight of it will be meaningless because you won't be able to believe it. I know. I've been there."—*The Strange Young Wife*

"Sweat stood across my forehead. My hands trembled. I was in the deepest part of hell. I was already dead and in hell. She was standing there in her nakedness, waiting for me."—*Brute in Brass*

"She was lovely as an angel with a hellish excitement in her eyes. The look in those eyes promised him hell and happiness, misery and torment."—*Don't Speak to Strange Girls*

"I forced her to turn her head. I tried to stare into the black depths of her eyes. The black depths of hell or the blackest heights of high heaven? I had to know which."—*Drawn to Evil*

"She looked at them with loathing. Something more than eight thousand dollars. Murder money. What had it bought her? A fast ticket to hell on earth, and nothing else."—*Fires that Destroy*

"He'd been high, but something about her had reached through the fuzziness in his brain. And he'd thought, God, how beautiful; a man could go through hell for that. And then he'd thought with alcoholic clarity: probably, she'd see that I did."—*The Naked Jungle*

"I'm a hellish guy, Miss Kapiolani. Mean. Brutal. I hate God's world, and everybody in it."—*Slay Ride for a Lady*

The characters in the two novels reprinted here all have first-class tickets to hell, and they seem in such a hurry to get there that they continually add more coal to the fires. The end can't come soon enough for these folks.

■ ■ ■

The lead novel is *A Woman Possessed*, originally published as a paperback original by Beacon in 1961, under the pseudonym Whit Harrison. It's been out of print for 62 years, and only Whittington completists have been able to read it. Now, thanks to Stark House, the cat's out of the bag: this book is pure Whittington, straight no chaser. Sweaty, grimy and relentless, *A Woman Possessed* stands up against any of his more celebrated and widely available novels.

Whittington is often praised for his speed, and *A Woman Possessed* is indicative of the driving pace of his plots. But beneath the frantic pacing, Whittington was a master wordsmith. Take the opening sentence: "From where he stood swinging the grass sling with the road gang in the ditch, Ferrel kept watching for the blue car to show along the sun-struck highway." Whittington could have easily used "Dan Ferrel," or just "Dan"—but that would make him too common, too human. Instead, he uses "Ferrel," which of course conjures up "feral." Once domesticated, but now wild and uncontrollable. Before we know anything about his backstory, we already understand much about this character: he's a sweaty beast, driven by id and animal instincts, operating on primal urges rather than rationality, morality, ethics, or just plain common sense. In short—he's the perfect embodiment of a Whittington protagonist.

Talk about a ticket to hell, by chapter one of *A Woman Possessed* Ferrel is already in his proverbial Tartarus. "The sun was high; it was past eleven. It had to be. It felt like it. It felt like high noon in the hottest street in hell." Ferrel is a lowlife, in prison after being framed for murder, but guilty of countless other crimes. Upon hearing that his younger brother is giving up med school to pull a burglary with a lounge singer named Areva Storm, Ferrel takes advantage of ex-lover May Alonzo to help him escape while he's working with the road crew so he can save his brother, and get revenge against a woman who tried to put a bullet in him back in Houston. Escape is the plan—but not freedom. From the beginning, Ferrel knows how he will end up. "He shook his head, remembering Paul. He was never coming out of this alive, and he wanted her clear. He wanted her to break it off. It was the best thing he could do for her."

If Whittington had limited *A Woman Possessed* to Ferrel's perspective, it would have still been a better-than-average crime novel for its time.

But what catapults it to top tier is that the author opens the narrative up to the other characters. Pursuing Ferrel across the country is the prison guard from whom he escaped, Virgil Hawkins, a trigger-happy cop who is introduced as somewhat of a doppelgänger to Ferrel. A fellow con compares the two men:

> "Hawkins is a man got an itch. He's got an itch to pull down on his gun and shoot a man. He's got the itch to kill so bad it's killing him…No. [Dan] You ain't got the itch to kill. You just got an itch. That's how you're like Hawkins, man. You both got a bad itch."

Hawkins, characteristic of Whittington, is driven by his own psycho-sexual impulses: "Nothing happened. The heat. The waiting. The tension. It got to you…. Hawkins was breathing through his open mouth. It really got him, thinking about it. He was sweaty and shaking all over." Later, he chases after Ferrel with the same dogged obsession that drives Ferrel to seek revenge.

Among the most interesting character perspectives is May. A legal secretary engaged to her boss, she risks her domesticity and security in order to rescue Dan. Like the men in the novel, she, too, is driven by a self-destructive inner-fire:

> "She felt as though at any moment she might be wrenched away from that steering wheel and hurled straight into the hottest pit in hell.
>
> But she was already in hell, wasn't she? Dan Ferrel had put her in hell, hadn't he? Oh, she had gone willingly. *Tell me about hell, Dan. I'll love it, won't I, Dan? I'll go to hell for you any time, Dan.* Like now."

May doesn't fall into the simplistic noir dichotomy of good/bad girl. She's no angel, and she's no femme fatale. Instead, she's well aware of her actions and her desires—and she's also well aware that reciprocal love has nothing to do with it. "Holding the wheel in the blue car now, she was in hell. He had opened the door for her, and she had come running. And all this time, there was one question she wanted to ask. Did it really matter to him that she was in hell?" What makes May such a compelling character is her awareness of both sides of her psyche, and her struggles to come to grips with the potential consequences of giving in to either side.

■ ■ ■

The second book in this Stark House edition is *Prime Sucker*, originally published as a Universal Giant Edition by Universal Publishing and Distributing Corporation in 1952 (paired with a reprint of Idabel Williams' 1933 novel *The Hussy*). *Prime Sucker* was then republished in 1960 by Beacon in a spiced-up edition (in just eight years, publishers could get away with a lot more lurid passages than in 1952—and their audience had come to expect as much). This Stark House edition reprints the Beacon text with the exception of Chapter Fourteen, which is restored to its original version (it was felt that the additions to this section broke with character and narrative continuity); this edition also restores Whittington's original chapter titles, which were omitted in the Beacon edition (and the Automat.Press e-Book).

The title of *Prime Sucker* tells you everything you need to know about its protagonist, Hank Ireland: he's a grade-A chump, he's gonna get screwed, and he's got no one to blame but himself. Chapter One sets up the downfall masterfully. Once again, Whittington's bullseye prose seals Hank's fate in the opening sentence: "Hank sat at the table and wanted George's wife. It was like being drunk, the way she made him feel." A sales manager, he accepts an invitation to a poker game at his colleague George's house. Hank's not much of a poker player, however, and between the alcohol and his hots for George's wife, Amy, he can't focus at all. "He'd been losing all evening. It wouldn't amount to much and he didn't mind losing. He'd been working too hard with no time off. He needed to relax like this. But after he had looked up and met her eyes, he'd lost interest in cards and he couldn't keep his mind on the game."

Despite having a wife at home, Ethel, Hank feels an insatiable and irrepressible compulsion towards Amy. "Hank had been on his fourth highball and he had looked up as he drank. She'd been watching him. Their eyes met. And there it was. Everything. It made his stomach churn. Her eyes told him just as plainly as if she'd spoken aloud, she wanted what he wanted. No. More than that. She wanted *whatever* he wanted."

You know where this is headed, right? So does Hank. "Oh God, he thought, I'm drunk. I've got to get out of here. I've got to get away from her."

But does he run away from Amy? This is a Whittington novel, so of course not. Instead, Hank grabs Amy in the kitchen and kisses her. And what a kiss it turns out to be:

"He caught his breath, feeling her body, the hot outline of her against him. He dropped the glass and heard it strike the imitation tile flooring. The glass didn't break. He didn't give a damn if it did. He didn't care what happened. He would break the glass and walk through it to get against her like this."

The Beacon version is even less subtle about the torment into which Hank is literally willing to walk:

"I'm drunk, Hank thought. I'm drunk and I'm dreaming. No woman could kiss like this, love like this. No mortal woman ever kissed like this before. This must be Venus. This is a goddess. Or a devil. A she-devil. An impossibly desirable nymph out of hell…"

The first chapter isn't over, and our protagonist is already on his way to hell.

What begins as a suburban melodrama quickly reveals itself to be a crime narrative of the blackmail variety, and at the center is Hank, a man who has every opportunity to save himself, and passes each one up.

Unlike *A Woman Possessed*, *Prime Sucker* is primarily focused on the perspective of its central male character, Hank. Nevertheless, Whittington doesn't neglect the two women in Hank's life, his wife Ethel, and his paramour Amy. Initially, Amy seems like a typical femme fatale, luring Hank into a web of deceit and illicit passion (not that he doesn't go willingly). As the narrative unfolds, she, too, is revealed to be ensnared in a plot from which she can't free herself. And Ethel stands out as the sole voice of reason in the book—she responds to Hank's infidelity with startling sobriety and frankness. (At least, in the original version she does; in the Beacon, she's much more tawdry.) Ethel understands what Hank refuses to concede: his passion is pathetic. "I don't hate you. It's just that you're a fool. And you—you're getting what a fool should get … You're wrecking your whole life … You're breaking my heart, Hank. And I can't help it, it's you I cry for. I don't even hate you. I'm so sorry for you." She may give him more sympathy than he deserves—but in Whittington's world, sympathy doesn't get you very far.

■ ■ ■

In a body of work as vast as Whittington's, it can be hard to know where to start. If you're already familiar with the author, then I needn't say anything more except that I think you'll find *A Woman Possessed* and *Prime Sucker* a worthy companion to his best work. And if this is your first exposure to the author, then you've picked the right book to dive headfirst and deep down into Whittington's world of warped desires.

—June 2023
Brooklyn, NY

Cullen Gallagher lives in Brooklyn, NY. His critical writing has appeared in the *Los Angeles Review of Books*, *Paris Review*, and *Not Coming to a Theater Near You*, as well as in the anthologies *Cult Cinema: An Arrow Video Companion* (2016) edited by Anthony Nield, *Screen Slate: New York City Cinema 2011-2015* (2017) edited by Jon Dieringer, and *Paperbacks at War: 20th Century Conflict from the Front Lines of Vintage Paperbacks, Pulps and Comics* (2021) edited by Justin Marriott. His fiction has appeared in *Beat to a Pulp*, *Crime Factory*, and the anthologies *Bourbon & a Good Cigar* (2018) and *Time to Myself* (2018). For more information, visit www.cullengallagher.com, or his blog Pulp Serenade (www.pulp-serenade.com).

A WOMAN POSSESSED

Harry Whittington

1

From where he stood swinging the grass sling with the road gang in the ditch, Ferrel kept watching for the blue car to show along the sunstruck highway.

It was hot. Even the khaki-clad guards were sweating, perched in the shade of the yellow trucks, guns across their knees. There was a truck parked at each end of the population—"population" was the cons' name for work gangs outside the prison—and a guard was hunkered in the squat shadows beside each truck.

Ferrel worked his yo-yo just enough to keep from attracting attention. A tall, angular man in his early thirties, Ferrel had let the population work slightly ahead of him.

He checked the highway again, feeling the savage expectancy drawing him taut.

"Dan." The rail-thin boy leaned on his grass sling and wiped the back of his hand across his mouth. "Dan, don't you think so?"

Dan Ferrel turned and glanced at the boy.

"I asked you, Dan. Don't you think Hawkins was?"

"Look, kid, beat it," Dan said.

"You didn't even hear me when I yakked. You got something eating at you?"

"Get lost, will you, Magill?" Dan bit off the words. In a moment Hawkins would get up from the shade and come toward them.

"What's the matter?"

"You trying to make the Rock, kid? You want to make the flat top? Bread row?" Dan barely moved his lips as he spoke.

Magill's face twisted in a grin. With those dark-rimmed glasses and that wavy hair, Magill looked like a timid college freshman. Even the striped blue prison pants and the sunbaked torso didn't make him look like a con.

"Now I know you got a burr," Magill said. "When did you get scared of the screws?"

Ferrel checked the road again, watched the heat waves shimmer on the black pavement as far as he could see—a long way, in this slash pine and cabbage palmetto country. He had to hold himself in leash. He wanted to swear at the kid, because the tension was like a hard knot in his stomach. And he wanted that kid away from him. He said, "Come on, get to work, will you, for God's sake?"

There was no sign of the blue car.

Ferrel felt the sweat chill on his forehead. He was tight and sick inside.

He clenched his fist on the yo-yo handle, cursing May Alonzo silently and bitterly.

He glanced up at the bright platinum sun. He could only guess the time, but he knew in his guts that it was past the hour they had agreed on. May had promised to drive the blue car past the work gang at eleven, just before the lunch break. The sun was high; it was past eleven. It had to be. It felt like it. It felt like high noon in the hottest street in hell.

"They got you chicken, Dan?"

Dan jerked his head around. He said, "Sure, kid. Chicken."

Magill swung his yo-yo, missing the weed tops by two inches. "You do think so, then, don't you?"

Ferrel took one quick gander along the highway. "Think what, for God's sake. Think what?"

"Man, you are on a jaggy! I asked you three times. Don't you think Hawkins was trying to shoot me in the back?"

"Yeah. Yeah, it looked like it. Come on, kid, let me alone."

He checked the guards. They had not moved—it was too hot to move. Then he turned his head slowly, eyes burning.

"What you looking for?" Magill said.

Ferrel felt himself go cold. He tried to laugh it off. "What's eating you?"

"You act like you're looking for the gent with your parole. You're itchy, man, and that's like a fact."

Ferrel swung his yo-yo, moving away from the boy. But he could not go far. He did not want to get in the population, and if he went more than twenty feet the other way, the guards would move him back in close. They loved herding a bunch-quitter. It was the only excitement they got sometimes, in a long, hot day.

"I know Hawkins was trying to kill me."

The kid was walking behind him, like a shadow.

"He's going to, if you don't shut up."

"No. He knows first chance I get, I'm going to lay it on to him for that trick he tried to pull. Trying to make it look like I'm on a break. Me, with less than a month to drag."

"Good—you got it made."

"I'd go back in the Rock, man, for one chance to cool that Hawkins. Just one chance."

"For God's sake, kid, will you get away from me?"

Ferrel understood what it was like on the rack now, when they turned the wheel tighter than a man could bear. You had to keep chilled, go on taking it, and you wanted to—only your body and your mind could not take it anymore.

This break had to succeed. He would not get another chance. Since he had heard the first talk about Paul, he had known he had to break out. He had lain in his bunk and thought about Paul—and tried to keep from thinking about Vera.

That was not easy. Two years … Only it was more than two years—it was two years since he had seen her last, but she was like something that had been eating away at his insides all his life. And then he had seen how it had to be, the only way he could possibly make it.

"For hell's sake, Dan, you on cotton?"

Dan felt the burst of laughter erupt from his throat. Cotton! That was the gauze the cons chewed when they cracked open a nasal inhaler. The cotton wadding was soaked in Benzedrine, and these punks thought it was a big jag.

The laughter stopped in his throat. "Good God, kid. You still here?"

"Man, you're getting like Hawkins."

Dan glanced over his shoulder at the empty blue eyes behind the thick lenses. "Yeah?"

"Yeah. Hawkins is a man got an itch. He's got an itch to pull down on his gun and shoot a man. He's got the itch to kill so bad it's killing him."

"You think I want to kill somebody, kid? I mean somebody besides you?"

"You already killed somebody, didn't you, Dan?"

"That's what they say."

"No. You ain't got the itch to kill. You just got an itch. That's how you're like Hawkins, man. You both got a bad itch. What's itching you?"

Ferrel winced. "Shut up, will you, kid?"

Magill laughed, and the sound was sharp enough to carry in the sun-cooked silence all the way to the far wagon and Hawkins in the shade.

Ferrel closed his hand on his grass sling, wanting to chop Magill down. If Magill brought Hawkins here when that blue car was in sight, he would kill him. He had wasted too much time now. He had to get out of here.

He saw Hawkins stir in the thin oblong of shadow, up on the highway shoulder. Hawkins jerked his head up, squinting his eyes in the pockets of fat, staring at them. He held himself rigid a moment, then settled back against the truck wheel.

Ferrel exhaled, feeling weak.

He tried to keep his head down, but he could not do it. He had to check that highway one more time.

His head came up, and he stared along the black ribbon of asphalt through the saw grass. Nothing. Empty. Hot and empty and dancing in heat waves.

After this final moment of hope, he felt the rush of agony. She was not coming. Something had happened to May. She couldn't make it.

He stood there with his face tilted slightly, the sun hard and relentless on his cheeks and his unblinking eyes. He felt his mouth pull into a thin smile.

All right, so she was not coming. Wasn't it better to know that for once and all, right now? He had tried hard, but there was nothing he could do out here on the eight-spot.

He looked around. The sense of emptiness inside him gave everything around him a look of unreality. Like animals, the other cons worked in the ditches. Most of them had peeled off their shirts, and sweat stood on their sun-darkened chests.

Dan wiped his hand across his prison shirt, leaving a wet dark streak. He was not working shirtless, because he had been dressed for the trip. Only that was off. She was not coming.

"Time to eat," Magill said.

Dan glanced at Magill, not knowing what else he had been saying, only that he had been talking, steadily, without stopping. It was a game with Magill. Magill liked to see how far he could push Hawkins and the other guards.

Suddenly Ferrel did not care anymore. The flood of calmness that swept through him left him weak and indifferent. He would have laughed, but he was too tired.

"Sure." His voice was flat. "Time to eat."

Magill stopped working and leaned on his grass sling handle, staring up at the two yellow trucks and the guards beside them.

Magill lifted his voice, yelling, "Hey, Hawkins. Hey, you lard tub. You gone to sleep, Hawkins?"

Hawkins came up tall, booted legs apart. He was a thick, barrel-chested man who had gone to fat. His jowls sagged. His neck folded over the limp collars of his shirts. His belly looked like a hogshead of beer. But he could move fast. He was young, and he was mean. He was always looking for trouble.

"Get back to work, you little pimp." Hawkins' voice was thick and heavy in the heat.

The other men on the eight-spot—the work gang—stopped swinging yo-yo's and laughed. They didn't know or care what they were laughing at. The sun was blisteringly hot; they all hated Hawkins; they would take any chance to stop working.

Ferrel felt his legs go weak. He had to lean hard on his grass sling— he was afraid he was going to fall.

Staring up at Hawkins, Ferrel saw the car coming along the highway, like a mirage in the heat waves.

Only it was no mirage. It was the blue car. He knew that, even at that distance—he knew that car.

"Oh, hell!" He whispered it, barely aware he had spoken. Hawkins was still standing there, gun up across his arm, still undecided whether to walk down to them and lay that gunstock across Magill's skull, or forget it.

But whether he forgot it or not, Magill's taunts had brought him up to his feet, gun ready. And beyond him, the blue car was racing toward them. May was driving fast, too fast for him now, and Hawkins was standing there with his gun ready, not even knowing what he was ready for.

2

May Alonzo was talking to herself. Her teeth were chattering so badly that the sound they made was louder than the words she was mumbling. But it did not matter. She was not listening to what she was saying—she had said it all so many times before.

She clung to the steering wheel of the blue car as if it were her last solid grip on the world she had known for twenty-three years.

She felt as though at any moment she might be wrenched away from that steering wheel and hurled straight into the hottest pit in hell.

But she was already in hell, wasn't she? Dan Ferrel had put her in hell, hadn't he? Oh, she had gone willingly. *Tell me about hell, Dan. I'll love it, won't I, Dan? I'll go to hell for you any time, Dan.*

Like now.

It had started the day she had gone to visit Dan at Prison Farm Twenty-Eight. She remembered that day vividly. She had got her pass and gone to that bare room with its long pine tables and the crowds of women, some of them with children. *It's Sunday, let's go visit Daddy. Where is Daddy? Daddy's in that place with all the other men, and they'll let us visit Daddy on Sunday.*

She had worn a plain cotton dress that day, no makeup, no perfume. She would never forget the bitter twist in Dan's smile. "Always thoughtful, huh, May? You wouldn't want to torture a guy who was in the chain gang for life, would you, May?"

"I didn't want to upset you, Dan."

He laughed, and people turned to stare at him—a young man, strong, handsome and vital—and serving life. "Baby, you couldn't hide your Cuban beauty in sacks."

She looked at him and knew she could not have reached him even with a low-cut dress and ten-dollar-an-ounce perfume. Not even after all those months on that road gang. Something was eating at Dan—he was too full of hatred.

May sat on the pine plank bench across the narrow visitor's table. She was getting his message, all right—she always had, all her life. There was excitement in the very light of his gray eyes, the quirk of his brow, the sound of his voice.

She felt her heart pounding, and the pulse throbbing at the base of her throat. The room was crowded, hot and smelly with other Sunday visitors. Guards were relaxing at either end of the room. It was a busy Sunday.

Then she saw that Dan was sweating. It was hot in that breathless room, but she knew instantly that his sweating had nothing to do with the heat.

May said, looking around, "I got your letter, Dan. I came as quick as I could."

He smiled thinly at her across the table. "How stupid can a dame be, baby? You were free of me—"

She bit her lip, knowing she had never been free of him, not since the first time he kissed her, the first time he held her against him, such a long time ago, such a long empty time....

"You finally got free of me, chick. Why didn't you keep it that way? I didn't believe you'd come—"

"Dan, you knew I'd come, if you asked me."

"No, not till you walked in here—and that's quite a walk you have there, doll."

"Thank you."

"You don't have to thank me."

"I want to. You don't say nice things very often."

"I'm sorry, kid. I don't think nice things very often. I thought you'd get smart. Thought I'd get a nice letter back from you saying your husband and your three kids sent their love. Love, from May, her husband and three kids. Period."

"No."

"That's what you'd have done if you were smart."

"You knew I'd come. Just as you knew I didn't get married."

He stared at her. She saw something happen in his eyes, saw the way he winced.

"Don't wait for me, sugar. This is a ninety-nine-year lease I got on this place." He stared around them. "Until death do us part."

Tears clouded her eyes. "But you didn't do it, Dan. You didn't kill that man."

"Didn't I? The law says I did. Who in hell are you to say I didn't?"

"I know you didn't. You—swore you didn't."

"Yeah … When I thought it mattered. When I thought I had a chance."

"Oh, you could have been somebody, Dan. You had to throw it away. Paul's going to be a great doctor—and I know it's thanks to you. But you could have been better than Paul—better at anything."

"I'm better anyhow," Dan said. "Look, I'm doing this time with one hand behind my back."

She tried to smile. But then abruptly it all changed, everything changed. The room had been dull and hot. Suddenly it crackled with the hatred and the strength in Dan Ferrel. He was leaning forward, speaking tensely into her face, voice low and cold.

"I've got to get out of here, May. Got to. Something I've got to tend to."

She stared around at the other people in this room, suddenly different from them, set apart. She was frightened. Her heart throbbed against her ribs. Her mouth trembled.

She gripped the table until her knuckles were white.

"Oh, please, Dan—don't talk like this."

"I've got to."

"Please, Dan. Don't be a fool."

He sank back on the pine bench across the table. He exhaled heavily, glanced around him. Finally he smiled. "There's somebody else, May?"

"What?" She was so confused and upset, she did not even know what he was talking about.

"You're in love with somebody else."

She could not lie to him; she never had, and this did not seem the time nor the place for lying.

"I can't go on like this, Dan. You didn't want me when you were free."

"I didn't want you mixed up with a character like me."

"No. You didn't want me."

He shrugged.

She bit her lip. "I don't love anybody but you. But—I'm marrying Wes Kingsley."

His brow tilted. "Ah, a new one. I never heard of him."

"He's good and honest, Dan…. The simple kind of good that you don't read about in newspapers."

"Sounds wonderful."

She said, "Maybe not. But we are going to be married. He doesn't know anything about you, Dan."

She saw the way his gaze moved over her face. She saw the hurt and the need. That need was there, or he would never have asked her out to the prison camp. He wanted something desperately.

He exhaled heavily. "Okay, kid. I hope you're happy."

"You aren't going to—try anything, are you, Dan?"

"Forget it, kid. I'll think of something else."

He smiled, and she could not hold out against him. She begged him to let her help, and finally he agreed. Or had he known all along that she was going to help him?

Holding the wheel in the blue car now, she was in hell. He had opened the door for her, and she had come running. And all this time, there was one question she wanted to ask. Did it really matter to him that she was in hell?

She had lived through that first week in hell, waiting for the second Sunday. He would have it all set up by then.

She had been unable to eat or sleep. She was so afraid of the law, afraid even to double park. She wanted Dan to be free. But no matter how sure of himself he was, would be ever be free once he left that prison camp? Or would he only be dragged deeper, and drag her with him?

Lying awake at night, she dreamed back to the moments when she had thought Dan Ferrel loved her. She had been in heaven then, and the torment was almost as exquisite as the hell she was in now. If she was going to get Dan out of that prison, she had to make sure he was truly free, didn't she?

She thought it all out, and she drove her red Ford down to the docks where her brother berthed his sloop, part of the shrimp fleet.

Tony was glad to see her until she mentioned Dan Ferrel's name. Tony was four years older than she, with black rich hair and black eyes—a handsome man, until anger twisted his mouth and narrowed his eyes.

"Forget that Ferrel. He's in the can. He should have been there years ago. You forget him."

"He's not guilty, Tony." Her voice quavered.

"Not guilty of what? Of killing that hoodlum outside the restaurant? They proved he was guilty—they proved he had to be guilty. If Ferrel didn't kill that gunman, who did?"

"I don't know, Tony."

"No. And nobody else knows, either. He's been a gambler, a lawbreaker since the first day I knew him. You know what was the matter with that guy? He wanted everything—and he wouldn't wait. Whenever he wanted, he took. That was Dan Ferrel."

She stared at the deck of Tony's sloop, knowing it was true. It was the way Dan had treated her. He had seen her ... he had wanted her.

She shuddered, wondering if any other girl had ever been as easy for any man? Dan loved flashy cars, and flashy women, and he was always in trouble. That was true.

She looked around the boat, and the others like it along the wide docks. They smelled strongly of shrimp. She supposed you got used to it. All she could think was that Tony could take Dan and her on this sloop. He could set them down in Cuba, and from there, they could go anywhere. The world would be wide open and they would be free.

She lifted her face, looking at Tony. She longed to tell him the truth, but she knew she could not. She was afraid now to tell him that she was going to help Dan escape from prison.

"If Dan did get free?" Her voice faltered. "Would you help him?"

"Help him? How? Do you know what it means to help a fugitive escape from the law?"

Her face burned. She knew. She had been over it a hundred times in the sleepless nights.

"You could let him on your boat. They never check the shrimp boats. You could let him off in Cuba—"

"What about my crew?"

"They wouldn't have to know, not the truth. If you were careful."

"Me? Oh, I'm careful. I won't get within ten miles of this Ferrel. And you stay away from him, May. You hear? You stay away from him."

He would not discuss it anymore.

But she could not stop, either. It was the only way she knew to be sure that Dan would be free. She came back, again and again. Finally, she said, "If I begged you to help him, Tony? Would you do it? For me?"

He spread his hands, helplessly. "For you, I'd do what I could. But let's not talk about it. They got Dan Ferrel where he belongs. Let's pray he stays there."

Time was suddenly a toboggan.

She was being carried along, hurtled along, whether she wanted to go or not.

It was Sunday again. She returned to Prison Farm Twenty-Eight. She had not slept. She knew she looked terrible.

Dan was too full of his plan; he did not even see her. Or maybe he was afraid to look at her—maybe he did not want to see what he was doing to her.

"There'll be a blue car. Parked outside your apartment house next Wednesday morning. You understand? You leave your keys in your car. A red Ford, is that right?"

She nodded, unable to speak.

"All right. This pal of mine, he'll leave the blue car outside your place, and he'll take your Ford."

"Why?"

"Will you trust me?"

She merely moved her head. She was in it, whether she trusted him or not, so it didn't matter.

"You got a gun, May?"

"My God, no."

"You know where you can get one?"

She shook her head.

He shrugged. "Okay. There'll be one in the blue car. It'll be in the glove compartment. You just make sure that it is there before you take off, understand?"

Her head moved again, she didn't know which way. It was as if she had no will of her own any more.

"Can you get me a suit of clothes?"

This time she nodded. She would love to see Dan in a suit of clothes again, a free man. Like all the other men, only handsomer, smarter and stronger. *Tell me about hell, Dan. I'll love hell, won't I, Dan?*

Time raced, and there was no relief from her thoughts. If only she could have stopped thinking....

The worst part was Wes Kingsley. He had a law office, and she worked in it. She had to see him every day, and she had to lie to him every day, and she could not lie to him at all, because she felt as though he could see right into her—that he knew when she was lying.

Even the suit of clothes. She had bought it, thinking about the way it could have been if only Dan had stayed with her, stayed out of trouble—out of the big trouble. She would have loved to help him select his suits and his ties and his shirts. But she went around alone, buying them, and then because she had to go back to the office, she had to take them with her.

And that meant she had to lie to Wes some more.

If only Wes were not so good! He was a gentle, serious man, with vulnerable blue eyes behind dark-rimmed glasses. She could have loved Wes, deeply—if only Dan did not own her soul. *Tell me about hell, Dan.*

She had to tell Wes the suit was for her brother, and that led to a dozen other lies. She was breathless and sick with her lying. But, she told herself, lying got easier all the time. It was easy when you began to lie, and really learned how. Then it got hard to stop.

Wednesday dawned hot and breathless, long before May Alonzo was ready for it. But it did not really matter when daybreak came. She had been up for hours. She was ill, really ill. She looked at her hands and saw them shaking.

She dressed carefully. She would wear no simple print frock this time. She wanted Dan to look at her. She wanted him to see the woman who had gone into hell for him.

As soon as it was daylight, she ran to her window and stared down into the street.

The blue car was parked there, waiting, just as Dan had said it would be. She stared at it, afraid she was going to be sick.

Was she even going to be able to drive the car at all?

For the dozenth time she sat in front of her mirror and touched a brush carefully to the black waves of her hair. There were blue shadows under her eyes. But what did she expect? Either she got her sleep, or she looked like the devil. Her mother had told her that all her life.

She tried not to think about her family. What a sick and ugly mess there would be if she were caught with Dan!

She pressed both hands against her stomach, feeling the knot of cold pain there.

At last it was nine o'clock, and she was dialing the phone, though she did not know how she did it, because her hands were shaking, hanging at her wrists as if they belonged to someone else. All they could do was shake. *Shake, damn you!*

"Hello, Wes. Is that you?"

"Where are you, honey? I've looked all over the office."

"I'm sorry, Wes. I'm sick." This, at least, was no lie. She was sicker than she had ever been. "I called to tell you, I won't be in today."

Tell me about hell, Dan.

"I'll come right over. You get in bed, honey. I'll get in touch with Doc Thomson, and be right over there."

"Oh, no, Wes. Please, don't."

"Why not?"

"I—well, I'm going to see a doctor—"

"I'll go with you.

"I don't want you to, Wes. You stay at the office. I'll be all right. If you'll just—"

She stopped speaking, and she could feel the chill on the line between them. They could both feel it.

"Just what, May?" His voice was low. "Just let you alone?"

"Please, Wes. It's just that I'm sick."

"And it's just that I'm worried."

"I'll call you, Wes."

"When?"

Oh God, when? She stared around the room.

"I don't know," she said. "As soon as I've seen the doctor and get back home, I'll call you. All right?"

"It'll have to be all right," he said, and hung up.

She was already driving the blue car up the approach of the Lafayette Street bridge, when she saw that the spans were separated—the bridge was up.

She would have seen it sooner, but she had not really seen anything since she had walked down the steps from her apartment, out into the street where the blue car awaited her like the ferry on the banks of the Styx.

She had got into the blue car, wearing a blue dress that clung to her round hips, the olive ripeness of her breasts. As soon as she was in the car, she was overwhelmed by the scent of *Daring*, at fifteen dollars the half ounce. *Daring. Be daring.*

She pressed the back of her hand against her mouth.

She was trying to remember everything. She hung the suit on the rear seat hanger. Then she opened the glove compartment, and caught her breath. The gun was there, lying flat and black and ugly on some Kleenex. She did not touch it. She slammed the glove compartment closed.

Her hands were shaking worse than ever.

Now when she looked up and saw the stalled double lane of cars, the drawbridge reared against the sky, she felt her teeth begin to chatter.

She rolled up close to the bumper of the car ahead. She saw the drivers of several cars standing in the street, griping. They were sweaty, and she could see the frustration in their faces.

She did not have to ask them. The drawbridge was stuck.

She looked around wildly. Dan had gone over all of it so carefully. He had figured out when she should leave the apartment, how long it would take her to drive out of town, down the highway to the area where the road gangs were working. He had shaved it so close. He had done that intentionally: he did not want her to get there too early and have to hang around. He did not want anything to attract attention to her.

She stared at the rows of cars, stretching out longer and longer behind her—at the bridge span, at the men talking together. Dan had been so careful. He had figured everything into his timetable ... everything except a stuck drawbridge.

She told herself that she should feel relieved. She was not going to be able to make it now. Dan had warned her, there was one good time for a break, and it had to be exact. If they missed, there would not be a second chance.

Well, by the time she got there now, it would be too late.

May stared at the bridge. But abruptly she was seeing Dan, standing on a sun-blazing road shoulder, waiting for her. She had to help Dan.

Suddenly there was only one thing she wanted in life—to be free. She wanted to be free of this dread, this sick fear that twisted her insides … maybe, even, she wanted to be free of Dan.

Without even knowing what she was doing, she twisted the ignition key, hearing her engine roar when she gave it too much gas. She saw the men glance up. Then they twisted their necks to look at the stuck draw bridge, and when they looked back, she was twisting the wheel, backing and turning the little blue car, making a sharp turn in the middle of Lafayette Street.

She had just got the car twisted around diagonally, its front bumper touching the rear of the car ahead, when she heard the shrill police whistle.

Her insides turned to jelly. She straightened up as if she had been struck. The shrill whistle echoed inside her head. Suddenly it occurred to her that this car might be stolen. She had no registration for it, nothing—except that horrible gun in the glove compartment. If that cop stopped her, she would be in trouble before she could even get to Dan.

May jerked the wheel around, twisting it with all her strength. She stepped hard on the gas.

The little car lunged forward, bumper squealing against the next car, but she was free, turning in the street. She saw the cop running down the incline from the bridge, blasting that whistle.

She was talking to herself, but she did not even know what she was saying. She kicked the accelerator and the blue car leaped, swinging around, down Lafayette away from the bridge. The whistle was still loud, but it was falling behind.

She glanced at the speedometer. She was going over fifty, in a twenty-mile zone.

She began to laugh, choking with laughter. Wouldn't it be funny if they arrested her, and she needed a lawyer to defend her?

She could always hire Wes Kingsley, couldn't she?

She was laughing and crying at the same time, because it was so funny. She could disgrace her family, ruin her own life, fail Dan, and drag Wes into it, too. She was a doer. Not bad for one day. It was funny as hell!

Time raced past her, and she tried to catch up. Dan had warned her never to exceed the speed limit, not even by the usual five-mile spread. But the road signs warned that speed was radar timed; the lawful speed was forty-five miles an hour. She was doing sixty.

The wind whistled past the window. She had to go so far out of her way after the Lafayette bridge was closed. No matter how many speed laws she broke, no matter how much she tried to hurry, she felt time was slipping away from her.

She watched the highway behind in the rearview mirror, waiting for the scream of patrol sirens.

Then she was stopping for the red traffic signal at the intersection of Highway 48.

She was almost there.

She swallowed back the sickness in her throat. She was aware she was still talking to herself. *Please God, just this once. Help me, God, just this once. Get me out of this, God, and I'll never sin again, not even the smallest sin. I'll be good for all the rest of my life.*

She turned the car out onto the wide black highway.

And now she could not make her foot press down on the accelerator.

She was late. She had to hurry, but she could not. She wiped her sweaty hands on her dress. Such a lovely dress. Dan was going to look at that dress and tell her how lovely she looked.

She glanced at the speedometer. She was doing forty now on a highway where the legal maximum was sixty-five. It was all crazy. Dan was crazy to think she could do a thing like this. What was she doing here? Why, she was afraid of a policeman's whistle—she had been completely unnerved since that cop had blown his whistle at her on the bridge.

Abruptly in front of her were small rectangular signs: SLOW DOWN. MEN AT WORK.

She felt her arms go weak. Ahead, she saw the yellow state prison farm trucks. She saw the convicts working in the ditches, the blazing sun reflected from their bent backs.

Dan had warned her to slow down as she approached the signs, and keep letting the car slow down until she finally reached the area between the two trucks.

She glanced at the speedometer. She was driving faster now. She went past the MEN WORKING signs going too fast. She could not slow down. All she could think of was that she had to be free of this nightmare. The only way to be free was to step harder on the gas, drive swiftly past this place—not to look at Dan, not ever to think of him again.

She jerked her head up. The car was swerving toward the right shoulder. She was driving too fast. She was too weak to pull it back on the pavement. She looked up, eyes wild, looking for Dan, and not seeing him anywhere.

3

Virgil Hawkins sweated.

Even the gun across his knees was hot. He could feel its weight and the chafing pressure of it against his legs through his khaki uniform pants.

He closed his finger on the hot trigger, feeling the aching need for violence, and that other sick desire that choked him up when he put it in words even in his own mind: the need to kill.

He glanced around almost guiltily, afraid the pressure was showing, afraid the cons could read it in his eyes.

"Hot. God. Hot."

He spoke aloud to himself, watching the cons swinging their grass slings down in the ditch. Animals. They called those grass slings yo-yo's, and they worked with them like animals, chopping away at the weeds in the ditch.

He reached into his back pocket, and then without taking his finger off the trigger, he mopped his handkerchief across his brows, blotting at the sweat that seeped under his hat band.

He heard a sharp laugh, and tilted his head, fixing his sun-swollen eyes on the cons in the ditch.

They barely moved. From the shortened shade of the yellow truck, he watched them sourly, seeing the sweat on their faces and shirts, on their bared backs and streaking their pants.

He wanted to yell at them. They had been working all morning in that slimy ditch, and he could not see anything they had accomplished. But he swore under his breath. He did not speak to the prison population in that eight-spot down there—it was not worth it. If he spoke to them, they would simply stare at him like the animals they were. If they had no other reason to hate him, they hated him because he was a free man. And they had better reasons for hating him. But none of them had the guts to stand up to him.

His hand tightened on the gun. If only one of them would stand up to him, just one. He got excited thinking about it, more excited than his wife ever got him anymore.

He wished he had not thought about Dotty. Her and her nagging about a vacation. The sound of her voice irritated him more than the heat rash in his armpits.

He glanced toward the other guard in the shade of the far truck. Kemper was almost as bad as the cons. He just sat there with that gun.

He wondered if Kemper would fire on a con if one of them made a break.

He swallowed, thinking about what he would do himself. He thought about it all day on the job, and nothing happened, and the heat and the waiting built up in him. And when he got home to that shack Dotty called a home, she started on him about a vacation. God's nose. She was like a fat, white slug. She got fatter every day, walking around on bare, flat feet, doing less and less around the house, talking about a vacation. He had one coming, but he dreaded the thought of being with Dotty all day, every day for two weeks. Every day out here, away from Dotty, even in this hellish heat, was a vacation for him.

There was another reason he was afraid to take a vacation. In this heat, something had to happen. He could feel it, and he sweated thinking about it. The heat was going to get to these cons, the heat and the pressure he kept on them, and they would plan a break, and they would try it, and then it would happen.

He was almost breathless, thinking about it.

He stroked his thick throat with his fingers. No, it was never going to happen. He was doomed to sit here and rot in the sun, and not one of them cons would have the guts to stand up to him or even look him straight in the face.

There was a time when even that was an offense in these work gangs. You didn't like the way a con looked at you, you could change his face with your gunstock.

It was not like that now. Since the civil rights trials had started upstate, with ten cons testifying about inhuman treatment by six prison guards, the word had come down from the prison director: *Walk easy with these cons.*

He spat into the grass at his feet. Wasn't that a tight wad of crud? Cons being allowed to testify in a law court against guards? What those jerks in the courtrooms didn't know was it took tough men to handle these animals. Some of them were killers. Turn your back, they'd kill you, any of them.

His hand tightened on his gun. He waited, hoping something like that would happen. Each morning he cleaned and oiled this baby, tested the telescopic sights, getting a gnat in that crossed line. Each night he polished off the sweat where his hand had gripped the barrel all day. And every day it was the same thing. He sat in the sun and watched the men, each one of them separately, thinking how it would be if he tried to break.

Nothing happened. The heat. The waiting. The tension. It got to you.

So finally you began to think about killing one of them. Seeing the way it would be, dreaming it in your mind to escape the heat and the waiting. It was like a daydream, only it was with you all the time—that need to throw down on a running man, to get him in your sights, press the trigger, keep pressing it until he writhed on his face in the dirt.

Hawkins was breathing through his open mouth. It really got him, thinking about it. He was sweaty and shaking all over.

He heard that sharp laugh again, and looked up. His gaze touched the two cons who were loitering behind the rest of the population. He could yell at them, but they were nearer Kemper than him, and Kemper would get sore if he yelled at them.

One of the two was that lifer, Ferrel. For a long time now, Hawkins had felt that Ferrel would be the one he would throw down on. Ferrel had given him lip. Ferrel's hard gray eyes had dared him to use gun butt or chain link on him. It would have been a pleasure, and except for the order that had come out since those damn fool civil rights trials upstate, Ferrel would long ago have gotten a chain link across his teeth. Hawkins had thought Ferrel might make a break for it, but in the past two weeks Ferrel had been even more spineless than any of the rest of those sheep down there.

Then Hawkins' gaze touched the other con, and he felt his breath quicken. That Magill was something else again. A young punk that liked for you to push him, because he'd hit back at you even if it bought him a stretch on Bread Row.

He felt his eyes cloud over. He'd elected Magill, once, to die. He had felt like God, planning it, seeing how it was going to be.

He had ordered Magill out of the population one day when the heat was fierce, hell-white and breathless. The eight-spot had worked around a marshy sump, and he told Magill he could go back there and clean it out alone.

Kemper, the stolid, fell for it.

It all fell in line, just as Hawkins had known it would. He could feel his heart slugging, the way no woman had ever made it beat. He could hardly breathe as he marched Magill ahead of him, away from the population and back to the weeded sump.

Kemper had said he would guard the population alone while Hawkins watched Magill in the sump.

Hawkins stood on the ditch incline overlooking that sump, feeling his arms going weak. This was it. He had maneuvered the young punk into a spot where he would make a break if he was thinking at all. The thick underbrush would be too much of a lure for a punk like Magill. He would never be able to resist the chance to run.

Hawkins stood there, sweating, waiting.

He watched Magill's boots sink into the bog and slime of the sump.

He licked his dry mouth. Even if Magill did not make a break, once he moved three feet more into that undergrowth, Hawkins could always swear he had thought Magill was going to make a break. Magill's record would be all he would need to substantiate him. Magill was a troublemaker, and he had tried to break before, and he was a loner.

Hawkins' heart pounded. Nobody could ever prove that Magill had not tried to break.

Hawkins even looked forward to the investigation. He could see himself swearing he had thought Magill was making a break. Some of the tension would be out of him then—after he had killed a man—and his voice would be calm, and he would even sound as if he had hated doing his duty.

He stood there waiting, watching Magill hacking at the shoulder-high underbrush with the machete. The sick, sweet pain moiled in him, like the need for a woman, only more terrible because there was the frantic knowledge that at any moment now it was going to happen, that terrible burning, spurting sense of relief that was going to burst inside him when he slapped that gun against his shoulder, found Magill's left shoulder blade in his telescopic sights, fired and snapped that bone the way you would a rotten stick, and the high-powered bullet would drive into Magill's heart.

He felt the sweet ache, and the longing, and had almost a feeling of hurting tenderness toward the boy down there. He was going to kill Magill.

His hand tightened on the gun. A man might say he was going to kill without reason, but he would be wrong: there were many reasons. Magill was a punk. He was vicious, an animal that was going to be set free on civilized people. He despised Magill when he looked at him, when Magill talked back to him—that cutting voice and that innocent face, those wide guileless blue eyes. He had thought it all out, he had thought about nothing else for days in this heat, and finally Magill was down there and now the moment had come.

Something happened. Somebody yelled from the near end of the population, a hundred yards away in the eight-spot. He glanced around. It was Ferrel, calling something to Magill.

It was nothing, just a casual, "Watch out for snakes in there, kid."

The words had no hidden meaning, even to Hawkins, who knew every slang and every code the cons used in the Rock or out on the eight-spots. But they had a strange effect on the kid working in the sump.

Magill straightened, waved an arm at Ferrel, and then turned facing Hawkins on the incline.

Hawkins felt his body wracked with a convulsive shiver that he could not control.

He tried to speak, tried to order Magill back to work in the sump, but when he spoke his voice failed him—it went out of control as though his throat were constricted, the way it got breathless when he had the urge for a woman.

Magill stared up at him, the sun glinting on those thick-lensed glasses.

Magill stepped up out of the sump and backed away from him, along the incline toward the eight-spot.

Magill knew Hawkins meant to kill him. Maybe he had not figured it out until Ferrel called to him, but he knew it now.

Magill's face was bloodless. He did not speak, just went back to the eight-spot.

For a long time Hawkins stood there. He was not able to move at all. Finally, when he was able to turn around and walk, aching with frustration, he moved back to the shade of the truck.

Kemper asked him what was the matter, but Hawkins did not even answer.

Now Hawkins stood with his gun up across his arm. He yelled at Magill to get back to work, but Magill just laughed at him again.

Hawkins stood beside the truck, staring at Magill and Ferrel down there, standing apart from the population. For a moment he figured maybe Magill and Ferrel were planning a break.

He shook his head. He knew cons better than that. Magill was a loner, a punk. Ferrel would never trust his life to a partner like Magill. Ferrel was not smart enough, or rich enough, to stay out of prison, but he was too smart to buddy with a punk.

He exhaled heavily. Then he saw Ferrel toss his yo-yo into the grass and move up the incline toward the road.

He waited, squinting.

Kemper said, "Where you going, Ferrel?"

Still moving in that lazy panther stride of his, Ferrel nodded toward the water barrel that was roped to the front bumper of the truck near where Hawkins stood. "Water," Ferrel said.

Hawkins saw Kemper nod, and he sank back against the truck because the shade had shortened another ten inches. There was not a breath of air in the whole barren countryside.

He heard a car approaching from behind him, but did not turn. Cars passed every few minutes on this highway. He could tell it was traveling too fast. The signs indicated a ten-mile limit. He never saw more than three cars slow down to that speed in a whole day, damn them.

He moved his head. He could no longer see Ferrel, but he could see his squat shadow jerking along the road rim. He did not have to watch Ferrel—Kemper could see him from where he sat.

He heard Ferrel at the water barrel. By stepping away from the truck a foot or so, he could have looked across the hood at him, but he did not move. He listened to the clink of the tin cup against the metal spigot, the clatter of ice disturbed inside the barrel by a large air bubble.

Then he saw a few drops of water splash on the shoulder grass as Ferrel tossed out the last mouthful from the tin cup. This was an infraction, but Hawkins did not move. You couldn't shoot a man for wasting ice water. The hell with him.

Then he got the old sense of something wrong, the intuitive feeling of trouble that had developed in his last ten years with the state prison department. He did not know what it was. It was everything and nothing.

That speeding car had slowed down. The driver was finally coming to his senses, he reckoned. And Ferrel had not moved away from the water barrel. Magill had thrown aside his yo-yo and was staring up the incline toward the truck where Hawkins stood, and Kemper too had straightened up against the other truck down there.

He heard the whisper and the tension and the wrongness, and he recognized it. He knew what it was. It was a break.

4

Ferrel forced himself to stand motionless on the edge of the hot black highway.

He glanced at Kemper, at Magill, at the men in the eight-spot, at the white blast of the sun, at the car speeding and swaying toward him on the roadway.

He saw that something had alerted Kemper. He saw Magill had an itch. Trouble was brewing—Magill could smell it.

The gang in the eight-spot was working—sheep in the ditch, chomping away at the saw grass and sandspurs.

Hawkins was the man who troubled him. Hawkins could smell out trouble ten miles away.

It flashed through his mind that there was one thing he could do. It was what he had to do. Maybe he had known all along it was what he would do when the chips were down.

He jerked his head around, staring at the blue car. He knew he had to wave her on past, wave her by him and forget it.

Nobody would think anything of his waving at the girl alone in the blue car. He had never done anything like that before, but the young punks on the eight-spots always waved at the girls, or winked, or stared, depending on the quality of their guts.

He cursed himself. He had no right to mix May up in a caper like this in the first place. He hoped to God someday May would know the truth. If it had not been for Paul, if he had not been desperate for Paul's sake, he never would have dragged her into it.

His heart pounded. What was going to happen to Paul if he waved May on past? For two months now, not one letter from him, and word on the grapevine said Paul was quitting medical school with less than two years to go, chasing a dame, wrecking his life. He did not know any way to stop Paul, unless he could get to him. He had spent the better part of his life keeping Paul moving on that narrow path, and by now it was a habit. It was more than a habit. It was the thing that drove him. He had fouled up, but Paul was not going to, not so long as Ferrel was breathing.

He wiped the sweat out of his eyes. But was there any chance to pull this one out of the fire? He did not see how he could do it. It was too near noon now. The highway patrol checked in here just before the eight-spot broke for chow. They came lazing in from both ways, but those boys could move fast when they got word on their car radios.

He stared at that blue car. It was his chance—his only chance, his last chance. May was driving fast. She had raced past the rectangular signs warning her to slow down, and now the car was wavering as if it had gone out of control.

Then he saw she was slowing down, braking the car. Any other time, Kemper and Hawkins would have bought that squeal of brakes. A lot of drivers remembered to slow to lawful speeds when they saw the guns in the guards' arms.

They were not going to buy it now.

She was bucking along, giving it too much brake, too little gas. The kid was scared senseless. Maybe she didn't even know what she was doing now.

She was doing ten miles an hour as she approached the truck where he stood, and she was staring at him, her gaze fixed on him as if there were no one else on earth.

For Dan, suddenly everything was in slow motion.

He moved his head once more, checking Kemper, Magill, the work gang. Then he saw May's face through the windshield. Her face was ashen, twisted, mouth misshapen.

As she rolled past him in the blue car, May leaned across the seat, reached over and slapped down the door handle on his side of the car. The right door opened, but the wind pressure of the moving auto kept it from swinging out far enough to be noticed.

In that second, he bought it.

He turned, lunged around, crouching low so that Hawkins would have to run all the way to the front of the truck to get a shot at him, and he ran zigzagging along the road so that Kemper would have to hesitate to get him in his sights.

He went racing along beside the blue car. He had gambled that this was all the time he would need.

He reached for the door handle, snagged it. At the same instant, he heard Magill yelling.

He leaped into the car, hitting the floor hard, and for a moment he lay crouched there, waiting for the gunfire.

It crackled behind him. Hawkins came running around the truck and out into the road.

Dan spoke from the floor. "May, gun it!"

She stepped on the accelerator, and the car lurched forward.

He heard the guns crack behind him, and he could hear the work gang screaming and yelling in the ditches. They had gone wild. He had known they would, and he knew Hawkins and Kemper realized what would happen. If they turned their backs, those cons would break, even when they did not have a chance in the world. The need for freedom died hard in every con out there.

Dan pulled himself up and stared around the open window frame at the trucks being spun away from him at ninety miles an hour on the wind.

"It's all right, baby," he said over his shoulder. "You're going to be all right."

The two guards had run out into the road, but they were too busy with the work gang to fire after the blue car anymore. The population had gone insane. It was as if Magill, running up and down the shoulder in front of them, was their cheerleader, working them into a frenzy. They were throwing shovels, moving around, slinging yo-yos both ways in the ditch, toward the road and out into the woods.

Hawkins took a dozen running steps after the blue car, gun up against his shoulder, He fired one more time, but Kemper was yelling at him, waving him back to the bedlam the cons were stirring up.

Hawkins stopped, standing with legs apart in the middle of the road, the sun like a spotlight on him, staring first after the disappearing blue car, and then at the convicts rioting in the ditch.

Kemper had run to the truck radio, calling for help. And then they were too far away. Dan could not see them anymore in the heat waves behind the car.

He turned, pulling himself up in the seat. He sat there a moment, breathing through his mouth, his eyes wild and his chest heaving.

May was watching him, breathless, her eyes sick with terror.

After a long moment, Dan pulled his head around, looking straight at her, but not really seeing her at all, and the scent of *Daring* at fifteen dollars the half ounce was lost in the smell of danger inside the blue car.

Dan gave her a sour, twisted smile. He reached out and covered her trembling hand on the wheel.

"You're going to be all right, baby. In just a little while, you're going to be out of this."

Her voice was odd. "Dan, are you hurt? Are you all right?"

Dan stared at her, really aware of her for the first time. He saw it all then—the blue dress she had worn, the hours she had spent on her black curls, the agony that stretched her lovely mouth out of shape. For him—all for him. Always thinking about him, always worried about him. She had been like that since the first time he had laid eyes on her, and she had been just a teenage kid then. She had been Paul's crush, high school stuff, until she saw Dan, and then she had changed. After that she hardly knew Paul, she knew nobody except Dan Ferrel—and all the king's horses and all the king's men couldn't change her back again.

He cursed inside himself. Maybe every man had one woman like May Alonzo, but not all men treated them as he had treated May.

"Slow down, kid," he said aloud, keeping his voice even and low. "You're breaking every speed law known to man."

Dan stared out the window. The land no longer looked heat-stricken, barren and pitiless. When you were free, and looked from the window of a fast-moving car, it was lovely. The stands of oaks were moss-touched and sun-slashed. Beyond the trees the bay lay flat and brown, and far across it was the span of bridges, the trees of a causeway, and there was a sailboat out there—free. Almost as free as he was.

"Dan."

"Yeah, baby?"

"Dan, I can't."

"What's the matter? You can't what?" Dan pulled his gaze back from the bowl of the bay, the land lush and sun-green around it.

"Drive, Dan. I can't drive anymore. I'm shaking all over. I'm afraid. I might—faint."

Dan nodded calmly. He was watching, eyes narrowed, for a yellow turnoff sign. They had to cut away from this highway, and fast.

"Slide over, baby."

"Now, driving like this?"

He smiled his flat, twisted smile. "Just lift that beautiful round fanny up as far as you can, cha-cha it this way, and I'll slide under you."

She tried to smile, pulled herself up, slid over. "Oh, Dan, how can you talk so easy, when you know what a jam we're in?"

He slid past her, the fabric of her dress whistling against his sweaty pants as she moved. Then she was in the right seat and Dan had the wheel, watching the road, keeping inside the speed limit.

He found the road he wanted, wheeled suddenly off the highway and stepped down hard on the gas. She thought he had forgotten her, but suddenly he laughed with that old animal exultance that made her dance and writhe inside.

"Who's in a jam, baby?" he said. "We're together, ain't we?"

5

Ferrel kept the blue car at forty-five.

The secondary road carried them across a far arm of the bay. The bridge clattered, the sound reverberating inside May's head. They had not passed a town, and she had thought this whole country was metropolitan. They raced past a few farms, some country filling stations. Nobody even glanced at them.

May sagged back against the seat, completely played out now that Dan was driving—now that she had nothing to do anymore but wait— wait, and think about the roadblocks that were being set up for them, the scream of patrol sirens that was going to split through her aching head at any moment.

The secondary road was so narrow that two cars could barely pass. But it was too public for Dan. He found the hard-packed orange-colored road he had been looking for, swung the blue car onto it.

They moved steadily into deep, thick marsh country. The bay trees, elder and marsh oaks grew hard against the road. May had never known there was such a wild country so near the three huge cities she had known all her life. But Dan knew it well. He knew just what he was doing, where he was going. Maybe he had worked on these roads on the prison gangs. If he had, he had memorized every turn.

Silence pressed in around them in the car. The road narrowed, became two ruts.

"Are you trapping yourself, Dan?" May asked. "Are you going into a place you won't be able to get out of?"

His mind was on something else. He grinned at her absently. "Trust me, baby."

Oh, I do, Dan. Tell me about hell. I'll love it, won't I?

Dan reached over, pressed the button. The glove compartment snapped open.

May stared at the black automatic. It looked like death itself. If somebody had asked her just then to picture death, she would have described the ugly, black automatic.

But Dan was not afraid of it. He leaned forward, closed his hand on it, brought it over to his lap. He gestured with his head and she slapped the glove compartment closed for him.

"Why, Dan?" Her voice was flat.

"Why what, doll?"

"Why the gun?"

"Smith and Wesson, sweetie. Thirty-two. Stock load. Fast action—"

"Why do you need it?"

He laughed, winking at her. "Why, baby, didn't you know?" He patted the gun on his lap. "It's this gun that makes you ten feet tall."

"Do—do you need to be ten feet tall, Dan?"

His eyes clouded. "Right now I do." He stared straight ahead of them, along the narrowing, shaded road that seemed gray with darkness in the high noon.

Dan had driven off the narrow dirt road, leaving the ruts and driving relentlessly forward through mud and elders and gum brush until finally the blue car stalled and the undergrowth behind it slapped back straight, almost concealing it from the little lost sand-track trail behind them.

Dan got out. He told May to take down the suit and get everything else that belonged to them out of the car.

He opened the door on her side, standing ankle-deep in the bog. "Come on." He held out his arms.

Carrying all her belongings, she slid across the seat. He lifted her, swinging her out after him and carefully closing the door behind her. She wondered why he was so careful, shutting the door of an abandoned car. Then she remembered and admired him. The dome light would burn if the doors were open. A small light like that could be seen for miles in the black swamp night.

He was so smart; he could have accomplished so much—if only ...

He turned, carrying her like a child, and yet she weighed a hundred and twenty-four solid pounds. Round hips, full breasts, rounded thighs.

He was unaware of her weight … He was unaware of her.

Her heart lurched when his strong hands closed on her. He was moving through the underbrush toward a clearing. He was so strong, so vital; it was as if there were a charge of static electricity in his hands and body. And it had been so long, and she had loved him so terribly!

She squirmed slightly, hoping he would feel the warmth of her body, that somehow she could communicate some of the need she felt for him.

He glanced back at the car across his shoulder.

"Leave anything that belonged to you?" he asked.

She bit her lip. Had she left anything of herself in that little blue car? Nothing, except the scent of the perfume she had chosen with such care and such extravagance. She knew he was worried that the police might find some trace of her in the car. But how could they notice that perfume? Dan had not seemed to notice it when he was enveloped in it.

"No," she said. "I didn't leave anything."

They came to a clearing, and her red Ford was parked there waiting. At first May could not believe what she saw. The car was like an old friend, and tears of relief came to her eyes.

Dan opened the front door, hung his new clothing over the top of it. Casually, standing there, he began to strip off his prison uniform. Carrying the denim shirt and trousers, he walked back to the rear of the car, took the cap off the gas tank. He twisted one leg of the trousers into a rope, stuffed it down the tank and withdrew it dark and dripping. He repeated the process with the other trouser leg, then with the shirt. He put the cap back on the gas tank, then carried the gasoline-soaked garments over to a large flat rock, and dropped them.

"Got a match?"

She fumbled in her purse, handed him matches. "You're going to burn them?"

"Every scrap, doll," Dan said. He lit a match, tossed it onto the heap of clothing. The flame blazed up with a rush, high and smoky, then clear orange in the sunlight. Dan stepped out of his shorts and tossed them into the fire. Naked, he walked back to the car.

May swallowed at the throbbing pulse in her throat as she watched him. No man had even been so comely to her. His body was like something sculptured in bronze. Why couldn't he turn, look at her, see what was in her eyes?

She knew what Dan would see if he would only look into her eyes. The need, the desperate, hungry terrible need that had been developing all the time since he had loved her last. She could never forget, even when he was gone from her with some other woman, in some other town—

even when he was sentenced to life in the chain gang—she could never forget the way he could love her, the way he drove her insane, left her clawing and biting and screaming at him.

Why didn't he look at her now?

She needed him so terribly. She had been through hell, and nothing would calm her now except his arms and his body, and his loving. How could he know so much about loving, what a woman wanted, and needed, and had to have, while other men could know so little?

Standing with his back to her, Dan picked up the fresh, clean undershirt and shorts she had brought for him. His back muscles swelled as he stood with head bent, pulling the price tags out of the new clothing. His legs were like dark pillars.

Her heart thudded in her body. She walked up to him, behind him. "Dan?"

He turned, looking at her. Trembling, she put one hand up to the smooth, bronzed side of his neck, feeling the skin warm under her palm. He said nothing, but his gaze turned somber. He dropped the clothing slowly on the seat behind him, then his arms were around her, his big fingers clutching her hair to pull her head back, as his mouth came down to hers.

May was straining herself to him, clutching him, her mouth seeking, demanding. Her breasts were crushed against his hard, bare chest.

Stifled, she broke away, leaned her head dizzily against his shoulder. "Oh, Dan … Oh, Dan, it's been so long!"

"For me, too, doll." His voice was husky, curiously tender.

Standing away from him with an effort, smiling up at him, she raised her arms, fumbling for the buttons at the back of her dress.

"Let me, doll," he said, stepping forward.

"No, I want to." She held him away. "Just look at me, Dan … keep on looking at me."

The dress was open at the top. May lowered her arms, reached up behind her back, found the strap of her bra and unhooked it quickly. Then she pulled the dress over her head, shrugged off the loosened bra, and stood before him proudly, nude to the waist. She saw Dan stiffen, heard his breath catch. Then his hands were on her cool, shaking breasts, with their brownish tips that swelled to his touch. The dress, the blue dress that she had put on so carefully, fell unnoticed to the ground.

Hardly aware of what she was doing, May tugged off her half-slip, her panties. Now they were naked together, and Dan's urgent hands were kneading her flesh as they strained close, mouths locked. The touch of him was heaven, and yet the fury in her body would not let her rest against him. She wanted to press herself into him, kiss him and love him, his whole, hard, muscular body. She wanted him now, this minute, whether they ever got free or not. She would want him on the raw, new-piled earth of the grave itself....

His hands were guiding her. The rear door of the car opened; he was pushing her back. The upholstery of the seat touched her thighs, and she fell, pulling him down with her.

They were both gasping for breath. Dan's face was darkly flushed, his gray eyes bright. "You should have stayed away from me, May," he said hoarsely.

"Yes."

"You never should have come out to that road camp to see me. But I was desperate—I had to have help."

"No." His hands were on her, caressing, tormenting her. "Long before that. I should have stayed away from you before you ever—"

"Ever did this?"

"I should have run, the first time I saw you," she moaned. His weight descended on her, and she writhed. "Oh, Dan—oh, Dan!"

"That's what you should have done, all right, if you'd been smart."

"If I'd been smart ... Oh, yes! Oh, Dan—please—Dan—oh, God—Dan!"

A woman, at last. All the banked passion accumulated over the months suddenly poised like a grenade in Dan's hot loins. He gripped her under-thighs and lifted her to him and his manhood pounded her. Shrieking, she answered with heaving hips, thrashing and throbbing, digging clawed fingers into his back and his thighs. Back and forth, the surging; back and forth and stabbing, and then the grenade went off in a burst of light and exquisite glory.

6

They were moving along in the increasing flow of traffic on a tree-shaded drive leading west into Los Reyes. The nearer they got to the city, the more houses lined the two-lane thoroughfare.

May was driving. She tried to hold the car to a steady thirty-five, but she couldn't do it. She felt that the police were behind her, that she was running, that she would be running all the rest of her life, and never be free.

"Take it easy, May." He had to keep slowing her down.

May glanced at him. His head was lolling back on the seat, his hair growing in a widow's peak and flaring deeply at the temples.

He was staring at nothingness, his gaze fixed on something she could not see.

She looked at the clock on the red dashboard. It was one P.M.

It was hard to believe so much had happened in less than two hours. She had heard on the car radio that Dan kept flicking from station to station, that roadblocks had been set up on every artery in three counties. The authorities believed it was only a matter of time until Ferrel and the black-haired woman would be taken into custody. But Dan had everything planned so carefully, they had moved around within the Los Reyes roadblocks, and now they were almost inside the city itself.

Her hands tightened on the wheel. Two hours ago she had been a woman afraid to break the smallest traffic law, and now she had helped a man escape from a road gang, she had watched him burn his clothes and bury the ashes, spread the rock with pine needles, hiding even the scar of the fire. She had seen him stand before her in a well-cut suit, looking healthy, tanned, like a million other men. Only he wasn't. He was a fugitive.

And all of that had happened in less than two hours.

She said, "I've rented an apartment for you, Dan, under the name of Don Pearson."

He spoke casually, from deep in his thoughts. "Sure, May. Thanks."

She glanced at him, troubled. "What are you going to do, Dan?"

His head came up. His grin was wide, and it frightened her. "I'll think of something."

She reached over, closing her fingers on his arm. He had to be aware of her—she had to make him come out of that shell of hatred and look at her.

"Dan, I've already thought of something."

"Fine, kitten."

"Are you listening to me?"

"What else, you Cuban Brigitte Bardot?"

"Have you looked at me?"

"Baby, I'm drooling."

She sighed. It sounded good, but it was just a string of words, popping one after the other like firecrackers. He always knew the words.

"I've made some plans for you, Dan. For us."

"You shouldn't have, sweetie."

"I had to. I—went through hell today. I don't want you caught."

"We got a quorum on that."

"I want you to get away. There's only one way you can do that. You have got to get out of the country."

"Sounds good—but impossible."

"Dan, listen to me. Remember my brother?"

"Tony? He never approved of me."

"He still doesn't."

Dan sighed. "He's right, too. You ought to listen to your big brother. Tony knows what he's talking about. I'm a no-good. This murder they pinned on me—I'm not guilty of that—but I am guilty of almost everything else. The works."

He stared at the dark row of parkway trees on the boulevard, and against that darkness, the scene ruptured, white and hot and bloody, glowing with neons. He had stepped out of the front doors of the Spanish restaurant Las Noches on West Twenty-second. It was in the Spanish quarter of Los Reyes, and that was where he worked the numbers racket, and the floating crap games, the fluid-drive poker parties. Everybody knew him out there, but not everybody loved him.

From a black-dark doorway across a narrow side street, North Avenue, that intersected West Twenty-second where the huge multi-colored neons of Las Noches spilled on the pavement, a man stepped out, calling Ferrel's name.

Ferrel's head came up. And the man stepped across the sidewalk, moving in that other-worldly gait of the needled, the hooked. But dope addict or not, the goon was armed, a gun in his hand, and he was dangerous, like gangrene is dangerous.

Ferrel never knew exactly how it happened. He spoke sharply to the girl with him, and she turned and ran back through the doors into Las Noches.

The gunman was at the curb over there. There were cars lining the side street. Dan could not tell if any were occupied or not. It did not seem important at the moment. Nothing mattered but the gun in the hophead's hand.

Dan went for the gun in his shoulder holster, thinking maybe this stranger was somebody imported to kill him.

The man yelled something, and Ferrel stopped, chilled.

"This is from Vera." The hood had a flighty, strange voice. "She said to tell you that, first."

The hood was already firing, the gun spurting orange that was brighter than the neon above him. The sound of the gun was like rattling thunder, reverberating off the buildings. The needle had made the gunman wild, but he was good enough. A slug caught Dan in the shoulder and sent him spinning back against the red brick wall of Las Noches.

He stayed there a moment, shaking his head, trying to clear the fire out of it. The gun in his hand was heavy. It was all he could do to lift it. Dimly he could see the man across the street, and he fired, but he did not have the gun up. The shot went into the gutter. But the sound of his gun was suddenly double, as if two guns had fired, and then the gunman across the street went spinning backwards. He was dead by the time he hit the cement.

For a long time, Dan stood there against that wall, staring at the man who lay unmoving across the narrow street.

His head was spinning. He could hear police sirens, and nearer, the whistles of police. He turned and ran.

May's voice was tugging at him now, softly, insistently.

"Are you listening to me, Dan?"

"Sure, baby."

"We can get away. Tony still runs that shrimp boat fleet out of Tampa."

"He's a good boy. Even if he does hate me. Maybe especially because he hates me."

"He can put us down in Mexico, Dan. Way down the coast. Near Vera Cruz."

"I wouldn't let him."

"You let me, Dan."

"I'm taking care of you, baby, every minute."

"Don't waste what I've done, Dan. I—It's been hell, but I won't mind—if we can get away together. It's no risk for Tony, or I would never have asked. They never check the crews of shrimp boats. Think about it, Dan. You and I—anywhere we want to go. South America—anywhere. Together."

He stared straight ahead. He tried to think about South America, about buying passports, and living easy and free, and never running anymore. For a moment, his mind was going along with it, filled with it, and his whole body relaxed. May was a lot of girl, more than enough for one man in one lifetime. She was made of love, and devotion, and he could lie in her arms, and he would never have to run again. Then he thought about Paul.

She saw his face go hard, saw the bitter twist of his mouth.

"Don't throw it away, Dan. Please."

He shook his head, remembering Paul. He was never coming out of this alive, and he wanted her clear. He wanted her to break it off. It was the best thing he could do for her.

"Oh, Dan. If we lose this chance—"

She stopped. Behind them was the sudden wail of a police siren.

May shook all over, as if she were chilled.

Dan sat up straighter. He glanced through the back window.

When he looked around again, his gaze touched May. She was looking straight ahead; her hands trembled on the wheel. Her cheeks were as white as the lilies in a funeral spray.

Dan pulled the gun from his pocket, laid it on his lap. He had ridden far enough with May. He looked at her one last time, looked at the straight line of her nose, the black depths of her eyes, the full Cuban redness of her mouth.

She stared at the gun, then, and her head moved. Her voice trembled. "Dan, don't."

"I can't let them take me, baby. But you're not mixed up in it yet. You slow down enough to let me step out, and I'll burn candles for you, May—as long as I live."

Before she could slow the car, two state police cars approached them from the rear, moving so swiftly they swayed in the wind. Cars going both ways pulled off the highway and stopped as they passed.

May pulled the red Ford hard right. With sirens wailing, both police cars raced past them. Dan was sitting there, stiffly waiting, but neither state patrolman even glanced toward the red Ford.

"Sure. How could they know about this red car?" Dan exhaled heavily, shoved the black gun back into his jacket.

May was trembling. She stepped on the gas again. He touched her arm. "Hold it. Keep slowing down."

"Dan, you're not going to leave me?"

"Honey, it's the best thing ever happened to you since your bust got to measure thirty-nine."

She tried to smile. "Oh, Dan, stay with me."

"Honey, I can't. Be glad I can't."

"Why can't you?"

He laughed in a cold way. "Somebody has found that blue car."

"Already? How could they? How do you know?"

"Those boys. They found it, all right. That shaves it closer. I better leave you before we hit the first roadblock. There's no way yet for them to tie you to that blue car."

"They might, Dan."

"They can't. I wouldn't have let you in this caper if I hadn't figured it all out. That car was stolen—"

"Stolen! Oh, Dan, how could you do that to me?"

"I didn't want to. I had to." His voice was cold. "You were safer in that stolen car, baby. Freshly painted, stolen license plates, filed serial numbers."

"I couldn't have done it, if I'd known."

His voice was soft. "I know. So stop this thing, doll, and let me out. You're in the clear up to now. I want it to stay that way."

"Dan, you've got to promise me we'll go away together. You haven't got a chance staying in Los Reyes."

"I can't promise you anything, May."

"We could be happy. Why are you throwing it all away?"

Dan looked at her again. "I wish I knew. Now stop the car."

May pulled the car over on the shoulder. The shade trees were thick. The afternoon sun laid mottled patches across the street, the car, the land.

Dan was staring up the road. Far up ahead he could see where the two patrol cars had blocked the street from both sides and were letting the traffic through one car at a time. Cars were slowing, lining up almost back to where May had stopped.

She caught his arm. "I've got to see you, Dan. I've got to know you're all right."

"What's the address of that apartment of yours?"

Dan had opened the door on his side of the car. He held it ajar, waiting. Frantically, May fumbled in her purse.

She brought out a small card with her address and phone number scrawled on it. He glanced at it, nodded, then stepped out of the car.

He glanced through the window at her. His smile was strange—bitter, unhappy, and something she could not read at all.

"I'll see you, May. If you're that unlucky."

She nodded, tears blurring her eyes. She fed the car gas and moved slowly away toward the cars lined up in the roadblock.

Dan Ferrel paused a moment, watching the red car pull away, glanced back toward the next car. He did not believe it was close enough for anyone in it to swear to seeing him step out of May's auto.

To be sure, he walked slowly along the shoulder toward the roadblock until the car had approached and passed him. The people in it were not even looking at him.

He stood a moment, looking around him, then glanced at the card May had given him.

With a quick, deliberate motion, he ripped the card across, then tore it to bits.

He dropped the scraps of paper on the walk as he crossed it, heading up a winding, shell-paved side street. He looked up, knowing the street went nowhere. It had to be a dead-end, or the patrolmen would never have set up the roadblock ahead of it.

But it was good enough for now. He did not need open streets, to get where he was going.

He had walked less than half a block on the side street when he heard the whine of a siren on the highway behind him.

He felt a stab of panic. He glanced back, saw the black-and-white Los Reyes police car turning into the street behind him. He jerked his head around, moving faster.

He felt as if he were wearing a target in the middle of his back. Where had he fouled up? They couldn't have been seen him step out of May's car. He had accomplished it quickly, and the roadblock was still almost half a mile ahead.

He moved faster. Maybe they had seen him walking along the shoulder of the road when he was checking on the car behind May's. That must have been it. They had seen a man alone out here, and the place was swarming with cops by now, and they were checking out every lone man they saw. That had to be it. But he could not take a chance. He was not about to stop to talk to them, and it couldn't end here on this street.

He turned abruptly east, toward downtown Los Reyes, going off the street and across the yard between two cottages. He ducked between the two houses, ran through the backyard, crossing an alley, and kept going, even when he heard the cops yelling at him from the street.

7

Paul watched Reve come around a sand dune capped with wild wheat, and walk slowly toward him across the deep white beach. She was wearing a strapless black swimsuit that molded her figure as if it had been painted on.

He had been troubled and drawn taut with worry, crouched there in his swimsuit on the army blanket, awaiting her. The beach was empty— endless and lonely as far as he could see either way, except for sandpipers, some shrill-crying gulls and a pelican sulking on a beached log.

He had the whole lonely beach all to himself, and his mind was made up—he had to tell Reve the moment he saw her.

He stared at the sun on the water until the brilliance was like a lance driven into his skull. There was no sense trying to go on like this.

But when he saw her, everything changed.

He felt his heart beat faster, and the excitement of her black-haired, blue-eyed beauty drove the worry away, and all he could think was that she was the loveliest thing he had ever seen.

"Holy Moly," Paul whispered, grinning.

He got up on his knees as she came near. She sank to her knees on the blanket, close to him, so close the same breeze caressed their bodies.

"What did you say?"

"I said wow. Like cool. Like, I've been here an awfully long time, but this was worth waiting for."

She smiled, and the sunlight dimmed for him. "I'm sorry I'm late. I am a working girl, you know."

"I know. I was a working man, and a student. That was before you."

She touched his face. "You don't regret it, do you, Paul?"

"I don't regret anything. Sometimes, though, I wish you'd meet me in civilization. Do you realize you never do? Always some lonely place like this. Are you ashamed of me?"

She laughed. "You know what I am. I'm jealous of you."

"That's silly. No woman ever looked at me until you came along. All I did was work. Work and study."

"Still, I like to have you all to myself, lover."

She caught his hand, pulled him to his feet. They ran out into the water. He heard her laughter, and his own answering laugh, and yet it was as though he were only half there, as if a part of him still hung back.

He grimaced. What was the matter with him? St. Peter was trying to pull him through the gates into heaven, and he was resisting. He tried not to resist, but he could not forget that she never wanted to go to any public place with him.

She danced, bobbing on the waves in his arms, staring at him oddly. And that made him uncomfortable—he felt she could always tell what he was thinking. He felt so vulnerable, so young and immature. Why couldn't he be a little like Dan? His brother knew how to handle women, dames, dolls and beautiful ladies like Reve; Dan was at ease with all of them. Why not? Dan had not wasted his life in science labs, and libraries, and the musty corners of state universities.

"I love to be with you." Reve was clinging to him and the water was thrusting her body with a tormentingly regular and gentle motion against him. "We don't have to go places where it costs money, darling. I sing in nightclubs. Would it thrill me to waste my time in one with you?"

He did not try to answer that. Instead, he caught her in his arms and pressed his parted lips over hers. At last she pulled away, gasping. "Wow. Like cool. Like it's been an awfully long time. But this was worth waiting for," she quoted him.

They floated in the waves, carried along, close together.

"I don't care where we are," Paul said. "As long as we're together. Not very original, but like sincere."

"What were you thinking?"

He traced his finger along the rim of her bathing cap.

"I was just thinking how odd you are."

"Odd?"

"Black hair, blue eyes. Isn't that odd?"

"You don't like it?"

"Like it? I love it. Every woman ought to be made like this."

She pressed closer to him, and for a long time they did not talk. They did not need words. They had everything: a lonely stretch of white beach, a warming sun, and arms and hands and mouths.

She was next to him on the army blanket, lying with her head down the slope instead of up. Her face was close to his, upside down; he saw the gleaming waves of her hair, and her delicate eyelids closed against the sun. Her mouth was faintly, smiling, and she was beautiful.

Shifting his position a little, he could see the pointed hills of her breasts in the wet black suit. She lay still pretending not to know he was looking at her. He got an arm over her, gently cupped one big breast. Her eyelids opened, and her blue eyes looked directly into his, serious, searching. Under his hand, through the cool wet wool, Paul could feel the firm softness of her flesh. But there was something in the way, some kind of stiffening in the suit.

"Reve—" he said.

"What, lover?"

He rolled over part way, turned enough to lean down and kiss her. Her mouth was cool under his at first, then it opened slowly and it was fiery hot. Her arms tightened around him. His hand slid over her shoulder and back, wanting the touch of her bare flesh. There was nothing in the world but their hungry mouths and tongues, and the closeness of their bodies, and the sound of their quickened breathing.

When the kiss ended, Paul pressed his lips against Reve's cool throat. She rolled over on her side, clinging to him. His free hand found the zipper at the back of her suit, pulled it open, and his hand caressed the silken skin of her back.

"Someone might see."

He raised his head, looked around. "There's no one. Not for miles." He looked down at her. She had rolled onto her back again, arms flung over her head. The top of the black suit was loose.

He stopped breathing for a moment. Her big breasts seemed hardly flattened at all as she lay there—they stood high and quaking, with pink tips that were like blind eyes in the sunlight.

"God, you're beautiful, Reve," he said hoarsely. She was flushed, excited by watching him as he looked at her. The wet swimsuit had left a film of water on her breasts, and when he kissed them, they were cool and salt-tasting. She murmured with pleasure, moving her body a little under his exploring lips.

Suddenly she pushed him away and struggled up to her knees. She was trying to pull up the dangling front of the suit. Blind with desire, Paul went after her. His weight threw her forward, making her put her hands down to support herself. Holding her close, Paul seized her swinging breasts, squeezed and shook them, while he kissed her back and nipped it with his teeth. "Paul, quit," she said in a stifled voice. "Let me go, we can't—"

But he yanked the suit down over her hips, then toppled her on her back. She lay tousled and panting, staring up at him. "Caveman," she said between her teeth. Under the passion in her voice, she seemed half angry, half amused. Paul tugged the suit all the way off her, struggled out of his own trunks and threw himself on her.

Her lips were sweet and hot—her body writhed with pleasure under his hand. Then they were gasping together, on the hot sand, with the breeze whispering across their naked bodies, and the gulls crying far overhead. Paul sucked at her breasts. Her long limbs writhed, wrapping themselves around him, and he felt the slithery sleekness of her belly against his loins. He stretched convulsively, his mouth going up to hers, his fingers clutching her throbbing buttocks. Her smooth thighs made a furrow beneath him. He stabbed mightily, frantic now, and felt his whole manhood submerging in wet sweetness.

They thrusted and thrashed, and with a mighty heave exploded over the brink of bliss.

"Something is troubling you, darling," Reve said. "Tell mother."

Paul sprawled on his back and watched her shake her dark hair out in handfuls. He thought about the way they had met, how mysterious fate was in letting even the best things happen to you. She had a flat tire on her little convertible right in front of the cottage where he lived. He was studying at the front window, and for a few moments he watched her standing helplessly holding wrenches and jack. He had never seen a girl look so helpless. By the time he had fixed the tire for her, they were laughing and talking as if they had known each other forever. She had insisted on helping him—mostly she just got in the way, but she got smudges on her face, blackened her hands and mussed her dress. He asked her into his place to wash up. He was nervous because they were alone in his cottage, and he had never had a girl in this house alone before, and because everything was a mess. But she was at ease—she thought the place looked "cute—just what you'd expect of a big helpless man." She walked around looking at things, and he stood there looking at her.

She paused before the only picture he had of Dan. "My big brother," he told her. She turned slowly, brows tilted above those pale blue eyes, smiling at his six-two, hundred and ninety pounds. "He must be a giant, if he's your big brother."

Paul laughed. "He's not bigger. He's not as big. Very slender, from late hours and high living. He's just older, that's all."

She was so at ease in his house, that he was almost at ease himself. Only he felt that everything was going to crack under him like eggshells, every step he took. He felt big and clumsy, and he seemed to brush against her every time he got near her, and he cursed himself, thinking he was being fresh. Finally he asked her to stay for supper with him, just hoping to prolong everything long enough for her to refuse. She stayed. They ate barbecued chicken, delicatessen potato salad and potato chips with beer from TV trays in the front room. They did not turn on the TV.

They talked about each other. He told her about his job afternoons and evenings at the research labs, his days of drudgery in his second year of medical school. "Not very exciting," he said. "And sometimes I think it's never going to end."

She told him about herself. She sang in nightclubs. Her name was Areva Storm—it really was, she said, smiling, when he raised a brow at her. It was a violent, unreal-sounding name, like something a press agent might dream up, until you saw her perform. Then you knew the name belonged to her.

He went alone one night to the club where she sang. She had never invited him, and he had stayed away as long as he could. He sat as if in a trance. He was so bewitched, he did not even applaud.

"You're magnificent," he told her, the next time she came out to the cottage to see him.

"No," she said, and those pale eyes were suddenly chilled, like a diamond, hard and chip resistant, because she had been hurt all she was going to be hurt. "It's all an illusion, lover. You take three parts martini, a gown that's little more than a G-string, songs that don't sell anything but sex, and a lot of tricks you pick up—and people don't notice that you haven't got it, not really. You don't have a voice. But in a place like that, it doesn't matter."

Her voice was bitter. He wanted to say something to make her feel better. But he did not know how.

She lay down beside him on the army blanket, flat on her back with her thighs, her round little belly, her full breasts catching the light.

She stared upward at the faded sky.

"Have you thought about what we talked about, Paul?"

He pushed himself up on one elbow, staring down at her. Thought about it? He had not thought about anything else. The first time she had mentioned the robbery, he had been shocked, almost stunned.

"Oh God," he whispered.

He had looked at her, feeling the world rock crazily under his feet. "Reve, you're crazy!"

He had never thought he would fall in love with a girl like this, a nightclub singer, bright and lovely and yet wiser than he was. She was the kind of girl Dan had always paraded on his arm—a sign of status with Dan, like his new Cadillac convertibles.

But he did love her. There wasn't anything in the world he would not do to keep her. Maybe he was more like Dan than anybody believed. Maybe Dan's kind of life was what he had always wanted, only Dan had stopped him cold, drawn an invisible line and warned him never to cross it.

He looked at Reve—at Areva Storm—and he knew that the real wonder was not that he loved her, but that a girl like Reve would ever fall in love with him. But she did love him. She came to the cottage whenever she could steal away, even going without sleep so her schedule would match his.

"Why am I crazy? I'm not crazy to want money, and a chance to be somebody."

"A robbery, Reve! You and me? It is crazy."

"Is it? Or am I crazy to go on singing in nightclubs when I know I haven't got it, when I know I'm never going to be any more than I am right now? Oh, it's not too tough now— I'm only twenty, but what's it going to be in five or six years? I'll have to trade the G-string gown for bubbles, or feathers, or something else to use in a strip act—"

He grabbed her arms, "Don't talk like that."

"I'm just stating a fact. Or would you rather I'd marry one of these rich old goats who promise me a splashy wedding, an expensive honeymoon and a big divorce settlement?"

"Oh God, Reve, stop talking like that."

It was three days before he saw her again. He called her, and her apartment phone rang twenty times, and at last when she lifted the receiver, her voice was chill. "What do you want, Paul?"

"I want you, Reve. Can't you understand? I'm going nuts. I love you.

I want to see you."

He talked her into meeting him.

They didn't have to be together long before the same old dialogue started again.

"Sure, I love you, Paul. But I can't wait forever."

"Three years, Reve. I'll be through med school and through with the year of internship."

"Three years? My God."

"And after three years, what? You going into a plush, ready-made practice, Paul?"

"Why did I ever have to meet you?"

"You don't have to see me, Paul. I'll stay away from you. I don't know how. But I do know I will."

The hell of it was, he knew it, too.

"No, you stay with me. We'll figure something."

She laughed. "I've already figured something."

"That's a crime, Reve. Can't I get that through your head? Robbery is a crime. Punishable by jail sentences."

"All right. If you're afraid, forget it."

"I'm not afraid, Reve. If I were just afraid, I'd say, sure, let's go ahead and do it. What does it matter—a shipping company office, a lot of loot, all insured? Let's take it and run. That's easier than losing you."

She remained rigid. "Why not, then? What do you care about a little crime? One robbery—and then plenty of money."

"I've got to live with myself, Reve. And you have, God knows. Even if we got away with it, we'd hate ourselves—we'd end up hating each other."

"But just think how comfortable and luxurious we'd be, hating ourselves, and hating all that money."

He had to laugh. "My God, Reve. I always thought they worked overtime making you—I didn't think there was anything missing. But there is. A whole cog. It's called a conscience."

"We were very poor, Paul. They couldn't afford one."

He tried to put his arms around her. "I'll take care of you, Reve. Please. Just give me time."

"Time is all right for you. But I haven't got time. I go every night to that nightclub, and I hate it, and I hate myself, and each night I feel a little dirtier than the night before. I'm not going on like that. The only way I know to get out of there is to have some money. The only way I know to have any money is to take it."

They were sitting in the living room of Paul's little cottage. It was a gray afternoon, with rain that beat in gusts against the windows. Reve was wearing a flowered halter that exposed her tanned shoulders and midriff. Her golden legs were bare under tight black shorts.

"This is nice, being with you here," she said, leaning back against the sofa cushions. "So peaceful—it feels like nobody could ever get in to bother us."

"Nobody can." He laid his palm on her cool, soft thigh. "Reve, I'm so crazy about you."

"I know," she said, holding his gaze. "Me, too, lover." Her thighs moved, opening slightly, then closed, imprisoning his hand. "Now you'll never get away."

"God, I don't want to, Reve." Impulsively, he bent down and kissed the smooth, bare flesh of her torso, between the halter and the shorts. After a moment he felt her stir, realized she was unfastening the knot of the halter behind her back. He looked up in time to see the pink-tipped globes of her breasts swing free as she pulled the halter over her head. She looked down at him, past those trembling mounds. Her face was flushed, her eyes bright.

With a gasp, Paul buried his face in her soft flesh. Her hands caressed the back of his head, stroking his neck, maddening him. He could smell the scent of her skin, hear her breathing as he kissed and caressed her body. He found the zipper at the side of the shorts, tugged it down, and felt the smooth bare curve of her hip under his fingers.

Suddenly she seemed to grow stiff. Her hands pushed him away.

"What's the matter, Reve?" He was bewildered.

She shook her head. "I'm sorry, Paul—I just can't." She bit her lip, fumbling for the halter on the sofa beside her.

"But what's wrong—did I do something?"

"No, it isn't that. I just suddenly felt—I can't explain it. Forget it, will you?" She arched her back, tying the halter. "Come on, let's have a drink."

They went into the kitchen and Paul made two Collinses. Rain rattled against the windows. Paul was upset, not understanding. "I don't get it," he said.

"Don't sulk, lover."

"You never acted like this before, Reve. Everything was fine, and then all of a sudden—"

"Put it down to artistic temperament." She grinned. "That's what they say in my racket when they mean 'bitchiness.'"

"Then you're not sore at me about anything?"

"No, I'm not sore. Maybe it's the weather." She sipped at her drink, looking at him over the rim. Her face was still flushed, her eyes bright. "Paul, you know I wouldn't hurt you for anything—if I didn't have to."

"I know that, Reve. I'm sorry, I just—"

"Don't apologize." She put her hand on his arm, leaned nearer.

He kissed her. At first there was that stiffness in her body, then it seemed to melt and she swayed against him. Her lips were hot and soft under his. He stroked her silken back, pressing her closer, until his own desire drove him frantic. His hands kneaded her flesh. "Reve, let's go in the bedroom."

She kissed his neck. "All right, lover."

In the shadowed bedroom, she held him off with gentle fingers when he tried to open her clothing. "Don't, lover. Let me."

She unbuttoned his sports shirt, helped him take it off, then tugged off the rest of his clothing. He moved to take her in his arms, but she held him away again. Reaching behind her, she quickly unfastened her halter and removed it. She stepped out of her shorts.

"Now lie down, lover—that's right, turn over, like this."

He lay on his belly on the soft bed, and in a moment felt the touch of her lips and her breasts as she bent over him. His mingled pleasure and frustration were almost unbearable. She kissed him and caressed him with her hands and body until he was wild with desire—and then, abruptly, she pulled away.

"I can't love you," she wailed. "Oh, I can't—much as I want to. Paul, it's this thing I've got on my mind—I keep thinking about it all the time. Last night at the club, there was this man. His name was Charley Muencher. Oh, it's a funny name, but don't laugh at him. People don't laugh at men who have as much money as Charley Muencher."

"My God, Reve—" Paul wanted to close his ears. She tortured him when she talked about the men she knew at the club. It made him sick to think about her, and the life she had when she was away from him.

"He wants to marry me, Paul. Tell me, should I marry him?"

She got up, and paced the floor in her bare feet, lovely, flushed, and so lost to him.

"Don't, Reve," Paul begged. "You don't have to torture me."

"Oh, I'm sorry. You don't want to hear about this man? He asked me to marry him. His yacht. His millions. His divorce settlement when the fun was out of it."

"Please, Reve. Stop—"

"Sure, Paul. You're right. He's fat—he's gross. Everything that makes me ill. I have to come running to look at your body, so strong, and muscular, and flat—and hard. But he has so much lovely money—"

"My God, don't talk like this."

"I'm only telling you. He's got money. Now. Today."

He sat up, shaking. "You wouldn't sell yourself."

"Not unless I have to."

"You're too lovely. Too decent. You couldn't do it—"

She held her splayed fingers before her, palms up, staring at them. "I can't go on like this, either. You talk about me—decent. How long will I be decent—even if I am now? Is it any worse to go on in that place night after night than to steal—once, just once—is it, Paul? Am I going to be any worse for one theft than I am for what's happening to me right now?"

Paul covered his head with his arms. He whispered, "Oh, God, Reve. Let me think. Let me think."

But no matter how much he thought, there was one answer....

They celebrated. They drove sixty miles to a seaside town. They drank wine and ate lobster, and got the butter smeared all over their faces. And Reve cried out, "It'll be like this, Paul. Just like this. For all the rest of our lives—together, having fun."

He tried to smile. He had agreed to it. What was the use of fighting? "You're stacked," he told her, in a sick attempt to laugh at himself. "You're stacked against me."

He held her close in her little car, returning to Los Reyes at night. He was content and warm in the car, moving through the night on the lonely highway. He wanted only to love her, to touch her and caress her, and feel her tight against him.

But she lay against his shoulder, staring at the roof of the car. "Just think, Paul, no more job in that smelly lab. No more trying to stay awake until three A.M. studying those books. No more waiting."

"That's what I try to think about it."

"Sure. Think positive. We can't fail. Why, I was in that shipping office. That big fat Charley Muencher. He insisted on taking me out there, showing me around. He blabbed so much, told me the whole setup. They keep a week's collections in a box in his office. And there's only an old night watchman to guard the stuff. Muencher's not worried about anyone trying to steal the money. It's all insured. Every last penny of it. Hear me, Paul?"

"I'm going to do it—I told you I was going to do it. But don't let's talk about it."

The bitterness was eating at him, corroding him, tarnishing everything, so that not even what they had together was as bright and lovely as it had been before.

Now she had set the night. Friday. And now on Wednesday afternoon he had lain on the beach sweating, waiting for her, and he felt the sun had sweat all the evil out of him. He had been crazy to listen to Reve— as crazy as she had been to think they could rob that company. He had to tell her that.

He propped himself up on his elbow, looking down at her on the blanket. He had never seen anything so lovely; he could not live without her; but he wasn't going to do it.

"We're not going to do it, Reve."

She tried to struggle up. He held her down with his arm across her breasts.

"Stay there, Reve. Now listen to me. We're going to have each other. The only way we can—"

"I've told you the only way we can." Her voice was flat.

"But you were wrong. We can get married. Now—right away. Get a license and wait three days, and we've got it made."

"Have we?" said that flat, distant voice. "And what do we live on?"

"We live in that cottage. And I work, and I go to school. And we wait—only we wait together. We can have everything, Reve, just slower, that's all."

She thrust his arm away. She sat up. "Thanks, but no thanks. I've been poor. I was born poor, and I grew up that way. I've had it. I won't have any more of it. Not even for you, Paul. Because I just can't take it."

He grabbed her arms, but she shrugged free, moving away from him. "I mean it, Paul. I don't want to see you anymore."

"I love you, Reve."

"Do you?"

"We were made for each other."

"Were we?"

"Stop it—stop being so cold. I'm only trying to save us from doing something crazy."

She shrugged. "All right, Paul—fine. I hope you'll be very happy and successful. I mean that, Paul."

She turned, standing up, reaching for her bottle of sun lotion, her bathing cap, her towel.

Paul was afraid he was going to be sick. He jumped up, pulled her against him. "Oh, my God, Reve, don't go. I can do anything else, but I can't give you up."

She was stiff in his arms. "I'm sorry, Paul. It's the way I said. Friday night—as we planned. Or I'm not going to see you again, Paul, ever. It's as simple as that."

8

Paul was twenty minutes late to work at the research lab on East Forsythe. He hurried through the security door, stopping just long enough to flash his clearance badge.

He saw the way they looked at him. He felt something tighten inside him. He wanted to yell at them, *All right—twenty minutes late. Sue me— put me in the electric chair.*

He said nothing. This was one of the jobs the university scrounged up for deserving students. He knew he was quitting. Friday was his last day. But he said nothing. He found his apron and went to the project they had assigned him—the slides, the microscope waiting, coldly accusing him of neglect. The hell with them. After Friday they could take their slides and their cultures and the whole bloody works, and—

Friday was going to change everything. Friday was graduation day.

Paul glanced around at the people in the lab. Somehow, until Reve came along, he had seen them as good, unexciting, dedicated people, looking for answers where nobody even really understood the questions. And he had been one of them. But not anymore.

He might have made it on time, even in spite of that long sick fight with Reve at the beach; but he had stopped by the cottage on the way to work.

His fist tightened on the cool metal of the microscope. Why had he stopped at the cottage? He knew by the way these people looked at his sandy, damp hair that he should have showered, but he had not stopped for that. He had stopped to look in the mailbox, hoping for a letter from Dan.

He had been worried about Dan for days. Every day he looked in that mailbox, and every day he drew a blank.

Well, what difference did it make? What could Dan say? Dan couldn't say anything that would change what he was going to do—what he had to do on Friday. It was easy to say he could tell Reve to go to hell, but he couldn't. Medicine, career—nothing had any significance without Reve.

Once he had made up his mind to that, the rest was easy.

Only, he kept thinking there would be a letter from Dan. It might help, somehow. There might even be something in it that he could read to Reve, and get some sense into her head at the last minute. He had to smile when he thought about Dan and his philosophy. "Always go to a fool for advice." That was Dan talking. "A wise man can advise you what you ought to do, what you should do, and what it is best to do, and if you're as smart and wise as he is, his advice might work for you. But if you want the answers, kid, always ask a fool's advice. A fool has made all the mistakes a man can make—and he can't tell you what you ought to do, but he can sure tell you what you better not do."

Dan had been at home when their mother died. Paul had been fifteen then, and he would remember that day as long as he lived. The look on his mother's face—the hurt, the way she stared up at Dan through the tears, clinging to his hand with fingers too weak to hold anything.

"Oh, Dan—it took a death in the family to bring you home."

Dan was thin then, but with a look of elegance and a smile that set you back on your heels. "I been busy, Mom. You know that."

"Busy chasing the chicks, Dan?" she whispered.

"You know a better business, chick?" Dan said, kissing her.

She sobbed suddenly, so weak and depleted, and so near death, though none of them believed it yet. She had turned away from Dan, from Dan's smart clothes and twisted smile. She grabbed Paul, pulling him to her.

"Oh, God, Paul, don't be like him. Don't think he's so wonderful, with his money and his chicks. Oh, God, I'm so afraid. I'm afraid to die, because of what will happen to you."

Dan touched her shoulder, soothing, his voice low. "You're not going to die, chick. A doll like you, how could you die? Besides, Paul isn't anything like me. He takes after you. And I won't let him change. Whenever he gets in trouble, why, he can come to me for advice."

She turned then, still crying, staring at Dan. "You? For advice?"

"Always ask a fool for advice, chick. He can tell you just what not to do. He's already made all the mistakes ..."

But Dan had been wrong. Their mother died—quietly, in her sleep, with Dan on one side of the bed and Paul on the other.

Paul wanted to quit high school and get a job. But Dan gave him a fool's advice. "You quit school, you got nothing. You're nobody, kid. And they kick you around. Stay in school. Get to be somebody—then you kick people around."

"I don't need it," Paul said. "I want a job. I got to take care of myself. I got to have some money."

"Tell you what, kid. Go ahead—quit school. But if you do, I'm going to kick you around, bad. I hate to do it, but you're going to be kicked around all the rest of your life anyway, so you might as well start with me, and get used to it."

Paul stared up at Dan—and he saw why people whispered that Dan could scare you. Paul had thought Dan was kidding. Suddenly he knew better, and he knew he was not going to quit school. He had a fool's advice.

So Dan brought their mother's sister, and installed her in the house to take care of Paul until he was out of high school. Every week, no matter where he was, Dan sent a check to run the place.

The night before Paul was graduated from high school, some old friends of Dan's showed up, and offered him a job selling numbers. "You can't get an income like this in any job you'll find," they told him.

Dan was at the graduation exercises. He just turned up without warning, looking smarter than ever, a little more harried, a little older.

"I made it," Paul told him. There was defiance in his voice. "Now I'm going to do what I want to do."

"Sure you are, kid," Dan said, smiling. "You've done fine so far. Got no complaints. Number two in your class. You dragged your feet a little there, but—"

"My God!"

"Look, boy, believe a fool. If you can get as close as second, you can be first. It's that simple—I know. I've made all the mistakes one guy can make."

"Well, it's over."

"What you plan to do?"

"I don't know. I'll find something."

"Like selling numbers?"

Paul's mouth sagged. "How did you know that?"

"Kid, I know everybody in that lousy racket. I know all about it. So you want to sell, huh? Low man on the pole. The one the cheap cops pick up when the pressure is on. You spend more time in jail than you do out. And for what? A few lousy bucks, and a dirty name."

"Where could I get a better job?"

"Number two man in your class." Dan shrugged. "I don't know. Maybe if you'd been number one in your class, you could have found something. But you had to drag your feet."

"My God, you talk like you know everything!"

"No. I don't know anything, kid. That's why I admire the number one guy. But there's one thing—"

"Yeah?"

"Maybe if you went to the university—"

"College?"

"Maybe you could make up for the fact that you loafed and you weren't number one here in school like you ought to have been."

"How could I ever get through college?"

"You mean money? Hell, kid, I got money. I got money that says you can be better than this number one guy. That you can be number one, at anything you want to be. I'll put out the money—just so you don't drag your feet."

During the next six years, they did not see each other very often. Dan wrote that he was out making some spectacular new mistakes, but that was because he had made his first mistake a long time ago, and now it was too late to do any better, too late to change. "But I got some real top flight advice for you, kid, on what not to do. Any time you want to hear it."

Then Dan was back home, in Los Reyes at least, though he stayed away from the cottage Paul had rented. And then suddenly Dan was in all the headlines. He had shot and killed a hoodlum in a savage "crime battle between two gun punks," as the Los Reyes *Tribune* called it.

Paul went every day to Dan's trial. He could not stay away. He sat in the back row and heard Dan's long record spelled out for the jurors.

The trial was odd, like a car that rolls along just slightly out of line, the frame bent so nothing is quite right. From the first day of that trial, it was obvious that the state's attorney could not prove the bullet that killed the man had been fired from Dan Ferrel's gun.

But Dan had pulled a gun. Dan had fired. The man named Spivoli was dead with a slug in him. The bullet had knocked Spivoli six or seven feet and spun him around. Nobody could later swear at what angle he had been struck.

What they had against Dan was circumstantial evidence. Dan had fired a gun; tests proved that. Dan had a bullet in him. Dan had a bad record. And that was how it went. Finally, the state's attorney suggested to an expert witness that Ferrel might have had another gun which he fired first, and which he then threw away. He had run from the scene of the shooting. He had had time to dispose of such a gun, hadn't he? The expert agreed all this could have happened.

Paul went to see Dan before they shipped him off to the state prison, and later to a chain gang road camp.

"Stay away from here, kid. Don't get mixed up with me. Some more of that fool's advice. You get to be known by the company you keep. So stay away from me."

"You're not guilty, Dan."

Dan smiled. "Want some more fool's advice, kid? Don't ever go into court without the best lawyers money can buy. That's another mistake I made. Costly—real costly."

There had been no letter. Paul went on to work, thinking about Dan. Dan was a great one to be telling him what to do. A great one to be telling anybody what to do. For weeks now, no mail....

He sat there, looking around the lab. What made him think he was any different from Dan? They were brothers, weren't they? Why did he think he could go on like this? What would Dan do, if he had ever really loved a girl the way Paul loved Reve? What would Dan have to say about love?

He would never know so long as Dan ignored his letters, that was for sure.

He grunted. He was no kid anymore. He was a man, and he could think for himself—and there was one thought he could not endure. That was the thought of the long empty time ahead of him without Reve.

But there was not going to be any empty time. He was going to have her—on her terms, if that was the only way possible. He was going to have her, and he did not care what he had to do to get her.

9

Dogs barked. Children screamed suddenly. A woman who was sunbathing yelled, as Dan moved across street and yard, going south and east in a wide circle around the highway roadblock, but always moving toward downtown Los Reyes.

He was breathing through his open mouth. He did not slow down, and he no longer looked over his shoulder, though he knew the prowl car cops had reported his running from them back there.

He no longer cared about that. That was miles behind him. He had moved fast and he had kept moving.

Dan stepped into the telephone booth near the intersection of Lafayette and Park. He closed the door, feeling the touch of the small concealed ceiling fan on his sweaty face.

He leaned against the side of the booth a moment, panting.

He watched the cars. The traffic was heavy along here, even in the middle of the afternoon. It seemed to him there were a lot of police cars in that traffic, but maybe there were no more than usual. He had learned one truth about running. When you were on the run, all you saw was cops.

He found some change in his pocket, picked out a dime, dropped it in the phone slot. He fumbled in his pocket and found the wrinkled, smudged piece of paper he had been carrying with him for the past three weeks. On it was scrawled a telephone number.

He held the paper spread out beside the phone and dialed, slowly, carefully. He could afford no mistakes.

He stood there with the receiver pressed against his ear, listening to the phone ringing. He let it ring and go on ringing.

At last he gave up. He glanced out at the busy street, cursing under his breath. He slapped the receiver back on its hook, fingered his dime out of the return slot.

He stepped out of the booth, still holding the dime in his fist. He had always been impatient. He hated waiting for anything.

He looked at the wrinkled scrap of paper. He folded it carefully, pushed it back into his pocket.

He grinned wryly. He did not know why he was so careful with that scrap of paper. There was no problem about his remembering the telephone number written on it. He wondered if he would ever be able to forget it.

He walked away from the telephone booth to the curb, looking both ways. A cab was waiting in a hack zone. He walked over, got in and slammed the door.

"Yes, sir? Where you want to go?"

"Riverlane Apartments," Dan said. "You know where that is?"

"Think so. On Terrace Drive, near the hospital."

Dan sank back in the car. His legs ached, now that he was resting them after that relentless plodding across town. The taxi pulled away from the curb and Dan laid his head back, thinking nothing at all except that he was tired.

His eyes were closed when the driver pulled the taxi up to the curb.

"All right, mister. Here we are."

Dan opened his eyes. He sat forward, fumbling some change from his pocket. He paid his fare and stepped out on the walk. The Riverlane was not far from downtown Los Reyes, in a quiet area, near the river and the express drive.

The cab pulled away and Dan stood a moment on the walk looking up at the tan brick building, the wan sun glittering in the upper windows. It was modest—not the sort of pad that Vera had nested in back in Houston. Maybe a lot of things had changed in two years—but with Vera, he doubted it.

He walked up the steps to the foyer, feeling a quickening beat inside his chest. He did not know whether it was the old hatred, or if it was just the feeling he always got when he was going to see Vera again after a long time.

His eyes narrowed and he laughed at himself, bitterly and silently.

He pushed open the heavy front door and went to the row of mailboxes with the tenants' names and apartment numbers on them. He found the name he was seeking. She lived in apartment 306.

Dan pressed the button fifteen times, holding it down with his thumb. Nothing happened.

The foyer was quiet, the whole building was silent in the hot afternoon, and this really was unlike any place where Vera had ever bedded down before. She was a girl who liked plenty of life, plenty of lights and laughter.

He glanced around the foyer, looked at the elevator a moment, decided against it. Instead, he walked to the stairs and climbed them slowly, feeling the harsh urgency mounting in him at every step.

Dan opened the doorway onto the third floor. He glanced along the corridor: it was empty. There were windows open at both ends, a fire escape showing through one of them. There were several apartments on this floor, all of them with doors closed, all silent.

He went along the carpeted corridor, paused outside 306. He stared, eyes chilled at the number, hating even the room she lived in.

He stabbed the doorbell with his thumb. He let the bell ring, though he could not hear it, here in the corridor. It gave him a mild pleasure to know it was wailing inside that room, even though Vera was not in there to be tormented by the ringing.

It occurred to him that she might have run.

No. She couldn't know—not yet. And even if she did know, it would not matter. She could not get away from him this time.

A woman with a small dog came out of a doorway down the corridor. She glanced toward Dan standing outside 306, but showed no surprise.

A thick potted palm was set by the window at the end of the corridor. Dan walked to the window, sat down on the sill. After a moment, he moved the potted palm away from the wall and sat down again, almost concealed behind the deep green fronds.

He felt the sun at his back, felt the weariness flooding through him. He stared at the door of 306, waiting. She had to come back some time. When she did, he would be here.

He heard the hum of the elevator. He had been sitting there almost an hour, leaning against the windowsill. He yawned repeatedly, but it was tension more than fatigue.

The elevator stopped. The doors opened and she stepped out. At first Dan did not know her. Who would ever be looking for a black-haired Vera Flynn?

But it was

Vera, all right. The look of that body, the way she walked, the click of those high, sharp heels.

He sat there, chilled, staring at her, hearing the click of her heels as she walked, and remembering her, remembering everything about her. She had not seen him yet, and for that moment, he sat there looking at her, looking for the girl he had known two years ago in Houston. She was there somewhere, all right, every betraying, two-timing inch of her.

He knew her, remembered her, even changed as she was with black hair. He knew her by the way his heart pounded, the way anger and hurt and desire churned inside him.

He stayed where he was, not breathing, until she put her key into the lock. She had some sort of a bag on her arm; her hair looked mussed, damp—right in character. Wasn't that the way she always came home in the middle of the afternoon—from last night's date?

As she turned the key, Dan came around the palm fast.

Vera turned and stared. Her eyes widened as she recognized him. Her mouth sagged open. She did not make a sound, but Dan knew she was screaming silently behind that rigid, starkly white mask.

10

Virgil Hawkins stood across Captain Tay Jones' desk in the frame administration building at Prison Farm Twenty-Eight.

"You want what, Virgil?" Captain Jones frowned up at him, left eye squinted against the cigar smoke curling up the side of his face.

"My vacation."

"Just like that?" Jones chewed the cigar across his mouth, squinted his right eye.

"Yes, sir. It's been due me now 'most two years. But I figured, way thing were, you people needed me pretty bad, and I kept putting it off."

Jones shook his head. "And now when we had a break, you figure is a real good time to ask for your time off?"

"Yes, sir. That there break is part of the reason I want to get off."

Jones laughed. "You got some idea you can run down that Ferrel, when the best police in the country has let him slip right through their fingers?"

"I know these cons, Captain. Now, you got to give me that. I know these here men. I know how they think."

"Hawkins, I can tell you this. That Ferrel would outthink you in a revolving door."

"Maybe, Captain. But maybe not. Like I say, I know a lot about these men. I know who they git their mail from, things like that. I know how to track down these men, 'cause I know how they think, and I know the people they know."

Jones stared up at Hawkins through the cigar smoke. "You didn't look real good up against Ferrel out on that highway today, Virge."

"No, sir. I got to give you that, all right. I didn't. But I could of got him, right there, if'n I hadn't knowed if I did, I'd lose some of them other cons."

"I'm finding no fault with what you and Kemper done, Virge. I'm just telling you that running a man like Ferrel down ain't your job."

"No, sir. But like I say, I know about these here men, and the people that come to see them, and the ones that write to them. I even know about the notes they kite out, even when they think I don't. You got to give me that. And then, there's this other thing. This Ferrel breaking from one of my work gangs, that don't look good on my record. Now, I tell you, Captain, I purely hate to have a blot like that on my record. That there's another reason why I'm asking you to give me some time off, starting today."

"What about the investigation, Virge? The men from the prison department will be here. They'll want to talk to you."

"You know where to find me, Captain. You know where I live, and you can git in touch with me mighty easy. You know how much red tape them prison board people go through—it'll be weeks before they get around to questioning me."

Jones laughed. "I got to give you that," he said.

Dottie Hawkins padded into the bedroom while Virgil was packing a clean shirt and some underclothes in a small canvas weekend bag.

Virgil tensed when he heard her coming across the bare pine floor toward him. She was barefooted, and her fat, flat feet made a slapping sound with every step she took.

He hated and despised the thought of turning around and looking at her.

"Where you goin', Virge?"

He talked into the open bag. "I got to be away a few days, Dottie."

"Where you going?" she asked again, her voice sharpening.

He straightened, jerked his head around. He winced, looking at her. Her brown, lifeless hair was caught in a loose bun at the back of her head and secured with a rubber band off the morning newspaper. Dottie always padded out every morning in her nightgown, her hair loose around her face. Then she wound her hair on her fist while she read the newspaper and drank the first of her dozen cups of black coffee, and when she got a knot of her hair in a bun, she snapped the rubber band from the newspaper around it.

"I tol' you, Dottie. I got work to do."

"Where?"

"Out of town."

"Where, out of town?"

"I don't rightly know yet. I go where they send me, Dottie." He blinked hard, thinking he would be glad to get away from her, the bulbous body in those stained, soiled dresses, the briar scratches on her bare legs. God, you'd think she would know how a man hated to look at a woman that let herself go to pot.

"You takin' your vacation, Virge Hawkins?"

"What makes you think that?"

"Be you? Be you taking your vacation, without me?"

"Dottie, now, damn it, you listen here to me. I got a job to do. I go where they send me. That's all."

It was as if he had not spoken. "If you are taking your vacation, Virgil Hawkins, you just better tell me right now. Hit won't take me hardly no time at all to git ready to go with you—"

"I tol' you, damn it, woman, I ain't. I ain't taking no vacation!" He was sweating. It was always like this when he tried to talk to her. She talked, but she never listened.

"If'n you are takin' your vacation, Virgil, and tryin' to sneak off somewhere without me, just don't you try to come back here, that's all. I work all the time, around here. I work and I clean—"

"My God, I'd like to see some of that. I really would. I'd like to see some of the cleaning you do. I'd sure like to see some of the work you do. You don't do a blessed thing but sit on your fat tail and keep the coffee perking."

"I'm the one been wantin' a vacation, Virgil. I been beggin' you to take me away from here somewheres. All the other wives go someplace. But you never take me no place. You make me stay home, and you never take me no place at all, Virgil Hawkins."

He shrugged …

It was after six before Hawkins could get into Sheriff Whiteside's office in Los Reyes.

Virgil spread his prison credentials on the desk before the sheriff. "That there's who I am, Sheriff."

Whiteside glanced up. He was a slender man, weighing less than a hundred and forty pounds. His hair was silky white. It had been a long day. The whole department was alive with phone calls and reports on the escaped convict. Whiteside had not even had time to stop for lunch. Now it was time for dinner, and it looked as if he would miss that, too.

"You the man that Ferrel escaped from, on Highway 48?"

Hawkins felt his thick-jowled face grow warm. He nodded. "Yes, sir.

It was a bad thing. I got to admit that. He caught us flatfooted."

"What you want here?"

"Captain Jones give me a little time off."

"Suspension?"

"No, sir. Nothing like that. I asked for this time off. You see, I know a lot about these cons that I guard. I keep a close tab on them. I mean, it always pays off. The people that visit them, that they write to, even the ones they kite letters out to. So I asked the Captain to let me come over and see if I could get on as special deputy with you—until this here Ferrel is caught and brought back."

He kept his voice level and his face expressionless. He did not add that he was going to hunt Ferrel down, even if the sheriff said no.

Whiteside frowned. "God knows, we can use some special deputies, especially if they know their job. You know when a con makes a break— really gets away—it's bad, as bad as it is rare—"

"Yes, sir."

"Most of them got no plans beyond the minute they make their break. If one of them makes a clean break, that means he's a smart cookie, and he's thought ahead. He can be a dangerous man."

"Yes, sir. That's the way I feel. That's why I wanted to go after him."

Whiteside looked at the bulge under Hawkins' cheap coat.

"You're not gun-happy, Hawkins?"

"What you mean, Sheriff?"

"I don't know. If I send you out for this man, we want him brought back alive, you understand that?"

"I'll give him ever' chance to give hisself up, Sheriff. You look at my record there. I got a mighty good record. You got to give me that. I've got a good record, and this here con's break today ain't going to spoil it. I'll find him."

Whiteside sat there for a long time. He looked at the credentials, and then up at the huge man across the desk. At last he nodded. "All right, Hawkins. I'll assign you to a plainclothes deputy of mine named Manton. You'll work with him. He knows the town, and you know that con. It just might pay off."

Hawkins walked out of the office, feeling the excitement and anxiety welling up like a painful sweetness. He was going to work with some deputy. That did not matter—all that mattered was that Dan Ferrel was running loose. And this time he knew. He would give Ferrel a chance to stop before he shot him, but Ferrel was not going to stop. Ferrel would turn and run, and nobody could ever say he had not given Ferrel every chance to stop.

He was breathing heavily as he walked, sensing the hard bite of anticipation, the tension, the blood throbbing in a vein that stood pencil-thick at his temple.

11

"Hello, Vera," Dan said.

A muscle twitched at the corner of her mouth. She looked both ways along the corridor. In that second she looked like a trapped cat.

She trembled suddenly, turning, and he moved swiftly, capturing her arm in a motion that was almost gentle.

With his other hand, Dan turned the key, pushed the door open, and with the slightest touch on her arm, forced her into her apartment ahead of him.

When they were inside, he gave her a sudden shove toward the small tan divan. She tried to catch herself, lost her balance and toppled on it.

Dan turned his back, removed the key from the lock, closed the door.

When he turned around, she was sprawled on the couch as she had fallen, like a cheap doll, dress high over her knees, golden legs tinged pink by a recent sunburn.

He kept his voice level. "Black hair becomes you, Vera. How long have you been a brunette?"

She went on staring up at him, unable to speak. He stood over her, glancing around the room—taking in the portable television set, the folding breakfast table in a corner, the alcove kitchen, the small bedroom through an open door, in the disorder he remembered so well—taking in everything except the gold of her legs, the upthrust breasts, the almost immoral suggestiveness of her velvety mouth. No man could imagine the kind of exquisite hell this girl offered unless he had had her. God help him, he had been there.

His voice betrayed nothing he was thinking, remembering. "Very modest pad, Vera—for a doll with a taste for mink—and morals to match."

Vera was a smart girl, too. When he did not kill her in the first two minutes, she knew he was not going to kill her—unless she pushed him too far. Some of the fear went out of her eyes; the rigid muscles in her cheeks relaxed. The fear in her eyes was replaced by a misty softness. God, how phony that look was, he thought—how many times had he seen that same look while she was mouthing the nakedest lies?

Then for a moment, there was a look in Vera's face that almost matched the bitter hunger he felt inside. It threw him off stride, and he refused to see it.

"Dan." Her whisper was soft.

She moved her tongue across her lips, looking up at him. His fists tightened. *Oh, no, baby.* They could always drive each other crazy, but it had never lasted past the beautyrest, not even at first—not even when he had been fool enough to think it did. He had heard about Vera, even at the first—there were always people anxious to tell him about Vera.

"Dan," she whispered again. She did not move.

He winced. For a moment he had no defense against her. He had been caged a long time, and what she had done to him in Houston was two years old, and now she was sprawled before him on that couch....

They stared at each other, their gazes locked, his gray eyes against the pale blue of Vera's. Two animals ready to be at each other's throats— a man and a woman who could not stay away from each other, though they made their lives a hell together.

Vera recovered first. Why not? She had been free on the nightclub circuit while he had been swinging a yo-yo in prison farm eight-spots.

She sat up slowly, slapping her skirt down across he knees. Her eyes glinted.

Her voice raked him with sharp claws. "What are you doing here?"

His tone matched hers. "I might ask you the same thing."

"What does that mean?"

"Who is Areva Storm?"

She shrugged. "One name's as good as another."

"Change them like the color of your hair, eh?"

She stared up at him. "I asked you—what do you want here?"

"Heard you were in town."

Her eyes got wary again, troubled, but she kept her voice level. "Did you?"

"I've heard a lot about you, Vera."

"How nice! I've heard a lot about you, too. Killing a man—getting life in prison. Violent Dan Ferrel. At least, you haven't changed."

He shrugged his coat up on his shoulders. "But you have, Vera, from what I heard."

"Oh?" She waited again, barely daring to breathe.

"Yes. I heard you were working a little sideline besides your usual singing-and-mixing at the clubs."

"I sing in clubs. I mix if I want to. Only if I want to."

"Sure. But I never saw you when you didn't want to."

Something flickered in her eyes. But this was an old dialogue with them; she was not going to start that again. "What do you want, Dan?"

"I want to know about this sideline."

Her hand clenched on the plastic beach bag in her lag. "What sideline? What are you talking about?"

"About you. I knew you went in for some mild prostitution—"

"Oh? Did you?" She bit her lip.

"Well, maybe you don't call it that. Sleeping with rich men for rich presents. But there's some name for it. It's just that I don't know the polite word for it—all I know is 'whore'."

"Sure. That's all you want to know."

"I didn't come here to talk about me. I want to know about this new gimmick of yours—armed robbery, isn't it?"

She caught her breath.

"I don't know what you're talking about … as usual."

"Don't you?"

"You always came up with the wildest accusations."

"Sure. But here you are in Los Reyes. A thousand miles from Houston—as the bat flies."

"You say things so sweetly."

"I don't feel sweet, baby. I'm standing here now waiting for you to start lying. Waiting for your first lie. Want me to help you? You came here from Houston to be near ol' Dan, eh? Down here waitin' for me, sugar?"

"Sure, Dan."

"Singing in clubs, while you wait? Not planning any little robbery on the side?"

Her voice dripped poison. "Where'd you ever get such a fool idea?"

He bent forward, face taut. "Not pulling any caper, chick?"

She stared up at him, eyes wide and empty, as empty as her voice. "Why, Dan, how could I? Alone?"

He straightened. "That's why I'm here. That's what I want to know."

"Why, Dan, you're still jealous."

His tone mocked her. "Am I, chick? Why, until I met you I'd never been jealous of anybody, anything. It's something I learned, trying to live with you. Maybe I learned it too well. Maybe it's not easy to change, once you catch it."

She tossed the bag to the couch beside her, shrugged. "Well, I'm not pulling any job, Dan. Not alone—and I don't have anybody to help me."

"No man to help you?"

"Strange as it sounds." She opened the plastic bag, found a pack of cigarettes, a lighter. She brought them out, holding them tightly, almost crushing the pack so he could not see her hands tremble.

He saw it anyway. His mouth twisted. "Thought if you were planning something, you might need an expert's touch."

Her head jerked up, and her eyes changed. Her face was abruptly drawn, a taut mask over something she did not want to talk about, something she was afraid of. She scratched a speck of tobacco from her underlip with her little fingernail, tilted her chin.

"Are you an expert at theft, Dan? I didn't know that."

"I've done a lot of things in my time—and I'm expert at anything I do."

She laughed sharply. "Sure. You're an expert—at beating women. You had plenty of practice on me."

For a brief moment neither of them spoke, and in their minds was the same thought, the same painful memory.

In Dan's mind, the memory was knotted sick and cold: he relived it in nightmares. It was the last time he had seen Vera in Houston.

He had been in a bar that afternoon because the kind of gambling he handled needed bar whisky, even in Texas.

He could not even remember the face of the man that told him Vera was up in their apartment playing house with Ollie Lamb. The man's face was a red blur. He sat on that stool, and everything in Houston was a sudden red blur.

He walked out, and went along the street in the sun. He passed people, walking slowly, whistling tunelessly between his teeth, not seeing the people, not knowing he was whistling.

He was thinking that lately he and Vera had fought mostly about his jealous rages. She accused him of spying on her. And yet, it wasn't true. If somebody brought a rumor to him and he did go looking for her, he never wanted to find her faithless, all he ever wanted was to find that she was true to him. He gave her every chance, every time, to be where she ought to be, doing what she was supposed to be doing, and often when he didn't find her where she ought to be, he had wasted time looking for her there first, and when he did find her there was no trace of her betrayal—except the look of guilt in her face, and the defiant denials.

What a lovely life!

When he reached the apartment house, he saw Ollie Lamb's big black Cad parked half way down the block. There were a hell of a lot of Cads in Houston, and he told himself that it could be some other black Fleetwood, even when he knew it was Ollie Lamb's—recognized the odd emblem on the license plate.

He walked into the building and went up the stairs, even though the elevator would have been quicker.

He put his key in the lock, turned it, found the inside latch was thrown. It did not take much to snap that latch. He didn't even feel the pain in his hand when he struck it.

The door slammed back and he stepped into the room.

They stood there where they had leaped up when he broke the latch—staring at him, neither of them able to speak.

Big, fat Ollie Lamb was wearing his shirt, tie still snug in its collar, his underpants, garters on his thick legs, silk hose and highly polished black slippers.

Vera was in a powder-blue chiffon shortie nightgown. It was more sensuous than nakedness; it gave a blue cast to the rise and depth of her breasts and the darkness at her loins.

He did not see either one of them very well.

Ollie Lamb's loose jowls quivered. He looked around for his coat and his shoulder holster. Ollie Lamb was a big man in gambling, but he looked fat and gross and sweaty in his shirt and underpants, and he looked helpless as a kewpie doll with his gun on the other side of the room.

His gaze struck his hat and trousers and shoulder holster on the club chair under the reading lamp.

Dan's gaze moved with Ollie's, and when he saw the clothes on the chair, he walked over to them. All Ollie could see was his gun on top of the jacket and pants. He managed to speak. "What you going to do?"

Dan glanced at him over his shoulder, but did not answer. He wadded up the two-hundred-dollar suit and the gun with holster. He stood a moment with them wadded in his fists. Then he walked over to the window of the fifth-floor apartment. He dropped the bundle out the window, did not even glance to see it hit the street.

He walked back to where they stood, unmoving.

He said, "What are you doing here, Ollie?"

When Ollie opened his mouth to speak, Dan hit him in the teeth. Ollie staggered back against the wall, blood spurting from his mouth.

He spoke through the blood. "You're never going to get away with this, Ferrel."

The blood was spurting fast now, streaking Ollie's imported linen shirt. Dan took a step toward him.

Ollie cringed against the wall, trying to press his fat body into it. He cried out, "I let you operate in this town. But no more, Ferrel. No more."

Dan's fists came up and Ollie screamed, a sound like a woman makes, and threw both his arms over his bloodied face to protect it. Dan drove his fist wrist-deep into Ollie's fat stomach.

Ollie folded, dropping his arms to press against his huge middle. He wretched dryly, gasping, toppling forward.

Dan caught him by the shirt collar, twisting it. He snagged him by the seat of his pale green underpants, waltzing him toward the apartment door.

He drove Ollie's head against the wall, opened the door, and then marched Ollie through it toward the stairwell. People were out in the corridors watching, and some of them laughed. Ollie tried to writhe free when he saw the stairwell. He grasped at the newel post, but Dan pushed him by it, throwing him down the steps.

He re-entered the apartment. Vera had not moved.

He stopped in front of her. "Aren't you going to lie?" His voice was low, but it was shaking.

"Dan, I couldn't help it."

"Oh, my God!"

"He was looking for you. Said he was going to wait."

"You made him comfortable."

"I didn't want to, Dan. My God, there's nobody but you. Haven't you got sense enough to know that?"

He caught the sheer gown, ripped it off her. He drove his fist into her stomach, and slapped her across the head when she doubled up.

She landed hard on her knees, grabbing him around the legs. Dan tried to pull free. She clung to him.

"Dan, please." She was wailing, sobbing, choking. "I didn't want to."

He bent down, caught her hair. His voice was wild and hoarse—he did not even recognize it anymore. He was insane. He knew wildly that he was insane. "Don't lie to me anymore. Not anymore."

"I'm not lying, Dan. I love you. My God, I'll make it up to you … do anything, Dan. I won't ever let anybody near me again—ever—Oh, God, Dan, believe me."

He twisted his fist in her hair until her eyes pulled in at the corners, slanting.

He slapped her with his other hand, back and forth across the face.

"Dan, you're killing me." She could barely speak.

"God, I hope so. My God, I hope so." He did not stop hitting her.

She clung tighter to his legs, pulling her naked body up against him, burying her red, burning face against him.

"I didn't want him—I hate him—"

"Stop lying. Haven't you got any sense? Don't you know I'm going to kill you if you don't stop lying?"

"Kill me. Kill me," she sobbed. "I love you—I'll make it up to you."

That enraged him still more. It was always like that. No matter what she did, she could always smooth it over, she could always make it up to him.

"He was with you on that couch. Naked with you. On that couch." His voice was hurting his raw throat now. "Why do you lie anymore?"

"He was trying to excite me. Doing anything to excite me."

"Doing a strip tease, bitch? Is that what he was doing?"

"I can't help it, Dan—I didn't want him—I only want you."

"Well, that's too damned bad."

His hand twisted. He brought his clenched fist up to smash it into her face again. But he stopped. Her face was swollen, welted, turning purple, and her mouth was bleeding, and blood was pouring from her nose and a cut along her eye. He stared at her, and did not even recognize her anymore.

But her breasts, her lovely, soft breasts. They were pure and untouched. The sight of them roused his desire and, angry with himself, he threw her to the couch on her belly. With insane intensity he pounded her soft buttocks until they throbbed and welled. She screamed bloody murder but he could no longer control himself. He let down his pants. He crawled on top of her, feeling the soft fullness of her mauled and reddening hips. And then he had her. He took her like a savage. She squirmed and lashed her legs with the pain of it, but with the excitement of it, too. Her screaming stopped and her breath came in great gasps as with hands on her breasts he exerted the madness of his manhood. He plumbed the deep velvety wonder of her in rocking fury, forcing her to the same burst of unbearable bliss that rocketed through his own loins.

"You stinker," she moaned. "You cruel, wonderful stinker. What you do to me—"

He thrust her away from him. At that moment the telephone rang.

She was sprawled on the floor, the remnants of the sheer blue gown hanging over her shoulders, her face pressed into the rug.

He stared down at her, and then looked at the jangling telephone.

He lifted the receiver. He could barely speak. "Yeah?"

"Is this the apartment of Vera Flynn?" It was a man's voice.

Dan glanced at her on the floor. "Yeah."

"Well, look, friend, is Vera around?"

"What do you want with her?"

"Well, this is Bernie Jacobs, her agent at Texas Artists. I got a rush call for her—a really big spot in New Orleans. Three-week guarantee. If I could talk to her—"

Dan glanced at Vera on the rug. His hand tightened on the receiver. "You better kill that booking, friend. Vera won't be taking any engagements anywhere for the next few weeks—not the way she looks."

Jacobs was still talking, but Dan replaced the receiver. He turned and walked out of the apartment.

That was two years ago, in Houston.

12

Dan prowled the small front room. Vera smoked, pulling long nervous drafts at her cigarette. Then suddenly, as if becoming aware of it, she ground it out viciously in the bowl of an ashtray beside her.

Dan spoke at last. "I had plenty of reason to beat you in Houston, baby."

She shrugged. "All right. And I've got plenty of reasons to hate you. But I only need one. I hate you because I hate you. So why don't you get out of here and let me alone?"

"Would you like that, Vera?"

"I got along fine after you left me in Houston. I lived fine, once I got rid of you."

"Did you?" His mouth twisted. "I hear Ollie Lamb got laughed out of Houston. Wandering through the streets with his pants down. They laughed him out."

Her voice was flat. "I never needed Ollie. Any more than I needed you."

"You never needed any one man. You always had a line of them."

She stared up at him in stony silence. He remembered she had always been like that—make her angry and she turned to granite, silent and immobile.

She got up and walked past Dan, almost brushing him in a careless gesture. She went to an all-band radio on a side table, switched it on, stood watching its dial face light up. The radio crackled, warming up, and he laughed bitterly. She had it tuned to the police band.

"Too bad you didn't get home sooner, chick. You'd have known I was loose. You could have run."

"I'm through running from you, Dan." She turned and faced him, the radio crackling behind her. "As far as I'm concerned, you don't even exist."

A man's voice came up in volume on the police band. "Dan Ferrel is thirty-two years old, six feet tall. Dark brown hair, deeply indented at temples. Gray eyes. No distinguishing marks. Last seen escaping prison work gang on Highway 48 in blue 1954 sedan. The car has been located in a swamp area near Los Reyes. Also found were charred remains of convict fatigues. A dark-haired woman was seen with Ferrel in the escape car. Ferrel has a long police record, is probably armed—"

"They know you, too," Vera said.

The radio rode over her voice. "He is believed to be in Los Reyes. All units be on constant alert. This is priority. Priority. Repeat—"

With a cold smile on her mouth, Vera reached behind her, tuned out the voice, but did not snap off the radio.

"They miss you, Danny boy."

"To know me is to love me."

She went back to the table, shook out a cigarette, lighted it. The trembling in her hands was less noticeable now. "Why don't you go back and give yourself up, like a good little convict?"

He walked close to her, stood looking down at the crown of her black hair. "Sure. As soon as you and I are checked out on this new guy you got."

She turned, then backed away a step when she realized he was standing almost pressed against her.

"Go on, talk crazy. Maybe back in Houston you had some right to say who I saw, what I did. You don't have that right anymore."

"Maybe I'm renewing my license."

"I told you. There's nobody."

"You told me that in Houston, too."

A small muscle worked in her jaw.

"Let me alone, Dan. Let me alone. There's nobody. But even if there was, I've got a right to live my life without asking your permission."

He ignored this. "I heard there was a guy. Who is he, Vera?"

She flared up bitterly. "You haven't changed. Tough. Got to have your way. Listen to nobody—Well, not anymore. Not with me, Dan—I've had it. In Houston, I was mixed up. I admit that. I wasn't cheating—but you wouldn't marry me. You kept putting me off. Other men offered to marry me—"

"Ollie Lamb?" His laugh was cold.

"All right. Ollie Lamb. He said he'd marry me. All I had to do was say so. I was afraid to run him away for good. You—might walk out on me—any night. And where would I be? I was afraid to trust you. What did I ever get from you but promises?"

He spoke in a casual tone. "I never made a promise in my life I didn't keep."

She talked over him, not listening to him. "I was afraid to trust you—and Ollie Lamb had plenty of dough. He offered to marry me—which is a hell of a lot more than you ever did. I was nice to him—and that was all."

"So nice." He tried to keep his voice flat, but the old memory still hurt, even after two years.

She laughed bitterly, moving away from him. "I was saving Ollie Lamb—for a rainy day, that was all. For that rainy night when you walked out on me. But I loved you, fellow. Oh, how I loved you. But you fixed little Vera, didn't you? Did you know I was a hospital emergency case after you got through with me? Or didn't you care?"

"I didn't care."

"Well, that's how I feel about you now. Now it's different. Now I know what I want."

She stared at him, her eyes ice-cold.

He took a step toward her, fists clenched. He felt the old rage wanting to smash that smile off her face.

Vera shrugged past him, went to the radio again. She turned up the volume.

"Repeat. All units. Dan Ferrel is believed to be in Los Reyes. Roadblocks have been set up at all highway exits. Code six-hundred-nine. Repeat. Code six-hundred-nine. All units. This man will be armed. He is a dangerous fugitive."

Dan strode to her and caught her arm, tightening his fist. But she showed no pain, merely twisted free.

"They do know my Danny boy, don't they?"

"Maybe they do, baby—but you don't. Or maybe you've got a short memory. I'm here for one reason. I want to talk to this new guy of yours. I don't waste time, Vera. You get on that phone, and you call this new guy. Tell him to come over here."

"Another little scene like in Houston?"

"Maybe. Quit stalling—call him." He jerked his head toward the telephone.

Her gaze met his. "You can't make me do that."

He stepped toward her. She took a deep breath, tried to slip past him, but Dan barred her way. He saw the fear in her eyes again, and felt a sudden emptiness. This was all she had left for him—fear and hatred.

He felt a sick need to hold her in his arms and kiss away that smoke of fear—hold her until everything evil melted out of both of them, and only their need for each other was left.

He breathed deeply. That was what he wanted—but that was what he had wanted in Houston, when he found her with fat Ollie Lamb. He was not going to let it stop him now, either.

"Get smart, sugar, just once. I'm in the pen for life. What else can they do to me?"

"They can burn you—"

"No. You did that to me, doll, back in Houston. I'm already burned out—a dead man. But I've got a lot of reasons for coming to see you, no matter what they do to me—when they get me again. You want to hear those reasons?"

She pressed her eyes shut, shook her head. "No."

"Why, baby, I'm in for life because they say I killed a hired gun punk. He drew a gun on me. Right here in Los Reyes, outside a Spanish restaurant called Las Noches. You know what he said to me, sugar, just before he took a shot at me?"

She shuddered, turned away. "No—"

His voice was relentless. "He pulled his gun and he said. 'This is from Vera. She said to tell you, first.'"

She chewed her underlip, staring at him with her eyes wide.

He laughed coldly. "But it's too bad, Vera. He didn't quite get me with that first one—"

She pressed her hands against her face.

"I never told them that in court, Vera. I never told them the doll I loved in Houston sent a hired thug to kill me. But we know, don't we, baby?"

She whispered, "Dan, I—"

"Don't worry about it, doll. It wouldn't have helped anyway. Self-defense was no plea for a bad boy with a record. I didn't even try." His voice lowered, becoming suddenly deadly. "And when they get me for killing you, I won't even tell them you could have stayed alive—just by leveling with me."

Vera stared at him a long time, with no sign of tears. Her face was expressionless.

Dan said, "So why don't you just call lover boy and get him over here?"

Vera stared at him a long time. Finally, she shrugged and pushed past him to the telephone. He turned, watching her. He snapped off the radio.

She opened the Los Reyes telephone book, thumbed through it.

His voice mocked her. "Come on now, Vera. You, having to look up your boyfriend's number?"

He took a step toward her as she went on moving her hand along the column of numbers.

She heard him, glanced up over her shoulder, almost frantic. Her face was white now, but she kept her voice level.

"He's at work. I don't know the lab number, where he works."

Dan waited. Vera shut the book, dialed. He sagged a little, aware of the tight constriction across his chest, and the weariness. He felt as though he had been running all his life—running scared.

Someone answered Vera's call, and she spoke in a fast, frantic monotone, trying to get it all said:

"This is apartment 306, Riverlane Apartments. Fugitive Dan Ferrel is here. He's armed. He's threatening to kill me."

Dan took two long strides, hit her on the side of the head. She went sprawling across the room, and the telephone bounced out of her grasp. She crumpled to the floor.

Dan stood looking at her a moment, then lifted the receiver.

A man's voice said loudly, "Hello. Hello. What's wrong there?"

"Nothing, officer. My wife is—disturbed. She's under a psychiatrist's care. She always calls the police—every time there's a new sensational case."

The man was saying something, but Dan did not listen. He put the receiver gently back in its cradle.

13

Vera sat up from the floor, shaking her head to clear it.

Dan's voice was sharp. "One more cross, eh, Vera? Right in character."

He looked around the room, then back at her. His mouth was twisted.

"No harm done, baby. Maybe inconvenienced me a little. I thought we could see your boyfriend here. But you fixed that. So come on. We get out of here, fast."

She shook her head at him. He laughed coldly. "Oh, we're still going to see him, doll. Don't you ever doubt that."

When she did not get up, Dan strode to her. He reached down, snagged her mussed, damp hair in his fist and yanked her up to her feet.

Vera caught her balance when he released her. She stared at him, eyes wild. In her face he saw how terribly the hatred had festered inside her during the past two years. Or was it all hate?

She wheeled suddenly and ran for the door. Dan took a long stride, caught her arm, swung her around.

As she came around, she brought her hands up, clawing at his face. He jerked his head back, caught her wrist, then her other arm, holding her at arm's length.

She writhed, mewling. She brought her knee up, trying to kick him, but he twisted her body. She moaned, sagging in against him suddenly.

Her breasts speared at him, flattening against his chest, and he could feel the raging pound of her heart against him, and even knowing it was the rage of hatred, his own heart quickened, responding. She pressed in, moving her hips, rolling her body against his body, pushing up until her mouth mashed against his. For a second he could not even see her through the sudden flare of red. He dropped her arms and pulled her closer against him.

He could feel her long fingernails clawing through his jacket, digging at him, and he felt the way she moved her body against his. He heard the sound of their frantic breathing, and the pound of blood in his temples.

And then, distantly, cutting through, came the sound of a police siren.

Dan lifted his head, freeing his mouth from hers. Still panting, he stared down into her flushed face. Even her kisses were phony—grabbing him like this was the same kind of double cross that calling the cops had been a moment ago.

He tried to pull away from her. She moaned, clinging to him, but he was not fooled anymore. The sound of the siren was louder now. He caught her by the shoulders and held her away at arm's length.

"You won't slow me down like this, Vera, so they can catch me here. We're getting out of here. You got a car?"

Her voice was flat. "No."

He shoved her aside, went to the couch.

The telephone rang, abrupt and loud. Vera shivered, moved toward it.

Dan gestured downward sharply. "Forget it."

She shrugged and turned away. The telephone went on ringing. Dan grabbed up the plastic beach bag from the couch, clawed inside it.

His fingers closed on a key ring. He brought the car keys up from the bag, tossed the bag at her. She caught it, drew it closed, stood there holding it.

The phone's ringing filled the whole apartment, shrill, maddening.

"All right, let's go." Dan jerked his head toward the door.

Vera shrugged, moved to the door. She did not even glance back. This place meant no more to her than any of a hundred other pads she had bedded down in during the past two years.

Dan walked past the telephone, lifted the receiver, replaced it. The ringing stopped.

He strode close behind her. She opened the apartment door, stepped out into the corridor.

"How long do you expect to stay free, wandering around like this!"

"Long enough."

She moved toward the elevator, but he caught her arm. "We'll use the stairs."

She shrugged again. He gripped her above the right elbow and they descended the stairs. As they rounded the landing, she moved toward the stairwell on the second floor. But Dan stopped her.

He glanced along the corridor. "We'll use the back stairs."

Her cold laugh mocked him. "You are running scared."

"I have, baby, all my life."

She glanced at him over her shoulder. "You just think you have," she said. "They're after you now, with guns."

"They always were."

"I hope when they shoot you, you don't die right away. A man like you ought to have time to think about it."

"Just move faster," he said, thrusting her ahead of him to the service stairs. "And don't talk so much. You're not going to delay me here until they catch me, no matter how hard you try."

She shrugged.

They reached the bottom of the stairs, crossed the square entry to the side door.

Dan tightened his hand on Vera's arm, forcing her to slow down. He pushed open the door, checked the service alley and the small parking lot beside it.

"Okay, let's go."

He pulled her after him, the heavy door whispering closed behind them.

Dan checked the keys on the ring as they walked. There were only three cars in the parking lot. One of them was an elderly Oldsmobile convertible. He glanced at the key, at Vera, at the Olds and moved her toward it.

He squinted against the orange brilliance of the late afternoon sun. It was bright, glinting, reflected in all the windows.

Vera moved slowly, making him propel her across the black-paved parking area.

The siren wailed, coming close.

"I warn you, Vera—if they pull in here before we get out, I'll use my gun on you first."

"Don't you always?"

But she moved faster, because he widened his steps. He opened the door of the aged convertible, thrust her into the seat.

He slid in under the wheel, put the key into the ignition. The engine burst into life.

He shoved the car into reverse, backed it, changed gears and moved toward the exit. He turned toward the Riverside expressway approach.

As the car straightened, a police cruiser skidded around the corner directly ahead of them, siren dying out.

Dan tightened his hand on the wheel. "Go ahead, baby. Make a move. It'll be your last one, so it had better be a good one."

14

Virgil Hawkins strode back and forth in front of the littered pine desk in Deputy Mannie Manton's office, feeling the impatience and frustration roiling around in his stomach.

"My God, Manton," he said. "We sittin' around here and Ferrel can be a thousand miles away. You got any idea just how many ways a man can git out of a town like this here?"

Mannie Manton was in his early fifties, a mild, thickset man with a shiny bald head and a big nose. He wore no uniform, carried his deputy badge pinned inside his wallet along with his credentials, a snapshot of his wife and several photos of his grandchildren.

He leaned back in his swivel chair, staring up at the special deputy the sheriff had assigned him. He sighed, shaking his head.

"Look, Virgil." His voice was mild. "You was assigned to help me, right?"

Virgil mopped at his sweaty face. He could feel the gun in his pocket banging his hip. "You need help to sit in this coop?"

Manton smiled faintly. "I'm not about to go running off in ten different directions just to please you, either, Virgil. First place, let's consider what we both know about cons on the loose—"

"I know plenty about this Ferrel. You got to give me that."

"I give you that. But cons make a pattern. Either they break and run, not knowing what they're going to do when they get over the wall, and they're caught the first time a posse gets on the trail. Or they break and run with help from outside—and some kind of plan for escape. Now, we know that Ferrel had help—"

"And I know where he got it."

"All right. That's why I'm glad to have you here. But simmer down. We ain't going out with guns drawn. We're going to use our heads. Because we know Ferrel has used his up to now. He got help, he had his escape planned, and part of that plan has worked. Now, let's consider something else."

"My God!" Virgil spread his hands.

Manton glanced up, something glittering in his mild eyes.

"You mind, Virgil?"

"No. Go ahead. Get it over with. He's making tracks while you're jawing."

"Sorry to waste your time. But I can only work my way. So let's get back to Ferrel. Either Ferrel intended to run—in which case he would have gone three other directions. Los Reyes is a cul-de-sac. A trap. A corner, Virgil. Now, if he came here to Los Reyes, he put himself in a corner. Why would he do that? Because he wanted something besides freedom. This Ferrel is looking for somebody—maybe for revenge, for some reason that's good to him. Now, can you tell me who he's looking for?"

Virgil scratched at the back of his thick neck. "Maybe I can."

Manton smiled. "All right. Let's come at it from the other end of the street. You say you know who this Ferrel was in contact with outside the prison farm. Right?"

"That's right. There was this one woman. Come up to see him. Three or four Sundays. Name of Alonzo, May Alonzo. She's a looker."

Manton scrawled the name on the pad.

"All right. What else?"

"He's got a brother here in Los Reyes."

Manton sat forward, leaning on the desk. He was scowling. He stared up at Hawkins a moment under his bushy brows, then checked the file on Ferrel that was spread at his elbow.

"A brother? Got no brother listed here."

"Just the same, he's got one. Here in Los Reyes. I seen letters from him. Read 'em. It's his brother, all right. A younger brother."

"Does he use the same name?"

Virgil massaged the nape of his neck, squinting. Finally he shook his head. "No. I don't think he does. I think the name was Connors. Paul Connors. But it's Ferrel's brother."

Manton scrawled the name on the pad below the name of May Alonzo. He underlined "Connors" three times. "You think the brother arranged the escape?"

Virgil grunted with exasperation. "I don't know, but I can find out fast—if you'll just let me out of here so I can find his brother and that Alonzo dame."

"We'll find the brother, Virgil. Just relax. And I'll have the address on the Alonzo woman in a few minutes. What else can you give me?"

Virgil rested his palms against the cluttered desk, staring down at Manton.

"He was kiting notes out to a hood named Degault."

"I know Degault. Could Degault have set up the escape?"

"Hell, man. I don't know, but—"

"—but you'll find out if I'll just let you out of here," Manton finished. His smile was wry. He made check marks beside the three names on the pad. "Look at it this way, Virgil. Suppose we'd gone bowling out of here the first time you wanted to. I wouldn't even have had this information.

What you want to do, jump in a car and just drive around—gun drawn?"

Virgil snarled. "I'm no more gun-happy than any other cop."

Manton frowned faintly at this. His voice was mild. "Nobody accused you of being gun-happy, Hawkins."

Hawkins flushed, wet his lips. "Well, I just don't cotton to sitting around here on our tails while that man gets away. He broke from my crew, Manton, and I mean to get him back."

Manton shrugged. "And I mean to help you. But the more we know about him and what's in his mind—"

"Lord God! How we going to know what's in his mind?"

"Simple. He escaped. He made good that escape. Then, instead of heading for parts unknown, he came in here to Los Reyes that's surrounded on three sides by water. He has to have a reason for doing that. Is his reason revenge? The man that he killed is no reason anymore. We never proved that anybody set him up to be killed outside the Las Noches. It could have happened. If the man that hired the gunman is here in Los Reyes, Hawkins, we might find Ferrel just by finding that man and staking him out. We might capture Ferrel without moving out of this office."

Virgil swallowed hard. He felt a sudden giddiness in the small, airless office. He wanted out of here. He wanted to find Dan Ferrel. He wanted to see Ferrel stand before him—see Ferrel turn and run ...

His hands shook. He clenched them and dropped them from the desktop. He tried to keep his voice level. "You make it sound real simple."

"It is simple, Hawkins. Either it's simple, or impossible. Now if you can give me some clues about what Ferrel griped about, who he blamed for his being in the gang, anybody—any name—"

Hawkins had stopped thinking. He was sweating, and there was only one thought in his mind: Manton was going to start using that telephone, checking on Degault, Alonzo, Paul Connors. They were going to sit in this small crib of a room while somebody else brought them the answers.

He shook his head, feeling sick.

Manton smiled. "Well, we got some things to go on." He glanced up. "You'll excuse me?"

Virgil nodded, hardly aware of Manton. He stood there, frustrated, feeling the trickle of sweat down his ribs.

He heard Manton's mild voice on the telephone. Manton was giving orders, requesting information, assigning men and teams to their jobs, and there was no more emotion in his tone than if he had been reading a grocery list.

Despite Hawkins' sick hatred for the mild, gray man across that cluttered desk, he felt a grudging admiration for him. Here was a real pro. Sheriff Whiteside was a politician, and Hawkins suddenly realized he would not be here in Manton's office now except that Whiteside was a politician, doing what would please a voter.

Hawkins felt the gun bump his hip again. A smart cookie like Manton, knowing it all the way he did, maybe he already knew why Hawkins had volunteered to hunt Ferrel down. He stared at the floor, afraid to lift his eyes for fear Manton would read that driving need to kill.

15

The night settled abruptly. The sky was bright orange with long purple fissures in it, and then the sun fell into the bay out beyond the mangrove islands, and Los Reyes was in twilight. Lights sputtered, coming alive in thousands of neon tubes; the traffic lightened between the after-work rush and the evening snarl.

Dan left the expressway, moved at twenty miles an hour along Bayshore. His face was shadowed, drawn, He kept both hands on the wheel. He had never realized before there were so many police cruisers in Los Reyes.

"Where do you think you're going?" It was the first time Vera had spoken in twenty minutes.

"Don't get frown wrinkles, baby. I'll handle it."

She laughed flatly. "Will you mind, Danny, when I'm gray?"

He did not look at her. "Hell, you might be gray now for all I know."

"For all you care, Dan?"

"For all I care."

When he pulled the Olds off the street into the pebbled drive of the Bay Sands Motel, Vera straightened up, looking around.

The tall motel sign winked at her in four colors. The Bay Sands was the swankest of the new motels along the Drive. It sprawled on an acre of expensive soil in deep-sodded grass, its wide swimming pool sparkling with reflected neon lights. The building was tan sandstone, everything fresh and new.

"You haven't changed. You even hide in style, don't you, Dan?"

"Why don't you come in with me?" Dan took the keys out of the ignition.

"I might yell for help in there."

He shrugged. "Go ahead. It won't get you anything but a fat mouth. If I have to run, I'm taking you with me."

He came around the car, opened the door for her. She got out and walked silently beside him into the motel office.

Dan parked the Olds outside the cabana farthest from the street. Still without speaking, Vera got out and crossed the walk with him. He unlocked the door. She stepped inside. The room was smartly furnished. She did not bother to look at it.

He took the key, closed the door, slipped the chain latch on.

She stood in the middle of the air-conditioned room. Her eyes were hard, but her voice was quiet. "Once, a room like this would have seemed like heaven with you. Do it to me once more, Dan. Once more, before something happens and it's too late."

"Vera, do you mean it?" He gripped her waist.

In answer, she let her hands glide over his buttocks, at the same time raising the red gash of her mouth. His lips came down hard. His tongue forced its way into her. She held the kiss, then twisted away from him—but only to divest herself of clothing. In a few moments she stood before him, lithe and proud in her creamy nakedness.

"I shouldn't," he groaned. "You bitch. You beautiful, hot bitch."

"Love me, Dan. Do it to me," Her tongue wetly flickered her red lips. Her hair shimmered darkly. Her golden breasts, tipped with dark blossoms, winked at him above her swaying torso, her long, eager legs.

He seized her then and flung her to the bed. His lips closed over one turgid nipple, then the other, his tongue caressing hungrily, his mouth working and sucking. His hands went around her soft hips and he smelled the woman-smell of her. "Show me," Dan rasped. "Show me you want me." He rolled over on his back.

She showed him. With lips and tongue and hands she showed him, until his chest was quaking, until the skin of his stomach screamed, until his thighs were on fire and his loins boiling. Then when he could stand it no more, he flung her from him, rolled her over; like a maddened beast he plunged into the velvety depths of her. He felt her receive him, heard her gasp as in warm, wild surges that matched his own she rode with him to piercing ecstasy.

During the lazy aftermath, he heard her stir. He opened his eyes. She had lifted a lamp. He moved just in time to avoid a fractured skull.

"Bitch," he said, and slapped her.

He cut the cord from the venetian blind, turned her around and made a quick knot, securing her wrists behind her.

He went into the bathroom, came back wadding tissues in a washcloth. He squeezed her cheeks with his fingers until her eyes watered and she was forced to open her mouth. He shoved the wadded cloth between her teeth. He secured the gag with a handkerchief around her head.

He led Vera back from the bathroom and toppled her into a chair.

"Now we'll get your boyfriend over here," he said.

She stared up at him, her eyes wild and murderous.

He walked over, sat on the bed. He opened the directory, traced his finger along the column until he found the name "Paul Connors."

She writhed in the chair.

He dialed. He heard the phone ringing. "Hello."

Dan winced. "Hi, kid. You're looking lovely."

There was a pause. He heard Paul's shocked intake of breath, and he thought at least Paul had not heard about the break yet.

"Dan, where are you? Are you calling from the prison?"

"No, kid. I had to give that place up—"

"Dan, what fool thing have you done? Where are you?"

"I've got to see you, kid. That's why I broke out."

Paul's voice was sharp. "Why didn't you write, Dan? You always have to do things the hard way? You could have written."

"Look, kid. Simmer down. I got no time. I did write. You never answered—"

"Dan, I haven't had any letters from you for weeks. Now listen to me, Dan. Before you get yourself killed, go somewhere and give yourself up, please. Don't get yourself killed, Dan. You gave yourself up once, don't get killed now."

Dan's hand tightened on the receiver. He remembered why he had surrendered to the police. After the punk winged him outside Las Noches, he ran, but he was losing blood, and he got scared, really scared for the first time in his life, and he panicked. He went to Paul with the bullet in him, but as soon as he calmed down, he knew he had fouled up for sure. The cops would implicate Paul, drag him into it. He had made Paul drop the Ferrel years ago, using his middle name through high school and college. Paul Connors. But the police would spoil all that, spoil everything Paul was trying to accomplish. He walked out on Paul, called the cops from a pay phone....

"Please, Dan, don't be crazy. Give yourself up before you get hurt."

Dan said, "Later, Paul. Right now, listen good. I got to talk to you. I want you to come out—"

He heard Vera moving behind him, and he jumped up from the bed, turning.

He was too late. He saw her lunging toward him and saw the heavy pitcher of ice water coming down toward him. He threw up his arm, but the pitcher landed across his skull. He sagged, dropping the telephone.

She hit him again, kept hitting him until the pitcher had sloshed itself empty and he was on the floor, unconscious.

16

Ferrel swung the yo-yo in a slow, steady rhythm that rocked the whole countryside with every move he made. Even the world itself tilted, and he reached out, clawing for support to keep from skidding off it into space....

He could feel the blast of heat from the sun and the pressure against the back of his head....

Hawkins must have struck him with his gun-stock and left him sprawled in the wet ditch....

He remembered some wild dream about a blue car, and May Alonzo rigid with fear, and then Vera pressed close in his arms, her mouth chewing at his mouth....

He pushed up slowly from the floor, and the pain in his head almost blanked him out again.

He fought back a need to be violently sick.

This time he took it easier, rolled over on his back and lay for a moment staring at the ceiling. It was no wild dream—it was a nightmare, and he was in it now.

He drew the back of his hand across his eyes, as if trying to crush away the clouded red web that almost blinded him.

He sat up slowly. Vera had really clobbered him. There was a girl that put her whole being into everything she did. When she loved you, you were in heaven, and when she hated you, she'd see you in hell.

He raised his arm, pulled himself up. The door stood ajar. Vera had not stopped to close it when she ran.

He looked around, wondering what time it was, and then distantly he heard the wail of sirens out on Bayshore. It did not matter what time it was any more. It was late. Maybe it was too late.

He stood up slowly, stood wavering in the center of the spoiled room. The heavy water pitcher was on the carpet where Vera had dropped it, and there was a wide wet lake spreading half across the room. Then he saw that some of the chunks of ice were unmelted, and that meant he had been unconscious only a few minutes.

He walked unsteadily past the chair where Vera had been tied. The cord was bloodstained. Vera had cut her wrists getting loose. The washcloth and wadded Kleenex were on the floor. What a mess this place was....

He thought again of Paul, and he moved faster, forcing back the sense of sickness. The hell with it. He could be sick when they put the governors on him in the flat top, or when they put a bullet in him.

He held himself taut, feeling if he relaxed a muscle he would burst into fragments. He shut the door, latched it.

The siren was nearer now. He strode across to the window, then leaned against its sill for a moment while the world returned to its axis. Then he rolled the window open as wide it would go. He broke the screen out, squeezed his body through.

It was hot in the night after the air-conditioned room. He stood in the humid darkness, looking around for a moment. There was a field of weeds behind the motel. Beyond was a dimly lighted street, and to his right, downtown Los Reyes glowed yellowly against the dark sky. He walked out into the weeds toward the street that would lead him somehow, eventually, back to those lights.

Ten blocks east of the motel, Dan paused outside a small corner drugstore. He stood at the window, studying the inside of the shop. He found the telephone booth he was seeking near the magazine rack.

He brushed the wrinkles from his suit as well as he could and went in. The clerks glanced up, then ignored him.

He sat down on the small seat inside the booth, closed the door. Weariness flooded up over him, and he had to force himself to open the book, find a number, dial it.

When a woman's voice answered, he said, "Send a cab. Davis Pharmacy." He gave the address.

He had walked as far as he could walk.

He sat in the booth as long as he felt it was safe, then he got up and crossed the store, walking as though the terrazzo aisle were a tightrope.

Outside in the darkness, he leaned against the brick wall, laying his head back gently and staring upward at the blackness above him.

A car skidded in to the curb, and he lowered his head, saw the taxi light gleaming on the car roof.

The driver leaned across the front seat. "Hey, buddy. You the man called for a taxi?"

Dan nodded, walked the impossible distance across the cement to the curb. The driver pushed the rear door open for him and Dan toppled into the back seat. He lay with his head on the seat rest, and the cab spun around him. He was afraid he was going to pass out, afraid the cabbie would think he was drunk and take him to the nearest police station.

He clenched his teeth, forced himself to sit up.

"You all right, buddy?"

"Yes. Just a little bushed. Been a long day."

"Yeah. Sure is hot."

The driver slammed the door, and the back of Dan's head felt about to fly off.

He felt a sudden urge to laugh. The prison guards, the cops, the whole law enforcement mob had tried to stop him, and they couldn't do it. Wouldn't it be funny as hell if it was Vera who stopped him?

He did not laugh. He was afraid to move or speak, for fear of blanking out again. If he blanked out, he would wake up this time in a jail cell.

The driver glanced hurriedly to his left, turned the wheel to pull out from the curb, then slammed on his brakes.

Ferrel sat forward, and for a moment neither of them moved. They watched a police cruiser whip past, roof light winking red, missing the taxi fender by inches.

The cabbie cursed steadily for half a minute. "Them damn cops. If we drove as wild as them hunkers do, we'd all be under the jail. Ain't that right?"

"Right."

"Tonight they been worse than I ever seen 'em, mister. I swear to you. I ain't turned a corner tonight it seems like I didn't meet cops."

"Maybe you got a guilty conscience."

"Naw, it ain't that." The driver pulled warily out into the street, looking both ways. "Some con got away from a road gang this afternoon. And they got him pinned down here in Los Reyes—"

"That right?"

The driver laughed. "Well, not pinned down exactly. They think they trailed him into Los Reyes. And they been running themselves silly looking for him all night."

Ferrel lay back on the seat. "That right?"

"Sure. But you know what I think? That guy—if he was smart enough to make a break, he'd be a hundred miles from here."

"Looks like it, all right."

"Sure. He'd have to be a jerk to get himself bottled up in a town like Los Reyes. Ain't more than three highways out of this burg, and you can bet they got 'steen thousand cops on all of them."

"Probably have."

"That guy would be a jerk to come into this town, all right. I can't see that anyhow."

"What's that?"

"A con trying to make a break. You ever heard of a one of them ever really gettin' away with it?"

"No. I guess not."

"You damn well know not. Cops are too smart nowadays. Poor jerk, hiding somewhere. What does he expect to wind up with?"

"I don't know," Dan said.

The driver glanced over his shoulder. "Where'd you say you wanted to go, mister?"

Dan gave him the address of an intersection a block away from Paul's cottage. Then he lay back, closed his eyes, and tried not to think about anything at all.

17

Paul prowled the small front room of his cottage. His sport shirt was streaked with sweat. It looked if he had been standing in the rain.

He heard cars distantly on the street, heard somebody's TV turned up too loud in the neighborhood. He stopped in front of the telephone and stood looking down at it, his hands trembling. Why didn't it ring? What had happened to Dan? Why had he suddenly stopped talking, dropped the receiver and then hung up? He did not even know where Dan was.

If only he knew that, he could do something to help him.

He kept on pacing. Why had Dan broken out of the prison farm? What was he trying to prove? He had not had a letter from him in weeks, and Dan had sworn he would refuse to see him if he ever came near the prison farm. "Nobody has got Paul Connors and Dan Ferrel linked up in the same family. And I want it left that way, from now on."

There was never any sense arguing with Dan on that subject. And now he had broken out of the pen, he was running around somewhere in the night, a target for every gun-happy cop in the state.

Paul wiped at the sweat oozing from his dark, curly hair. How could everything go wrong all at once like this? Here he was, planning a robbery—him, planning a robbery with Areva Storm, and he had never even stolen candy when he was a kid.

He stared around the small room. Had the walls moved in on him? There wasn't a breath of air, and tension was drawing him tighter and tighter. Why didn't Dan call back? Had they cornered him already?

He shut his eyes, squeezing them closed, trying to shut out the picture in his mind—Dan running, and cops holding guns on him, impersonal, business-like—guns blasting, blasting, blasting, and Dan not running anymore.

The phone rang and he lunged at it, knocking it off the table. He fell to his knees on the floor, grabbing the instrument, pressing it against his ear. He wanted to yell Dan's name, but he was afraid to. He fought the emotion that shook in his voice. "Hello."

"Hello, Paul." It was Reve.

His hand shook so badly, he almost dropped the phone. "Reve. Hi. What do you want?"

"What do I want? If you don't want to talk to me—fine."

"Oh, wait a minute, Reve, for God's sake, I'm just all shook up right now. I'm sorry."

"I called you about—you know—what we want to do."

He was too sick to think about that robbery now. "What you want to do," he said. "Reve, it's time we came to our senses."

Her voice was flat. "I have come to my senses, Paul. We've got to do it tonight."

"Tonight?"

"Yes. Everything has changed. We've got to do it tonight, or we won't be able to do it at all."

"Then don't let's do it at all! Reve, listen to me, something has come up. My brother—"

"I don't want to hear about your woes, Paul. You've put me off long enough. It's too late for any more arguments. Either you're going to do this with me—or we're through. I won't see you anymore. I'm in a corner, Paul, and I've got to have that money—now, tonight."

"Reve, my God, I—"

"Just say it. It's real simple. Yes. No. I can marry Charley Muencher. He still wants me, whether you do or not."

His sweaty hand slipped on the receiver. He realized he was still on his knees. He pushed himself up, sat on the edge of a chair.

"I want you, Reve. But right now, I'm in a hell of a spot, my—"

"You won't do it?"

"I can't, Reve."

"Then don't try to see me anymore, Paul. I mean this. I'm marrying Charley, and I'll sic the cops on you if you come near me—"

"Reve, stop talking crazy!"

"I'm not talking crazy. I'm talking plain sense. Either you help me with what I've got to do tonight, or we're through. It's that simple."

"Reve, I can't let you go."

"I don't want to let you go. So I'll be at the corner of Franklin and Jay, in front of the Kit Kat Club. I'll be there at two tonight, Paul, and I'll wait fifteen minutes. If you're not there in your car—"

The connection broke sharply, and after a moment a vibrant hum came over the line. Paul lowered the phone only far enough to stare at it in his trembling hand. He did not move.

He was still sitting there when he heard a sharp knock at the door.

He looked around, dazed. The knock was repeated, lower this time.

He stood up, replaced the receiver. He wiped his sweaty face with the hack of his hand.

"All right," he said aloud. "All right, I'm coming."

He opened the door, and stood staring blankly at the two men outside. They did not have to tell him they represented the law. He could tell from the way they looked. The man in front was stocky, mild-looking, gray-haired, in his fifties. The other was a huge lard tub of a man, much younger and almost as sweaty as Paul himself.

The gray-haired man showed Paul the badge pinned to his wallet. He did it in such a friendly way that Paul half expected him to invite him to look at the snapshots of his family.

"My name is Manton." He had a mild voice, too. "This is Special Deputy Virgil Hawkins. May we come in?"

They were already moving through the doorway. Paul nodded and stepped aside for them.

Manton jerked his head, and Hawkins lumbered past him to search the rest of the cottage. There were only three rooms and a bath. Hawkins turned on all the lights, checked the closets, looked under the bed. He came back out to the front room, and shook his head.

"What are you looking for?" Paul said.

Manton smiled. "That depends. Your name Connors? Paul Connors?"

"Yes, I'm Paul Connors."

Hawkins made a sound like a choked growl in his throat. Manton gave him a quick, hard glance. "You know a man named Dan Ferrel?"

Paul bit his lip. He felt his heart beating faster. What was the sense in lying to these men? They already knew the truth, didn't they?

"He's your brother, ain't that right?" Hawkins had a brassy voice, hoarse and loud—a parade ground voice.

"I'll handle this, Hawkins," said Manton. He turned to Paul. "Your real name is Paul Connors Ferrel, isn't it?"

"Yes."

Manton asked, "Have you heard from Dan Ferrel lately, Paul?"

Paul shook his head. "Not for weeks."

Hawkins snorted. "He's been writin' to you."

"Maybe so, but I haven't heard from him."

Manton said, "Well, I better tell you then, if you haven't heard. Your brother broke away from a prison work gang today, and we believe he is in Los Reyes—"

"Hell, the kid's lying," Hawkins said. "He knows where that no-good brother of his is."

Manton ignored Hawkins. "When was the last time you saw Dan,

Paul?"

"At—at his trial."

"I see. Well, now, Paul, it's a serious offense to aid or harbor a fugitive criminal, you understand that?"

Paul nodded.

"And there's more," Manton said. "You wouldn't want to see your brother killed?"

Paul winced, shook his head. "No. I hope—he'll give himself up—before he's hurt. That's God's truth."

Manton said, "Maybe if you cooperate with us, Paul, we can get him to return to prison—and he won't have to be hurt. Will you do that?"

Paul looked at the stocky, gray man. There was a look of honesty about Manton. Then his gaze moved to Hawkins.

He felt an ache across the bridge of his nose. If he helped Manton find Dan, men like Hawkins would kill him, despite all Manton could do.

"I'll do what I can," he said at last.

"You better," Hawkins said, "unless you want to go to the pen yourself."

"You play along with us, Paul," Manton said, "and stay out of trouble. And if you hear from Dan, or if he comes here, you get in touch with me." He gave Paul a card.

Paul stood there and watched them go. Get in touch— Who were they kidding? There would be stakeouts out there until Dan was caught.

He glanced at the phone again. But he was thinking about Reve, not Dan. He had to get in touch with her. If he left here tonight, the cops would trail him. It was all off—it had to be.

He grabbed up the phone, dialed Reve's apartment. She did not answer. He called the nightclub where she sang, and was informed that she had not turned up there tonight.

He put the phone down, shaking all over. If he went to her, he would lead the cops to her. If he did not go at two o'clock, he would lose her. He walked back and forth in the small room, trying to control the trembling that went through him.

He heard cars drive away, motors loud, but he knew they had left men staked out in the darkness. Those men were standing out there in the night, watching him.

He moved slowly around the house, turning off all the lights Hawkins had left burning. He went back to the front room, but did not see how he could stay there. He could feel those men out in the darkness, watching him, waiting.

18

The walls of the small room crowded in closer. When Paul heard a movement at the kitchen door, he jumped like a frightened child.

He stood rigid, listening. He heard it again. He wheeled around, ready to run into the kitchen. Then he stopped. He could feel the eyes of the police stakeouts in the darkness. They were watching every move he made. All he had to do was run into the kitchen, make any suspicious move, and he would bring them closer.

He heard the scratching at the screen again. Holding his breath, he glanced around the room. He picked up an ashtray, carried it into the dark kitchen, walking as slowly as he could.

When he stepped into the kitchen, he heard Dan's sharp whisper at the back door. "Don't touch that light switch."

Paul felt a convulsive shiver go through him.

Now, more accustomed to the darkness, he saw Dan's shadow, pressed hard against the kitchen door.

Paul put the ashtray on the drainboard, crossed to the screen door. He opened the latch.

"Dan, there are cops all over the place."

Dan stepped into the room, gliding into a dark corner. "All the more reason for leaving the light off. Lock that door, kid."

"If I stay in here in the dark too long, Dan, they'll come closer to find out why."

"Okay." Dan didn't move from the corner. He was breathing heavily. "You can walk back in the front room every few minutes. Try to keep it as natural as you can."

"Dan, are you hurt?"

"No. I'm all right." He stepped away from the shadows, searching the front room. His voice was hard. "Where is she?"

"What are you talking about?"

Dan stepped toward him. "Like you said, kid, there are cops all over the place. They're looking for me—I got no time to waste. Listen to me, and listen fast. I know you're mixed up with a broad named Vera Flynn—"

"I never heard of her." Paul's voice shook.

"You've heard of Areva Storm. Well, that's a fancy name for the same twist I knew back in Houston. She called herself Vera Flynn then, and I caught her playing beautyrest with a fat slob—"

Paul was trembling. "Shut up, Dan—"

"I beat both of them up, walked out. She's a phony, Paul. As phony as that black hair of hers."

"You're lying. I love her."

"And she's twisting you into a crooked deal. She's setting you up, kid, and that's all she's doing—"

"Stop it, Dan!"

"I got no time to argue, kid. She's the Miss America of the tramps."

"Don't!" Paul groaned. He stepped forward, swung wildly.

Dan stepped in close, caught Paul's arm, twisted him around in a half-circle. Paul was held there, arm twisted, helpless.

Paul's eyes filled with tears of rage. "Damn you," he whispered.

"Get smart. She's talked you into some kind of robbery deal. All I want to know is when, and where."

"Let me alone."

"Sure, kid. When you get smart enough to tell me what it is that Vera Flynn wants from you. I don't want to hurt you, Paul, but I will."

Paul said, "All right. You're running—from a prison break, wanted for murder. And you come here and judge me and the girl I love. Damn you, you got to know, I'll tell you."

Dan's voice was soft. "Sure, kid. That's fine." He released Paul and Paul staggered backward, standing in the doorway, inches taller than Dan, broader, younger, heavier and yet, he knew, helpless before him.

When he spoke, his voice was slow, tense, full of anger. He saw that Dan had stepped back into the shadows, as the devil himself might move back away from the light.

"We're in love, Reve and I. She's good and wonderful—but she's broke. We both are—and we're sick of being broke—"

"You been broke all your life, kid. You're not sick of it. You don't know anything else."

"Maybe I want something else—"

"Sure. I know what you want. I been with that twist myself."

"Stop it, Dan. Stop talking about her like that."

"Sure, kid. What about medical school?"

"What about it?"

Dan exhaled. "So come on with the gimmick. How is Areva Storm going to make you two rich for life?"

"This place she knows. She's been there—with a man—"

"What else?"

Paul sighed, feeling sick. "It's easy to get into. A lot of cash. Nearly a hundred thousand—and only one night watchman."

"And you fell for this stupid come-on?"

Paul's voice flared. "We know what we want. Why don't you let us alone?"

"I'll tell you why. Because one convict in this family is enough. If you haven't got sense enough to see what's wrong with that job, I can tell you."

Paul sagged against the doorjamb. "All right. So I didn't want to rob anybody—but Reve—Vera needs that money—and I need her."

Dan laughed. "And when is this thing set for?"

"Stay out of it, Dan."

"I don't want to work you over, kid. Now get smart. When is this caper supposed to start?"

Paul stared across the room. He was sweating worse than ever. The whole world was pressing in on him.

"She's meeting me tonight at two," he said. His voice was flat.

"Set it forward some, huh?"

"Yes."

"Did she tell you why?"

"No."

Dan laughed again. "Okay, kid. You leveled with me, so now big brother is going to show you what a fool you are. Telling you won't do—not when you've got the smell of Vera Flynn in your nose." He moved, checking the room. "What time is it?"

"Almost one."

"All right. It'll soon be time to go."

"Where?"

"We're going to keep your little date with Vera."

"Maybe you didn't hear me, Dan—this place is swarming with cops. They're all out there in the dark."

"Sure they are. The story of my life. Stick around with Vera—it could be the story of your life."

"We can't get out of here."

"We're going to. You're going to drive your car out of here, and you're going to pick me up at the corner of an alley two blocks from here on your way to our girl Vera."

Paul's voice rasped, "Dan, you must be nuts."

"Yeah. I must be. But you won't take a fool's advice anymore. Maybe you'll believe what you see."

Paul looked around, helplessly. "Dan, please. You're only going to get yourself killed."

Dan was moving toward the rear screen door, a shadow gliding through shadows. "See you, kid."

It was twenty minutes of two when Dan Ferrel caught sight of the small six-year-old Ford rolling along the street toward the alley.

He saw the other car, too, far up the street, but rolling along, lights out, in the darkness.

He stayed in the shadows until Paul was almost to him. Then he ran out into the street, moved along beside the car. "Don't touch that brake pedal," he said. "Slow it down as much as you can, but don't touch that brake."

Paul nodded. He reached over to open the door for Dan. His hand was shaking so badly he had to twist the handle twice.

Dan caught the door and propelled himself into the seat beside Paul. "Okay, kid. Let's go."

Paul's voice shook. "Dan, it won't work. There's a cop's car trailing us. They haven't got any light on, but I stalled around coming down here. I saw them."

"Sure. They're back there, kid. But all we got to do now is lose them."

"I couldn't do it, Dan. I don't know how."

Dan's laugh was sharp: "Slide over here. Get out from under that seat. Man, it's a good thing I came along tonight—you couldn't rob a kid in a carriage."

19

May Alonzo sat in her apartment staring at nothingness, and did not even know how long she had been sitting like that. Near her she had the radio turned low, and yet loud enough that she would hear the first news flash: *Dan Ferrel, fugitive, was shot and killed tonight at the corner of—*

The music played on, uninterrupted. Nobody cared about Dan except her. Where was he? Where was he hiding? Had they caught him yet?

She tried to shake off her depression, tried to turn her head and look at Wes Kingsley on the divan beside her. She realized he was talking to her, and had been talking for a long time.

She had no idea what he was saying.

She managed to turn her head and look at him. He was such a handsome, kindly man—so serious behind those thick-rimmed glasses—and he deserved so much better. She was not good enough for him. She was not good enough for anybody anymore. All she was now was what Dan Ferrel had loved and used, and thrown away.

She was aware that Wes was speaking louder. "I shot three lions on Franklin Street today just before lunch. One was wearing a black and white four-in-hand. One of them shot back at me. I remember he had a red beard and—"

She turned, staring at him. "Oh, Wes—I'm sorry."

"Welcome home, May."

She tried to smile.

"What's on your mind, May? You've been like this since supper. Is it about us?"

She spoke too quickly. "Oh, no."

"Oh, yes. You've been like this for more than two weeks, May." He caught her hands, held them, making her face him. "You went out to that prison farm to visit that old flame of yours—Dan Ferrel—didn't you, May?"

"How did you know?"

"I didn't want to pry, May. Tony told me. Your brother thought it was all over between you and Ferrel. He said Ferrel had hurt you enough."

"I don't know what you're talking about. I just went to see Dan."

"Why?"

"I've known him all my life, ever since I was a little girl. Why not? Why shouldn't I, if I want to?"

"That's a good question. Why not? I just don't like to see anyone make you miserable, that's all."

"Dan never—loved me."

"Well, right there, that proves he's nuts." He pulled her to him. "I wish you could get him out of your mind, May. I'm not much—not very exciting. But I love you. I'd try to make you happy—"

Suddenly the music broke off. May pulled away from Wes, hardly aware of him now, sitting rigid, listening.

"Police tonight are continuing the search for the dark-haired woman who was Dan Ferrel's accomplice in his daring escape from a prison road gang a little after eleven A.M. today. Police say they are working on definite clues, but so far have found no trace of the woman, or of Dan Ferrel who has eluded every police net set out for him."

Wes was on his feet before she could stop him. He went around her, snapped off the radio. "If we've got to have anything," he said, voice hard, "let's try murder and mayhem on TV. I'm tired of hearing about Dan Ferrel."

May was standing up. She did not know why—did not remember getting to her feet.

Wes put his arms around her. "We don't need news like that, May. If Ferrel gets killed, all right. It's nothing to us—is it, May?"

May stared up at him. "Oh, Wes—I'm not good enough for you. Why don't you just … go away?"

He laughed, holding her. "Because I don't care whether you're good enough for me or not. I love you. When you forget this character, you'll wake up and know you love me—"

"Oh, Wes, I just feel so miserable."

There was a sharp knock at the door. May went rigid. Wes frowned, looking down at her.

She turned and stared at the door. After a moment she moved away from Wes, went to the door and opened it.

Two men stood there. She held the door wider, said, "Won't you come in?"

The older of the two men showed her the badge pinned on his wallet. "I'm Deputy Sheriff Manton," he said. "This is Special Deputy Virgil Hawkins."

"What do you want here?" Wes demanded.

"Who might you be?" Hawkins said.

"My name is Wes Kingsley. I'm an attorney."

Manton glanced up at May. "You're Miss May Alonzo?"

She nodded.

"You know a man named Dan Ferrel?"

Wes spoke up. "She knew him once—a long time ago."

Hawkins said savagely, "She visited him in the prison camp, less'n a week ago."

"I know him," May said.

"Would you mind telling us where you were today, Miss Alonzo?"

"I can tell you that," Kingsley said.

Manton quirked a gray brow at him.

May said, "Wes—"

"She was in my office all day. She is my secretary, and she was with me all day—and this evening."

Manton said, "Is that right, Miss Alonzo?"

May swallowed hard. "I'm—"

"That's the truth," Wes said.

"Would you come down to the station with us, Miss Alonzo, and sign a statement?"

"She can sign it here," Wes said.

"Sure. But maybe it would be better if she just came along with us down to the station. Few things we can talk over on the way."

"I'm coming along," said Kingsley.

"Suit yourself. All right, let's go."

20

The neons around the entrance of the Kit Kat Club were dead by two A.M. Shadows were deep inside the lobby, and the girlie pictures were nothing but pink blurs in the night.

Vera was standing deep in those shadows, when Dan pulled Paul's car into the curb at exactly two o'clock.

She was already across the sidewalk, almost to the old car, when she saw that Paul was not alone. She stopped on the walk, looking around wildly.

Dan was out of the car before she could move. He closed his hand on Vera's arm. "Get in, baby," he said harshly. "Slide over, Paul. You can drive—no cops on your tail now."

Vera tried to writhe free, but she could not get away.

She shrugged and got into the car. She glanced once at Paul's stricken face, then sagged back against the seat.

"All right, kid," Dan said. "Let's go. You've got expert help now. Let's get this show on the road."

The warehouse showed a block-long, windowless wall to the dimly lit street. Around the corner, a single bulb glowed in the warehouse office. Paul pulled the small car up to the curb, he killed the lights, turned off the engine. None of them moved.

They sat in the silence.

After a few minutes an elderly night watchman, carrying a small unlighted flashlight, came around the corner of the warehouse. He paused in the shadows, glanced at the car. A cat slithered against his leg. The night watchman knelt to stroke the cat's arched back.

The cat whined. The watchman carefully pulled a foil-wrapped can from his pocket.

Vera and the two men sat and watched him pick a sardine from the can and hold it above the cat's nose until the cat came up on its hind legs and caught the sardine in its mouth. The watchman stayed there a moment, stroking the cat.

Dan's voice was cold.

"That the night watchman, sugar?"

Vera stared straight ahead. "Yes."

Paul's voice was sick and frantic. "It's no good, Dan—we can't do this."

"Oh, yes, kid. Most important job I ever pulled. Come on, get out, Vera. Make your play."

Vera sat there a moment, clasping her handbag in her lap as if it were the last solid thing on earth.

Dan caught her arm. She moved out of the car, the fabric of her skirt whispering on the seat covers. She walked slowly across the dark street toward the night watchman. Her heels clicked loudly on the pavement. But the watchman must have been hard of hearing. She was almost up to him before he heard her and straightened.

Dan's face was twisted. "Okay, kid. Let's go. Get your part of it done."

Paul shook his head. "I can't, Dan—I can't do it."

Dan shrugged. "Okay, get out of here. Get to that doorway and wait there."

Paul did as he was told. Dan turned, moving as swiftly and silently as the cat had moved in the darkness.

Paul leaned against the wall near the office entrance. He saw Vera speak to the old man, saw him fish in his pockets, take out a match. He struck the match on the seat of his pants, held it up for her. And suddenly Dan stepped from the shadows behind the old man. His arm rose and fell. The old man crumpled without a sound. The match dropped into the gutter, sputtered and went out.

Paul pressed the back of his hand against his mouth. He saw Vera grab the keys from the ring on the old man's belt, and then they were moving toward him across the street, Vera's heels clicking, Dan as silent as the whisper of the wind along the walls....

Vera unlocked the door, held it open. Dan moved past her and after a moment, Paul followed. Vera closed the door, and Paul felt as though he were entombed in a breathless hole.

Vera nodded toward a desk. Paul moved woodenly to it, opened it, dragged out a metal cash box.

"That it?" Dan said, staring at Vera.

She nodded. Her face was white. Dan moved past her, holding the door open. They went out, and Paul hurried, almost running to the car.

He had the car started before they got there. He saw the watchman stirring on the walk, trying to get up. They slid in beside Paul. He dropped the box on Vera's lap. His voice quavered. "Let's get out of here."

Dan sounded almost cheerful. "You're the chauffeur, kid."

Dan directed him to a lonely street near the river. There was not a house within three blocks of the place.

"Kill the engine," Dan said when they arrived. "Cut the lights."

"What are we doing here?"

"Hell's sake, kid, we're dividing the swag. Right, Vera?"

She stared straight ahead, did not speak.

Dan said, "Go ahead, Vera. Open the cash box." He put something in her lap. It was a screwdriver.

She hesitated, then fumbled with the lock. After a moment she shook her head.

Dan took the box from her. He jammed the screwdriver up under the edge of the lid, pried. The thin steel buckled. He forced the corner up and back, opening the box without unlocking it.

Then he shook the contents of the box into Vera's lap. Paul caught his breath. He heard Vera whimper. There were a few stamps, and four one-dollar bills on Vera's lap.

"Office petty cash box, kid," Dan said. "Ever see one?"

Paul stared unbelievingly at the box, unable to speak. Dan's face was twisted. "You begin to get the picture yet, kid?"

Paul still could not speak.

"Have I got to spell it out, kid? Why do you think this tramp made you meet her secretly, was never seen in public with you? She was setting you up, kid. Only one little change in the way we played it. She was going to turn in the alarm over there while she was with the old man—and you were going to be caught inside—"

"It doesn't make sense," Paul whispered.

"No, kid. Not unless you know Vera. Not unless you know how Vera can hate—oh, not you, kid—me. She tried to get me killed—"

"No," Vera whispered.

Dan ignored her. "Then when that didn't work, she had to ruin you, and everything I wanted for you—it was the only bitchy way she knew to be quits with me. Go on, Vera, tell him how you came to his place every day before he got home and destroyed my letters."

Paul's face was agonized. "But why?"

"Hell, kid, because I was kiting those letters out when I heard she was here, under a different name, setting you up for a phony robbery."

Paul stared at Vera. His voice shook. "I loved you. My God, can't you understand that? I loved you."

Vera would not look at him. It was as if she had turned to stone.

Dan spoke softly. "So why don't you get out and walk home from here, kid? It's a long way, but you'll have time to do a lot of thinking.... This is going to take a lot of thinking. But you'll make it, this time."

Paul sat there a moment. His eyes were blurred with tears. Then he nodded, got out of the car. Dan watched him until he disappeared, walking away into the night.

21

Dan and Vera got out of the taxi outside the darkened Kit Kat Club on Franklin. They had left Paul's car on a side street on the other side of town. When Vera saw the black well of the lobby, the deep shadows where she had stood waiting for Paul a little more than two hours ago, she began to tremble.

Dan waited until the cab moved away, then took Vera's arm, urging her past the darkened entrance of the Kit Kat and around the corner on Jay Street. Her Olds was parked half way down the block.

He opened the door of the Olds, and took her purse as he pulled her in after him. His hand closed on the small automatic he found there. She heard his bitter laugh, saw him drop the gun into his pocket. Then he took out her car keys and started the car.

Vera's voice shook. "Where are we going, Dan?"

"It doesn't matter to you, sweetie."

"What are you going to do?"

"To you?"

"Yes. To me."

"I don't know, baby. I'll think of something. What the hell? You tried to chop me down by hurting Paul. It didn't work. How many chances do you think you get?"

"You fixed me with Paul, Dan. He knows now. He's free—isn't that enough?"

"Not for you, sweetie. As long as you run around loose, I can always get a knife in my back, a hired bullet—"

"Give me a chance, Dan—let me go. I won't bother you anymore, I swear. I admit I was trying to frame the kid. I had to hit back at you, Dan—I couldn't live unless I did, after the way you hurt me."

"Getting me shot, getting me in the gang for life—that wasn't enough, you had to ruin a decent kid—"

"Oh, Dan, I didn't—I never had anybody try to kill you. I hated you, but I didn't know what to do to hurt you—not till I remembered Paul, and how proud you were that he was going to be a doctor. Dan, can't you see, you hurt me so terribly, I hated you so—"

"Too bad, baby, because it didn't work."

Vera was trembling. "Dan, no, I swear."

Something flickered at the edge of her vision. The faint yellow eyes of a car's parking lights were trailing them.

She glanced at Dan to see if he had noticed. He showed no sign. The lights were so dim that he might have missed them.

She waited holding her breath. Dan made a turn. At last she could resist no longer—she turned her head slightly. The lights were there, persistently following.

Dan said, "That car's been following us since we pulled away from the Kit Kat, Sweetie."

Sick with disappointment, she said, "It may be the police."

"No. I gave them a couple of chances to pull up. Who is it, sugar? Who's in that car?"

She stared at him. "Dan, I don't know!"

"Not one of your boyfriends? Not some little gimmick you arranged, in case something went wrong out at the warehouse?"

Vera was trembling. "Dan, no, I swear."

He shrugged. "Your word means nothing to me, doll. But we'll see. If he's no friend of yours, I can lose him." He laughed bitterly. "I've been losing people all my life."

Her voice was low. "Maybe you don't lose them—maybe you drive them away."

He said softly, "I haven't heard you beg yet."

"What?"

"You know I'm going to kill you, don't you?" He swung around a corner, snapped off his lights. He made two more turns before he turned the lights on again.

"You don't have to kill me, Dan. I've been dead without you. I knew that when I saw you today in my apartment."

He laughed at her.

She kept on talking.

"Even hating you, I knew how much I loved you. All I really wanted was another chance—for us. We could go away, Dan."

"It's too late, sweetheart. But if it's worth anything to you, I never stopped loving you—not even when I knew you didn't care any more about yourself than to lay Ollie Lamb—"

"Oh, God, Dan. Haven't you ever been wrong? Haven't you ever been mixed up? Haven't you ever made a mistake?"

"I'm batting a thousand in that column. That's why all this won't work. You've had it, baby."

She lunged at him suddenly, clawed at his face. He tried to shove her away, but she was like a frantic animal. "No," she screamed. "No, damn you! You hurt me! You drove me insane! But you're not going to kill me! Damn you, you're not!"

Her fingernails raked along his face. Then she grabbed the wheel, jerking it with all the crazed strength in her arms, wrenching it out of his hand.

The car spun to the right, off the street, bumping up across a curb and crashing against a stone pillar at the corner of a darkened service station.

Dan was thrown forward, then snapped back. The impact of the speeding car against the stone pillar was like a thunder clap.

For a moment he was stunned. He saw lights flash in the houses along the street, saw the flare of auto lights racing toward him, and knew the pursuing car had found them. He saw Vera spring for the door, trying to open it. He heard her mewling in anguish because the door was stuck. She was sobbing, fighting it, and then he saw it swing open, and she was throwing herself out, but for that instant he could not move.

The big black car skidded to a stop, brakes screeching close to the rear bumper of the Olds, trapping it against the pillar.

Vera looked around wildly as the near door was thrown open.

She stared. "Ollie."

The fat man twisted his body, stepping into the street. He held the gun out where she could see it. "Just stand there, baby," he said.

He came closer. She could smell the remembered reek of perspiration, deodorant, men's toilet water.

He was staring at Dan in the car. "All right, Ferrel. It's you I come to see. Come on, get out of there."

Dan slid out of the car, leaned against it. "Might have known it." His voice was flat. "You two—still playing house."

Ollie said, "Knew this broad would lead me to you. Too bad the police weren't that smart. They didn't know about you and Vera down here. But I knew, didn't I?"

Dan was staring at Vera. "Real clever little frame, baby."

Ollie Lamb laughed. "Figured all I had to do was watch the broad, Ferrel." He glanced around at the lights coming on in windows along the street. Then his voice went cold. "Sorry to have to cut this short. I got something for you, Ferrel. Something that hopped-up punk didn't quite give you outside Las Noches—"

Dan straightened abruptly against the car. "You sent him," he said. It was all abruptly clear. Lamb wanted him dead, and Lamb wanted him to think while he died that Vera had sent the killer.

"That's right, Ferrel. You should've stayed in the pen where I put you."

"My God," Ferrel whispered. He knew now who had been sitting in one of those dark cars on that side street outside Las Noches—waiting, watching to see himself avenged on Dan Ferrel. Lamb, sitting there, had seen the needled punk fail—Lamb had shot the gunman, and framed Dan for the murder.

Ollie Lamb's voice shook. "Get the picture now, Ferrel? You were dead—dead—the day you threw me out of this broad's apartment with no clothes on, out in the street for people to laugh at. They laughed me out of business—out of Houston—but I'm still alive, punk—and you been dead all this time, only you just didn't know it."

Suddenly Dan lunged forward. He was fumbling for the gun in his pocket as his shoulder struck Ollie Lamb's chest. He fired, the bullet going wild. A scream of sirens followed the roar of the gun. Somebody had called the police.

Ollie yelled in terror and rage. He chopped his thick arm downward. Dan fired from his pocket, and Ollie went staggering back.

Dan did not glance at Ollie again. He kept moving. At the corner, the sirens were screaming and the first cruiser headlights were swinging wide, as the police car skidded against the far curb, making the corner.

Vera stood as if in a trance. She felt Dan grab her wrist, and then he was dragging her along after him.

He dived through the door of the black car, pulling her after him. The engine was running. Dan put the car in gear and stamped on the accelerator. The big black car surged forward.

22

One of the cops in the cruiser behind them was firing around his front window. Dan swore. They were close—if they hit a tire, it would be all over.

He felt Vera moving on the seat beside him. He could hear more sirens up ahead. The night was wild with sirens, all of them converging on him.

He reached over, caught Vera's head, pressed her back down on the seat. "Stay where you are. You want to get hit by a stray bullet?"

"Does it matter?"

He saw a corner ahead, glanced at his speedometer. "Maybe it does matter," he said. "But I know a lot of things now I didn't know before. I feel a hell of a lot better—even in a spot like this." He jerked hard on the wheel, and the tires screamed. The car rocked, swayed as he fought the wheel. "I was wrong about—some of the things I hated you for, Vera—" The car tilted, careened along the curb, then straightened.

Dan heard the whine of brakes behind him. The cops had not dared to try that turn—they would have had to skid to a stop ninety feet down the street back there and make a long reverse before they could turn. He laughed aloud suddenly, snapping off his lights.

"Some of them," he said.

"All of them, Dan." Her voice was flat, drained of emotion. "No matter what I did to you—I loved you. I never loved anybody but you—not even when I hated you the most."

Dan did not speak.

His hands gripped the wheel. He went around another corner with tires screaming. Vera did not stir on the seat beside him. He felt tears burn suddenly in his eyes. God, how he loved her—how he had always loved her! She was in his blood. The only way they would get her out was to bleed him dry.

He made one more turn, snapped on his lights. Two cruisers were parked up ahead, blocking the street. They had him pinned down.

He stepped on the brakes, swung the car into an alley. As he turned, he saw a cruiser, its red roof light blinking, shoot along the street behind him. In a second, he knew, another patrol car from the roadblock would join them.

He raced out onto the next street, turned right. He knew he was staying inside the trap they had set up, but all he wanted was time— a chance to think. He slowed the car, driving without lights. He saw another alley, swung into it without touching the brake.

He had to get away—had to be able to hold Vera in his arms again, to love her, to keep her.

He turned left in each alley, going a few blocks on open streets until he saw lights ahead, then whipping into another alley. Now he was moving with a purpose again—he was trying to get as close to the docks as he could.

He glanced down at Vera, lying beside him on the seat. Two bad guys—getting one more chance. He wanted to laugh.

He swung the car into a wide street that led across town to the bay front, the shipping piers. He snapped on his lights, wanting just one thing now. He wanted to get close to those piers. If he could find Tom Alonzo's boat—get aboard …

Suddenly two green-and-white cruisers whipped out of side streets ahead of him, driving straight toward each other—trying to block him.

He stepped hard on the gas, driving straight at them. At the last possible second the police drivers hit their brakes and he went racing between them, their fenders gouging deep into the sides of the black car.

They were tailing him now, and he saw he was not going to make it. He could see the first long buildings of the shipping piers, but he saw the headlights of other cruisers ahead of him, too. Four sheriff's cars were converging on him now, two from the rear, two ahead of him.

He whipped the big car hard to the left, still moving toward the piers. It was no good now. They could never get away on Tony's boat, on anybody's boat—the cops were too close. But still he raced toward the piers.

The big car jolted off the street, up a loading ramp, straight toward a brick wall. He slammed on his brakes, skidded to a stop.

He got the gun from his jacket with one hand, grabbed Vera's wrist with the other. He swung open the door. The whole long ramp was lit up by police car headlights.

He heard brakes squealing as the cruisers skidded to a halt on the ramp behind him.

He did not even look at them. He pulled Vera after him, running— and suddenly he knew this was the story of his life—he had been running all his life, only never quite fast enough. He had never quite made it. But he went on running, dragging Vera after him, because running was all he knew.

He heard a voice on a battery-powered loudspeaker. "Halt, Ferrel. This is Deputy Manton. We order you to halt."

A gun went off and the bullet screamed across their heads.

Dan glanced back. He could see the deputies running up the ramp after them, guns drawn. Then Vera writhed suddenly, jerking free. He stopped, reaching for her, but she was running back toward the police.

"Vera, don't. My God, Vera—don't leave me."

Vera did not hear him.

Dan ran after her, caught her, wheeled her around. "No, Vera, no! We—"

A gun went off. Dan heard the sound, but felt nothing, and then Vera stumbled, a dead weight dragging on his arm. He stopped, staring at her.

She had fallen to her knees. Her head sagged loosely on her neck, her hair spilling toward the ground. She would have fallen on her face if Dan had not held her.

He heard the running feet come nearer behind him. He hurled his gun away, bent over and swung Vera up in his arms. He turned again, began to run.

"Halt!"

They did not need the loudspeaker anymore. They were all around him, and he had no more place to run. He stood there, panting, legs apart, holding Vera in his arms. Her head hung over his arm. Her body was limp and still.

The deputies stood there without speaking. After a moment, Manton strode between them. He carried a gun. His gray face was savage. His eyes were fixed on Virgil Hawkins' fat, sweaty face. The gun in Manton's hand was the one he had wrenched from Hawkins' grasp a moment ago.

"You low, moronic, gun-happy murderer!" Manton's voice trembled with rage. "I am going to break you for this, Hawkins, if it's the last thing I ever do."

Hawkins was pale. "I stopped them."

"I told you—all of you! No guns except for warning. We had them, Hawkins. We didn't have to kill anybody."

Dan backed up, leaned against a wall. He was barely aware of the men in front of him. Two of them took Vera from his arms. He saw them lay her down on the ground nearby.

A man kneeled over her. "She's dead," he said.

Manton looked at Hawkins once more. His face was twisted. "Get Hawkins out of here—right now. Put the cuffs on him. Get him out of here."

After a long time Manton said, "This the woman that helped you escape, Ferrel? She the woman drove the blue car?"

Dan looked down at Vera's body, at the black hair spilled on the ground. He thought about May Alonzo, and knew he owed her this. She would be free. He nodded. "Yes."

Manton stared at him, frowning. The hell with Manton! All the police knew was that the dame who had been with him in the blue car had dark hair. That was all they needed to know.

He watched them remove Vera's body, her dark hair hanging over the sides of the litter. He watched the ambulance speed away, its red tail light blinking in the darkness.

Finally, Manton nodded. "Well, that about wraps it up. That's all we can do here. Let's go."

A deputy touched Dan's arm. Dan moved away from the wall. Manton spoke to him, voice low. "That Ollie Lamb. Didn't die, Ferrel. Spilled the truth to us, though. You're not guilty of murder. Maybe we can do something for you."

Ferrel was staring out into the darkness, but the ambulance was gone; he could no longer see that red light blinking. His shoulders sagged. Free? Was that what Manton was saying? What for? What difference did it make?

He turned, glanced at Manton. He shrugged. They walked slowly toward the police cars, and they did not speak again. Ferrel lifted his head, looked around, feeling the sting of sunlight in his eyes.

It was dawn.

THE END

PRIME SUCKER
....
Harry Whittington

CHAPTER ONE
Cards on the Table

Hank sat at the table and wanted George's wife. It was like being drunk, the way she made him feel.

She was curled up on a divan across the room reading a magazine. She was wearing a pale blue house dress that fit tightly across her breasts and hips. The pressure was all the fabric could stand and it was too much for him. He wanted to touch her, to feel the give and warmth under the stress on that frock.

From his place at the dining table he could watch her over George's shoulder. He hadn't started out watching her at all. They were playing cards. Hank and George Miller and Fred Vaught and Carl Peters from the office. It was poker, solemn and serious. None of that seven-card or sissy wild-cards stuff. These guys played for blood, even if it was a dime limit. It was the first time Hank had ever been asked to play poker with them, the first time he'd ever been in George Miller's house. The first time he had ever seen George Miller's wife.

It wasn't that she was the most beautiful woman Hank had ever seen. She wasn't. At first she hadn't looked like anything special at all. Ethel was prettier. Ethel was Hank's wife. Ethel was at home sleeping right now and she had told Hank he ought not to come. And now he guessed Ethel was right again. Ethel didn't like poker. She didn't like him out nights. She sure wouldn't like his watching another woman and feeling the breath tight in his chest and feeling the effects of the whisky all out of proportion to the amount he'd been drinking. He was giddy with it. When he closed his eyes as he had to once in a while, the whole room went spinning around his head.

He opened his eyes again. The room settled into place and she was over there on the divan, her legs up, skirt prim across her knees. He wondered what it was besides the whisky that made him want her so much. His breathing was quickening again and he had to admit it. It had been like this ever since she'd met his eyes a little while ago.

Hank had been on his fourth highball and he had looked up as he drank. She'd been watching him. Their eyes met. And there it was. Everything. It made his stomach churn. Her eyes told him just as plainly as if she'd spoken aloud, she wanted what he wanted. No. More than that. She wanted *whatever* he wanted.

That was what did it. That was the kick in it. Hard and sudden. Like straight alcohol.

He felt himself getting warm under his shirt, warmer than the room was warm, warmer than the drinks would make him. He had picked up his cards, trying to concentrate on them. Somebody growled, "Wait till they're all dealt, can't you?"

He felt his face turning red and he dropped his cards as though they were hot. He looked up. She smiled and went back to the kitchen. That was all she'd done, all evening. Mix drinks. Bring them whenever anybody's glass was empty. The rest of the time she lay on the divan and read.

Hank shook his head. He couldn't see Ethel spending an evening like that. Waiting on guys from the office. Men she didn't even know, smoking and playing cards around her dining room table.

George Miller looked up from his cards. "I guess Hank is not much of a poker player."

"Like I told you," Hank said, "I haven't played for months."

He'd been losing all evening. It wouldn't amount to much and he didn't mind losing. He'd been working too hard with no time off. He needed to relax like this. But after he had looked up and met her eyes, he'd lost interest in cards and he couldn't keep his mind on the game.

He was unused to this tension over cards and it made him nervous. The whisky. The heat in the room. The thick cigarette smoke. Trying to concentrate on the cards. Trying to forget the way she had looked at him. Trying to forget *her* across the room from him.

The worst of it was, he knew. It wasn't just at him that she looked that way. Her brown eyes opened up the way to her insides. You looked in her eyes and you saw what she was. *I want whatever you want,* her eyes had said. And he knew in sickness that they also said, *I want whatever any man wants. Any man.*

Somebody spoke to him. Hank jerked his head up, trying to focus his eyes on the filmy faces before him. The light was reflected in Carl Peters' glasses. It almost blinded him. For the moment he couldn't see anything but that glittering light.

"What you say?" His voice was thick.

"Ante!" George Miller said. "It's your ante."

"My God. Keep your mind on the game," Fred said. "Are you in, or ain't you?"

Hank looked at his cards without knowing what they were and dropped them, face down.

"No," he said. "No. I guess I'm out."

He sat there for a moment watching them. He wiped his hand across his high forehead. It was sweaty.

"I need a drink," he said. "I guess I need a drink."

He pushed his chair back and stood up, steadying himself against it until the room quieted.

"Sit down," George Miller said. "Let Amy get it. Amy. Hank wants a drink. Get Hank a drink."

She dropped the magazine and swung her legs off the couch.

"He's got one," she said. "It's almost full. It's right there."

George was busy with his cards. "The hell with it," he said. "Maybe he don't want that one. Get him what he wants."

"No," Hank said. "It's all right. I'll get it—"

George didn't look up. "Amy!"

"All right, George."

"No, please," Hank said. He looked at her over their heads. "It's all right. I can find it."

He stumbled. Caught himself. Stood tall. The room wheeled. He looked over his shoulder at George. "Haven't had anything to drink for quite a while, either," he said.

George didn't even look up.

Hank pursed his lips and exhaled heavily. He shook his head to clear it. What a hell of a way to behave. First time he'd ever been in the man's house. First time he'd ever seen the man's wife, too. And he had to get *that* out of his mind.

His legs were wobbly but he made it to the kitchen. He leaned against the drainboard. Greyhounds were chasing an electric rabbit through the thirty-mile track of his intestines. He was going to be sick.

She had followed him into the kitchen. She was standing just behind him.

He turned a little, leaning his weight on the drainboard. He looked at her. The dark hair, wavy and caught in a net at the nape of her neck. Earrings. Big things. She looked like a gypsy. His eyes moved to the clean line of her nose, her full pouting mouth and the tip of her tongue worrying at it. Oh God, he thought, I'm drunk. I've got to get out of here. I've got to get away from her.

"Are you all right?" she said. Why did her voice have to be lower than other women's? Different, with a throb in it.

"Sure. I'm all right." Fine. Lovely. He was sick to his stomach. He wished to God he was home in bed.

"What kind of drink you want?" she said. "I'll fix it for you."

"No. No. I don't want a drink—"

"But you said—"

"No. I'm kind of fuzzy. Things are sort of mixed up. I want a drink of water. Ice water."

Everything would be all right if he had ice water. Good, cold water. God never invented anything that tasted better in a dry mouth, in a coiling stomach.

"Water?" She looked as if she were going to laugh.

"Yes. It's all right. I'll get it."

"No." Now she did laugh "It's just that you're the first man I ever saw who'd drink water when there was anything else."

She went past him to the electric refrigerator. He watched the way she walked. Watched! He couldn't keep his eyes from the taut lines of her hips, the effortless way she moved, the sensuous strain of thigh against skirt.

He knew he was moving toward her and he didn't even know why. He had picked up a glass from the drainboard and held it forgotten in his hand.

He stood and watched her open the refrigerator and take out a plastic water container. It was so cold that sweat stood in globules on its sides. But he wasn't looking at the water now.

Amy turned and pushed the door closed with her back. For a moment she leaned against it.

She didn't look at the water in her hand, or mention it. She looked up at him and took a backward step that pressed her against the facing of the refrigerator. She let her head tilt back, her hair jet black against the white enamel.

And there it was again. Her brown eyes. The bare windows revealing her naked thoughts.

He could feel the slugging of his heart. He took a step toward her. There were only a few inches separating them. He could feel the warmth of her across that space.

She smiled, pulling her lips back from perfect white teeth. There had to be a blemish. He looked for it and found it. One of her teeth was chipped. The kind of chipped place a woman could make opening bobby pins with her teeth.

"Kissing another man's wife in the kitchen," she teased. "Ah, me. In how many thousands of homes are they doing this tonight."

Confused, he stepped back.

She laughed again and caught his arm. "It's all right," she said. "It's like kissing a woman in a taxi. Everybody does it."

Her breath was hot with whisky. For the first time he liked whisky on a woman's breath. It smelled good. It was headier than the stuff he'd been drinking.

The good smell of that whisky on her breath did something for him. Made up his mind.

He stepped up close, pressing hard against her.

He caught his breath, feeling her body, the hot outline of her against him. He dropped the glass and heard it strike the imitation tile flooring. The glass didn't break. He didn't give a damn if it did. He didn't care what happened. He would break the glass and walk through it barefooted to get against her like this.

His hands closed on her arms. He could feel his chest flattening her firm breasts. He could feel their yielding. He pushed her head back and pressed his open mouth over hers.

For just a moment her lips were cold and hard; then, suddenly, like a gun being fired, they came to life, a life of their own, a life independent of her mind or her eyes or her body. The lips of her writhed and pulsed and pounded with her surging blood.

Her tongue darted into his mouth, exploring, seeking, reaching.

I'm drunk, Hank thought. I'm drunk and I'm dreaming. No woman could kiss like this, love like this. No mortal woman ever kissed like this before. This must be Venus. This is a goddess. Or a devil. A she-devil. An impossibly desirable nymph out of hell …

Before their naked tongues had touched, when the only intimacy shared had been that of their eyes—before the clothing that covered their bodies had rubbed together with inanimate desire and when only their thoughts had probed each other's secret places—then she had set him afire. But now that the intimacy was real and moist and warm, an intimacy of hands and lips and whiskey breath, he was blazing. He was a volcano full of fiery power, ready to erupt like an exploding star.

He could feel the sharp, hard claws of her scarlet fingers on his shoulder, driving through the fabric of his shirt, lusting for the taste of his flesh, digging deeply, as he longed to do.

Her mouth left his for a moment and crept along his cheek, her turgid breath strangely sweet in his nostrils.

He hung on, clung tight, moved his hands, pulled her tight against him. He could feel her breath, the tender wetness of her tongue on his ear lobe, the sharp pain as her teeth found him and spoke in their own way of the savagery of her wanting.

She stopped suddenly, and looked at the water container still in her hand. "I've got something here for you," she laughed. "Do you still want it?"

His hands moved, each in its own sweet direction, lingering, prodding, squeezing, caressing, finding.

"I want you," he groaned drunkenly. "Man, how I want you. More than I ever wanted anything else in the world."

"Then take me!" she whispered brokenly. "We came in here so you could. You know that's why we came in here together."

I'm drunk, Hank thought, but not that drunk. Not with her husband in the next room.

"It'll keep," he said. "Some other time." Then suddenly as her body moved, and as the sharp hardness of her pointed breasts burned a path of fire across his shirt front, his breath came hot again. Hot and fast.

She reached away from him, but only with one arm, to set the water container on the sink top.

Then her arms were around him again, and her lips were burning and their bodies were locked together in a conflagration of desire.

This isn't just a drunken pass at another man's wife in the kitchen, Hank thought. It isn't just a hot dame whose husband doesn't give her enough, trying to grab a quick thrill while his back is turned. It's too intense for that. I want her too much. She wants me too much …

He reached for her black gypsy hair, grabbed two handsful, twisted until she cried with happy pain, and pulled her head upward, grinding his teeth against hers, grinding her very soul into his.

He didn't know how long they stayed like that.

Finally she pulled away. It was abrupt and savage. But as confused as he was, he was aware of one thing. She jerked her mouth away first and then her breasts so they strained again under her dress. It was as though the rest of her was locked to him and it was impossible for her to pull away.

When she was gone, her hands pushing against his chest he felt cold, incomplete without her warm body locked to him.

Amy was looking at him. She wasn't laughing and her eyes weren't inviting him. Not anymore. Her eyes were baffled, and she looked a little afraid.

"My God," she whispered. "Oh, my God."

She slid from between Hank and the refrigerator. She bent down and picked up his glass. She poured him a drink of water. The container had one of those tops that pushed up, allowing the water to pour through. He was surprised it wasn't steaming.

Her hands were shaking. She spilled a little of the water. She handed him the brim-filled glass.

"There's your water." Her voice was cold. She replaced the container and went out of the kitchen, patting her hair back into place.

Hank took one sip of the water. He felt it burn his throat and chest. It stirred havoc in his stomach. He set the glass down on the drainboard.

He went back to the dining room and George looked up at him.

"What's the matter, Hank?" he said. "You look sick."

"Yeah," Hank said. "I guess so. I guess I've had enough for tonight. Better count me out."

"My God, it's just eleven o'clock."

"Yeah. But I'm not feeling so good."

Light glinted on Carl's glasses. He was figuring.

"You're out a buck fifty," he said. "Stick around. Your luck might change."

"No. Thanks, George, it was swell. I'm just a little woozy."

"Want me to walk out to your car with you?"

"No. No. I'll be all right."

George looked over his shoulder. "Amy, get his hat, will you?"

"He didn't have one," Amy said from the couch.

George looked up from his cards. "See you tomorrow, Hank."

Hank nodded. He had to force himself to remember to say good night to Carl and Fred. The sweat on his forehead had turned to ice water. He went around the table.

He got to the front door. He looked back at Amy. She was on the couch. Her legs were up. She was reading her magazine. She picked up a glass, sipped at it, set it down.

"Good night, Mrs. Miller," Hank said. "Thanks."

"Good night," Amy said. She didn't meet his eyes. She didn't even look up from the magazine.

CHAPTER TWO
The Guest Room

He let the front door slam. He looked at his car parked at the curb. It was a late model Mercury. It looked a long way off. Impossibly far. He wondered if he could make it.

He bit down hard on his underlip and started down the walk. The backs of his knees were weak. That made him unsteady and he weaved from one side of the walk to the other.

He reached the car, and sighed. He steadied himself against it. He knew he was going to be sick. He looked over his shoulder. He could see them in the house at the dining table. He could see the top of Amy's head over the back of the couch.

He staggered around the side of the car. He was pleased with himself. He had gotten out of there. He was in the dark where they couldn't see him being sick. He was very pleased ...

He drove the Mercury at twenty miles an hour. He passed a police cruiser, smiling and nodding at the cops in it. Of course they couldn't see him in the darkness of his car. It was a wonder they couldn't smell his breath, he thought. A cat raced across the road in the glare of his headlights. Hank slammed on his brakes, cursing.

He drove the car into the driveway before his six-room ranch-type cottage. Somebody had shrunk the garage doors since he'd left earlier tonight. Ethel, he assured himself. She hadn't wanted him to go. She'd shrunk the garage doors so he couldn't get back in.

He drove the car right up to the open doorway. Clearly, it was impossible to get that wide car into that narrow space. He killed the engine, removed the ignition key and got out.

The front porch light was on, the door was unlocked. He entered the house, locked the door and snapped off the light.

The house was in darkness. He knew this place like the palm of his hand. Come to think of it, who ever really gets to know the palm of his hand?

He loosened his tie, unbuttoned his shirt, feeling his way across the living room to the hall way. He crossed the hall, felt around and snapped on the bathroom light.

He finished undressing, letting his clothes fall on the tile floor. He picked up his underthings and dropped them directly in the laundry hamper. He washed out his mouth, brushed his teeth and stared at himself in the mirror. He grinned. "Sneaking a kiss in the kitchen," he said aloud. "What in the world are kitchens coming to? A man can't even get a drink of water anymore without fighting off some beautiful dame."

He stopped grinning and stared at himself again. He had that empty feeling in his diaphragm. He was remembering Amy's breath, warm with whisky. Her mouth, soft under his. The way she had pushed herself against him, the way he could feel her against him.

He remembered the way she hadn't even looked up when he'd left the house. "Well. So what? Now I'm out of the house, it'll be good old Carl Peters or Fred Vaught who'll get a drink of water and a kiss in the kitchen." He laughed angrily. "Hell, she might even get so hard up, she'll kiss her own husband. Oh, no. No. She wouldn't do a thing like that. Not really. I just said that for a joke."

He was sweating again. He wiped his hand across his face. He stared at himself in the mirror again. He inhaled, filling out his chest. He shook his head. Naked, he regarded himself in the mirror one more time.

"Her husband is a hell of a lot better looking," he told himself. He was just a guy who had been working too hard for too long. No parties. No playing. Just getting up to an alarm, and coming home a certain number of hours later. And running every minute between. A guy trying to afford a new Buick, a new home, trying to get a better job. The great American dream. Most guys could take a thing like the kitchen episode, a doll like Amy, in stride. He was out of practice. Rusty. "Forget it. She had her little laugh. Her little session in the kitchen. What you want for a buck fifty? Dancing girls?" He grinned. "Good night, Don Juan. Primmer donner." He smiled, pleased.

He left the bathroom light burning and went into his bedroom. Ethel was asleep. Her blonde head, in tight pin curls, was snuggled down in her pillow. Her body was curled across the bed. He would have to wake her to lie down.

He stood beside the bed and looked down at her. She was the youngest looking thirty-year-old he had ever seen. Everybody said that Ethel prided herself on how young she looked. She worked thirty minutes every night on her face. They'd been married ten years and it was a long time since she'd been anxious enough to get in bed with him to neglect her facials. Years. Come to think of it he wondered if she ever had. Maybe she'd done her face after she'd gotten him to sleep.

He thought back, ten years back, to the time when he had come home from Korea to meet, court and marry the sweet and gentle, blonde and shy young thing called Ethel, all within the period of two hectic months.

He wondered, does any man ever know what he's getting? Can any man look past the pretty face, beyond the tip-tilted, proud young breasts, inside the rounded curves, below the promise of passion? Do men realize that a bride is a gift, a pretty package, all wrapped in tinsel and ribbon, tissue and tape? All gift-wrapped in hair from the beauty parlor, lips from Revlon, odors from Lenthéric? All gift-wrapped in pretty skin? Do they know that the gift wrapping has a sublayer, that it's also made of frustrations and regulations, of lessons and repressions and whippings, of four-letter words scribbled on alley walls, of curious probings in public school girls' rooms, of forbidden gigglings, of mothers who have never let the umbilical cords be cut?

Ethel had been such a pretty gift package, so good on the outside, and with such pretty tinsel. And the gift of Ethel, when the very first wrapping was removed—the well-tailored clothes, the pink lace panties, the cup-shaped brassiere that lifted her a little more, and made her a little fuller than nature intended, the girdle that rounded her and made her bottom bounce just a little more provocatively—the gift of Ethel had been good.

Even when he had gone beyond, beyond the golden hair, beyond the tinkling laugh, beyond the soft and yielding flesh, the gift of his pretty young wife still had looked good.

And even beyond that. Beyond the glory of her virgin's breasts swelling and pulsing in his bridegroom's hands, her parted, moistened lips, her grunts and snorts of animal passion, her anxious, wanting hips, her alabaster thighs; even beyond that, the gift of his virginal harlot still had seemed good.

But on every woman, he thought, there are so many layers of wrapping, so many layers to remove before you reach the real woman, the naked, wanton, unashamed Eve. So many layers that grow less festive and more tarnished, uglier and browner as the years go on. So many layers until you reach the gift, only to discover that the loveliness wasn't in the gift at all, but solely in the wrappings—the wrappings of illusion.

He remembered the room and the night, remembered the rice falling from his hair as he bent down to untie his shoes. He saw the door from the dark bathroom open, saw his young, shy bride stand there, white against the darkened doorway, her golden hair wild and tumbled about her shoulders, her breasts straining, pushing their hard brown points into the lace of her nightgown, the ultimate loveliness where her downy stomach sloped lower to meet the Grecian perfection of her thighs.

"I thought you were going to wait inside until—"

Her face was pale. She looked at him like a frightened doe, but a doe that had suddenly decided to be a tigress. "I'm ready now," she said. "All ready and wanting. I'm tired of wanting. I've wanted too long."

"But you were so-so shy, before."

"I'm still shy. I'm a little drunk, too. So what? Should I wait some more? Don't you want me?"

His voice caught in his throat. He could feel his desire rising. "Want you? My God, how I want you!"

She reached down, caught the hem of her nightgown and pulled it slowly upward, wriggling her hips joyfully, suggestively, loosening her flesh from the cold caress of the fabric.

"Then let's not wait anymore." She smiled through the lace veil of her skirt. "Are you glad you waited?" she asked. "Look at me. Did you think that I had so much to give you? Did you think I'd have so much to give to a husband? Because I'm shy, because mother was around so much when you came courting, did you think ..." Her words were lost in the thunder of blood pounding in his head.

He was aware only of the gentle yet enticing motion of her body, of her breasts, first one, then the other, peeping free of the rising nightgown. He saw the nightgown as it pulled and tangled her hair upward, as it dropped silently to the rug.

Before he could remove his shoes or shake the rice from his hair, before he could get out of the striped-pants symbol of his groomship, she was with him.

With his shoes still laced, the clown's costume of his wedding night crumpled in a heap on the foot of the bed, they became man and wife.

He remembered how, hours later, she lay on her stomach, legs spread slightly apart, playfully kicking her heels in the air while he picked out the grains of rice that were embedded in her tousled hair or had fallen to the sheet. He remembered how his fingers searched for each grain, real or imagined. He remembered the shrill tinkle of her laugh as she squealed, "Silly, you won't find any rice *there*."

"So who's only looking for rice?" he answered.

He remembered the tip of her pink tongue lancing out to taste the sweaty palm of his hand. He remembered many things, some good, some that made him wonder now, as he recalled removing one more layer of the gift-wrapping from around the shy young virgin with the harlot's hips and hot-tipped tongue who had been his bride.

But this was many years, many layers of gift wrapping later.

He reached down to shake Ethel's shoulder …

"Hello," he said. "Are you asleep? Oh, no, don't get up. Don't even open your eyes. Just move your pretty little fanny over about two-and-one-half inches so I can lie down and rest my upset libido."

She didn't move. He leaned over and touched her bare shoulder, shaking her. She moaned a little and turned over on her back. Her breasts lay firm and full under the sheer bodice of her gown.

He touched them, closing his hand.

Her eyes came open and she stared up at him. She twisted away from his hands and flopped her arm across her breasts.

"You're drunk," she said.

"No fair. You peeked. You ever hear the story about the fellow came home plastered?"

"No."

"Lucky. You're just lucky. You always get out of hearing more things than I get out of hearing. Did I tell you how pretty you're looking tonight?"

"Get your pajamas on. Lie down. Go to sleep."

"Wait a minute. Are you attempting to becloud the issue, madam? Tell me. You want I should get on my pajamas, lie down, or go to sleep?"

"Please, Hank, honey. I'm tired. I'm sleepy and I want you to let me alone."

"Honey. But, honey. I don't want to let you alone. I came home to you. Don't you think that is wonderful? There were a lot of places I could go. Grouse shooting in Canada. You ever shoot a grouse? You ever see a grouse? There was a polar expedition just outfitting on the corner of Lemon and Main as I came by. They were using the spot usually reserved for the Salvation Army. When I reminded them of this, they offered me a full colonelcy to join them. But I—say, that's a beautiful gown you've got on. It looks so—"

"Stop it. You're drunk. I've never seen you so drunk." He sat down on the edge of the bed. He tried to kiss her. She twisted her face away.

"Your breath. It's terrible!" Ethel said.

He shook his head, smiling. "Now isn't that funny? What whisky can do to breaths? Some breaths it makes so fine. And some breaths it makes so mine. Is this place taken? You mind if I lie down here by you? You're built so pretty. I'm a building inspector. Plumbing. Heating—"

"You're nasty. Stop talking like that!"

"Honey. Words. They're just words. They don't mean anything. Until you make 'em mean anything."

"Oh, I don't care. God knows, I know you well enough by now. I know how awful you are. No other man would talk to his wife the way you talk to me. They wouldn't dare!"

"Well, my God, no wonder. No other man ain't me. I'm me. My God. I say the little things that people want me to say—that people expect me to say. They look at me and say, look at that Hank Ireland. You can look in his eyes and see that he is a devil. Suppose I speak like an angel? People would be disappointed. You would be disappointed. You would have married Ed Gantner. And would you have been disappointed. Oh, would you have been disappointed!"

"He would have treated me with respect. Like a lady—"

"You tell me who's more bored than a lady. And I'll tell you who's married to Ed Gantner!" He chuckled.

"Ed Gantner's a gentlemen!"

"Who?"

"Ed Gantner!"

"I never heard of him. Say, that's a beautiful gown you've got on. Nobody but you could wear a gown like that. You gotta have everything to go with it, or it's no good."

"Stop it, Hank. Keep your hands off me. I'm not going to have you coming in drunk like this to maul me. I wish now I'd gone on my vacation yesterday. Mother wanted me to go up to the lake with her. I wish I hadn't waited. I wish I hadn't been here to see you like this—"

"What's wrong with me like this? I'm beautiful like this. Remember?" He looked down at his naked body, sucked in his navel and grinned. "Body beautiful. Do they call you skinny? Study with Hank Ireland and develop the muscles that thrill. Maybe they'll still call you skinny. But they'll call you. At all hours."

"If you don't stop, I'm going to get out of this bed. I'm going to sleep in the guest room."

"Oh, no. Let me. Never let it be said I chased any woman out of her warm bed. I'll go to the guest room. Exiled to the guest room. Like an overnight guest in Wantaugh."

Hank stood up. "Good night, my love. I want you to know I've enjoyed every chilly minute of it. Call me sometime. Any time. It's been a pleasure being married to you. Sometimes it even seems like I'm not. Sometimes. Good night, Mrs. Ireland."

"Go on, Hank. Go to bed," Ethel said. "I want to go to sleep. And put your pajamas on. You look indecent."

Hank looked down at himself. "Who's to care?" he inquired.

He stood there looking at her for a moment. He turned around and staggered out of the room. He snapped off the bathroom light and stumbled the rest of the way in darkness.

He fell across the bed in the guest room without even turning back the spread. Ethel would raise hell about that in the morning. But that was in the morning. Meantime, he saw two giant earrings dancing in front of his eyes. Gypsy earrings.

"Good night, Mrs. Miller," he said aloud. "Thanks. And good night, Mrs. Ireland. Thank you, too."

CHAPTER THREE
Squaring Accounts

Hank awoke at six o'clock the next morning, sweated down. Mornings after were always rugged for him. But there had never been one like this in his memory.

He swung his feet off the bed. He sat there a moment with his forehead against the heels of his hands. It wasn't his head that ached. It was his stomach. There was an awful emptiness there. A sense of loneliness without knowing what he was lonely for. A sense of need without knowing what he needed. A feeling of lack and insufficiency.

Quietly, he got up, went to the bathroom, showered and dressed. He moved on tiptoe. He didn't want to talk to Ethel. She was going up to Lake Vital to spend a few weeks with her mother. She went every year. For the first time, be wished she were already gone. This morning more than anything he wanted to get out of the house without seeing her, or talking to her.

It was a silly way to act but he didn't see how he could face her. He didn't want her to see what was in his eyes this morning. What had she said last night? No other husband would talk to his wife like that. Treated like a lady. Coming in drunk to maul me.

He scratched his head. It seemed to him his marriage could use a few maulings. Maybe there was too much respect and too much caution, and too much working twenty-four hours a day for more money and respectability. Anyway, he didn't want her to see what was in his eyes this morning. They'd been married ten years and he had never consciously hurt her. He had done a lot of things he hadn't wanted to do to keep from hurting Ethel.

He winced. It looked like he had done damned few of the things he had ever wanted to do. He was in a rut. He didn't have a life at all. All he had was a set of habits that he put on and took off like the shirts Ethel bought him, neck size sixteen.

She was his wife. And this was a morning after. It wasn't a matter of wanting to leave her or anything like that. He loved her.

He stood perfectly stiff, thinking. At least he had loved her. The memory of the way they had been in love was still pretty clear in his mind. It was just that they had been married for ten years and she said she knew him so well. And he didn't understand her at all …

He had always known what he wanted. He knew where he wanted to go and what he expected of life. Ethel was a part of that life. It was just this morning. Hangover. He didn't want to talk to her this morning.

He was buttoning his shirt when she opened her eyes. "Where you going?" she said.

"Work." He didn't turn around. "I'm going to work."

"What time is it?"

"I don't know. Forgot to wind the clock."

"You've got your watch on."

"Forgot to wind it, too."

She sat up in bed. "Are you going to be silly, Hank? Are you going to act foolish because of last night?"

"No."

"Well, you are. You're standing there like a stubborn little boy."

"A man is a little boy grown tall," he quoted. His voice was heavy with sarcasm. "I don't see how I can help being what I am."

He started out of the door.

"Wait a minute," she said. "I'll fix your breakfast."

"No. I'll buy it downtown. I'm not hungry. Go back to sleep."

"I'm perfectly wide awake now."

He stopped in the doorway, looking back at her.

"Well that's just too bad," he said. "Because now I don't give a damn."

There was no place to go when he got downtown. It wasn't even seven o'clock. His office didn't open until nine. There wasn't any place to eat breakfast but a greasy joint on a side street, An all-night cafe where people ate with their hats on. People who didn't care how much grease there was on their eggs, or how boiled their coffee was, or how airless the surroundings.

He drove around. The sun was already metallic. His shirt was sweated across the shoulders. He left his car in the parking lot near his office building and walked across the street to the park.

He found a shaded place and sat down on one of the wooden benches. A cop sauntered past and a newsboy went whistling by on his bicycle. A little man in a gray suit led a black cocker spaniel on a leash. It got to be eight o'clock and the shade shortened around his bench. His head ached and his eyes stung. His stomach was infested with crawling insects.

He tried to think about Ethel, but all he really thought about was Amy Miller. A nice-looking girl passed on her way to some office and he tried to think about her. But it always came back to last night. What he had wanted was in Amy Miller's brown eyes. And he had known it and she had known it.

It had happened fast all right the way lightning strikes. No foolishness. No frills. Just two people looking at each other in a crowded room. And *knowing....*

He clenched his sweated fists. Last night he had looked at a woman and wanted her and today the whole world looked different. His outlook had changed. He had been perfectly content. In a kind of cataleptic state of contentment. He was in a rut, but he had been so busy making it a bigger and better rut that he hadn't even realized he was tired out and bored and suddenly scared.

Oh, what a hell of a way to feel! He wasn't a kid anymore. He was thirty-one. They made excuses for kids.

There wasn't even the excuse that he was unhappy with Ethel. He wasn't unhappy. He was just hamstrung and he was bored. Boredom. He couldn't even remember how long it had been since they'd had anything else.

The sidewalk was getting busier now. People passed him, hurrying to work. Trying to buy a gold-plated lining for their little rut. All of them looking like they knew what they wanted and knew where they were going.

He knew only one thing. He had been a sleepwalker for a hell of a long time.

He got up and joined the hurrying people. In an air-conditioned restaurant on the ground floor of his office building, he ordered orange juice, coffee, bacon and eggs. But when they brought it, he couldn't eat it. The smell of the food made him ill.

He pushed it all away from him untouched. He left a tip for the waitress, paid his bill and went up to his office. And the funniest part of the whole thing was he was twenty minutes late to work....

When he came into his office, his secretary said to him, "Mr. Herviman is waiting to see you."

He sat down behind his desk and looked at her. Very pretty, very serviceable, the way a secretary should look early in the morning. She was blonde. A little heavy. "You still married this morning, Lucile?"

She smiled. "Afraid so."

He shrugged. "All right. Send in Mr. Herviman."

He managed to stand up and smile when Mr. Herviman came in. If he held on tight to the edge of his desk, the pigeons in his belly would roost for as long as a minute at a time.

Mr. Herviman was a stocky, gray-haired man with a flushed round face. He smiled at Hank with his mouth but his eyes were frowning. Hank told him to sit down and Herviman took the chair at the side of Hank's desk.

"Good to see you, Mr. Herviman," Hank said.

Herviman's Stores had been one of Hank's biggest accounts before they made him sales manager at Thompson's. Herviman knew Hank from those days and liked him. Probably that explained why he had come to him with his trouble instead of going to old man Thompson himself. "Afraid there's a little trouble, Hank."

"What is it, Mr. Herviman? Anything we can do, we certainly will. You're too good on account of ours for us to let anything happen to upset you—"

"Well, it has upset me. And it wasn't necessary. And it isn't the first time it has happened."

Hank leaned back in his chair and tried to smile.

"Let's start at the beginning, huh?"

Herviman managed a smile. "All right. It began when they sent a new salesman to replace you. This man Miller—"

"George Miller?" Hank felt a sinking sensation in his belly.

"That's right. Twice he's gotten big orders from my managers by promising quick delivery on scarce items. In both cases, my men have contracted for goods at premium prices in order to get the delivery he promised. In both cases, by the time delivery was made, the goods were no scarcer with any other jobber and the prices were a little lower."

Hank sat forward. It was a neat trick. A good way to get big orders. Find out what your customer needed and then promise immediate delivery. The fact that the distributing company didn't even have the quantities demanded on hand was minor. Good orders brought bonus checks. It was a trick Hank never used. But then he had never been pressed for bonus money the way some salesmen were. The way George Miller was.

"If you'll give me the order dates and items ordered, we'll check, Mr. Herviman. It may be that Mr. Miller was correct in making the promises—"

"Twice?"

"Well, accidents do happen. Let's find out. If he marked the orders rush, and we had the merchandise, then the mistake was in the shipping—"

Herviman's hand was trembling. "Well, the mistake wasn't in the shipping department. That man Miller is no good. He will promise anything to make a sale. He continually misrepresents. I'll wait until I hear from you on this matter. But only because I've always found you fair and because I've always been able to trust you. But if it happens again, I'm going after his skin. I—I'm not going to continue doing business with a man I can't even trust!"

Hank's shoulders sagged. He had known this was coming. He had seen it coming. But why in hell did it break this morning.

When Herviman was gone, Hank buzzed for Lucile.

She came in. She was carrying her shorthand pad and pencils. Very efficient.

She sat down in the chair Herviman had just vacated. She crossed her knees. Hank didn't bother to look this morning.

She frowned. "Are you ill today, Hank?"

He scarcely heard her. His smile was mechanical. "Look," he said, "when George checks in, will you tell him to come in to see me?"

"Herviman?"

"Yeah."

"Boy. That George Miller plays 'em fast and loose. Will you do me a favor when he comes in here?"

"All right. What is it?"

"Remind him that yesterday was payday and that he owes me ten bucks—"

"My God. You, too—"

"Well, you sure can't resist him when he turns on that old charm. He turned it on me and had ten dollars from me before I could remember to shake my head from side to side. But I really need it and he doesn't even seem to remember—he borrowed it."

Hank raked his hand across his forehead. "I'll get it for you this time, Lucile. But don't lend him any more."

"Don't worry. Since I lent him that ten, I've heard from everybody else in the office. He's owed some of them for months. What does that guy do with all our money?"

Carl Peters was the company bookkeeper. He was about thirty. He had studied to be an auditor, but his job as head bookkeeper for Thompson's looked so secure he was afraid to throw it over. A fleece-lined rut for Peters, Hank thought.

Carl's hair was light brown and he must have bought the cheapest haircuts in town. His head was clipped up close in the back and around his ears. His hair stuck out on the sides. His glasses were thick-lensed.

He sat down at the side of Hank's desk. He had a handful of papers with figures scribbled all over them. He didn't say anything. He straightened his glasses on the bridge of his nose with his finger and flipped an expense account on the desk in front of Hank.

It was signed by George Miller.

Peters shook his head. "I've read some action stories in my time," he said. "But here's one that really gets around. Entertaining two customers at lunch. Seventy-five dollars!"

Hank's hands were shaking. He picked up the expense account and let his eyes move down it. "My God," he whispered. He breathed out and then he said it again. "My God."

"That thing's got to be okayed by somebody," Peters said. "I'm ashamed to show it to anybody and ask for an okay. I hate to have anyone think I'm that dumb."

"Has the cashier paid it?"

"Sure. That's Thompson's orders. Pay 'em out. He likes to get a guy across a board. You know that. Let 'em pull something like this and then force them to produce itemized statements or kick back. The only other thing is to get it okayed before Thompson sees it. If he sees an okay on it, that's as far as the old boy will go."

"Did you talk to George about it?"

"No."

"Why not?"

"Well, when you get to talking to him, there are so many things to talk about. Shortages. Unbalanced accounts. He's spending more money than he's turning in. At least he's not turning it in." He dropped the rest of the papers on Hank's desk. "I don't say that George is worth saving. But he's a hell of a swell egg. I hate to see him get the axe if there's anything anybody can do."

"My God. I don't know what I can do."

"Well, I don't either. I thought since you were a friend of his and his wife's—"

"Wait a minute. Last night was the first time I ever saw her."

"That right? George told Fred and me that you were a friend of theirs. That's why he wanted to ask you over when Andy got sick and couldn't make the poker game."

Hank was getting sicker by the moment.

"Look," he said. "Leave the stuff here. I'll go over it. I'll talk to you this afternoon."

Carl stood up. He was relieved to get this mess off his shoulders. He hurried out of the office.

Hank sat there looking at the papers before him. A complete record of how a man had snarled himself up by spending money that didn't belong to him and then tried to repay it with an exorbitant expense account and bonuses on big orders that couldn't be delivered as he promised.

He closed his eyes and pressed his fingers against them. He could see Amy as she had looked at him last night. Tilting her head back. Parting her lips. And then the look in her eyes that she didn't mean for him to see: the startled look, the baffled fear.

He opened his eyes and looked at the statements before him. Things like this were what he hated most about his job. He guessed every job seemed pretty bad at times. This one paid well and the hours were good. Just the same, he would be glad when he could break free. He and Ethel's father were going to buy and operate a country newspaper. Hank had promised Ethel that he wouldn't say any more about it until they were out of debt. When the house was paid off, his last debt would be cleared and Hank would be free. He was saving the money that he was going to sink into the weekly newspaper and printing plant with Ethel's father. Ethel's father loved the mechanics of printing and publishing and Hank wanted to run the business and editorial end of it. What a dream! What a wonderful day that was going to be. He couldn't discuss it aloud at home but sometimes Ethel's father dropped into the office, and they talked together like two boys whispering in a classroom.

Maybe that was what was the matter with him. He had been working so hard to pay the debts that Ethel made for him and still be able to save a little money that he hadn't realized he was leading the same kind of life a squirrel lives on a treadmill. That paper was still a long way off.

His fist closed over the paper on his desk. In the meantime he had to talk to George Miller. George Miller who had fast-looking girlfriends, gambled, drank, lied, borrowed from everybody, padded his expense account and lived one hell of a spree, got some fun out of life. How he envied George Miller. George was out helling around right now. And Hank had to do something about George's fouled up statements. And in the meantime, there was the memory of a girl he wanted. And he had to get her out of his mind.

CHAPTER FOUR
Winona Dream

"Mr. Payson to see you."

"All right, Lucile. Send him in."

The secretary turned around in the doorway to call, but Ethel's father was standing there right behind her. He grinned at her, a rakish little devil-may-care guy of fifty-three.

Hank stood up, smiling. He came around the desk.

"My golly, Justin! I was just thinking about you. How the devil are you, anyway?"

Justin Payson waited until Lucile withdrew, closing the door after her. It was as though the state of the little man's health was a secret. Confidential. Restricted.

He shook Hank's hand warmly, looking him over.

"Good lord, Son," he said. "You look sick."

"Hangover," Hank said, "Hell, I was up till after eleven last night." Ethel's father laughed.

"Why you rakehell, you!" he said. "Did Ethel lock you out?"

Hank looked grim. "Not with the key," he answered.

Payson smiled and sat down. He picked up his trousers as though there was a crease in them. There wasn't. He looked wrinkled as if he'd been sleeping on a park bench.

"I know how it is," he said. "Ethel's mother was often like that. I read that a great many women are that way. I've often thought that if there were any suitable substitute for women, men would soon do away with them."

Hank smiled, feeling better. It always gave him a lift to talk to Ethel's father. The little man was a printer by trade. He'd gone out on strike against a newspaper fifteen years before. When the newspaper rehired the union workers, it refused to take back Ethel's father. He'd been pretty bitter and outspoken during the strike against the management. When the union forced the newspaper owners to rehire Payson, they made him so miserable that he quit in less than a year. He'd spent the rest of his life yearning after a printing plant of his own, one that he could run the way he knew it should be run.

"I've been out of town for a few days," Payson said. "I took a run down to Winona."

"What's that? A dancing girl?"

"It's a town. A county seat. Twenty-five hundred souls. One of the nicest little newspaper and commercial job plants I've ever seen. We could buy it. I know we could. Why, in a year we'd be strutting like pigeons."

"Did the owner want to sell?"

"I've never found one who'd admit he did, and there never was one who didn't if the right price came along. We've got to get together on this thing, Hank. Put up our money—if it's nothing more than a down payment—"

"Right now, I can't." Hank spread his hands.

Payson seemed to wilt physically.

"It's like this all the time," he said. "When will you be ready, Hank? Are you getting in a rut? Is security getting to mean more to you every day?"

"Damn it, you know better than that. I've promised Ethel. What else can I do? You were married to her mother. You ought to know what they are like."

Payson sighed and looked down at his rumpled clothes. His suit was brown single-breasted and needed pressing badly. He needed a haircut. It seemed to Hank that he had never seen Ethel's father when the little man didn't need a haircut. His tie was old and stained and his shirt collar was wilted.

Payson lifted his head. His eyes were a faded blue. In them there was a look of inexpressible sadness. Loss.

He nodded. "All right. We'll wait. A while longer. Maybe there'll be another buy along as good as the *Winona Star*. But I don't see how. A weekly newspaper in a county seat. Legal advertising and political printing. It's a basis. The rest is gravy. And in a progressive small town there's plenty of gravy."

Hank shook his head. "I'm sorry," he said. "I think Ethel would leave me if I tried to break off here at Thompson's before her house was paid for."

"All right. All right. I know how it is. I'm afraid she would, too. You're a smart young guy, Hank, and I don't want to see you throw over what you have. A guy needs a wife. He—he goes to seed without one. He— he's forever lonely. He's forever lost—without one. Wandering around, eating in restaurants, sleeping in strange hotels—"

"Forgetting to get a haircut."

Payson smiled. "Yes. That, too. I know that it won't be long. And I ought to quit coming up here bothering you like this. But this thing is all I have—you know—"

"I know. And I want it as badly as you do."

"No. With me it's something else. A newspaper plant would be my whole life. I haven't anything else left. That's why I want you to walk carefully, Son. Don't lose things, carelessly, like I did. Things you think you can replace. Things you think you can do without."

Hank didn't smile. "Haven't you ever tried to make it up with Ethel's mother?"

"No. Why, Son, what have I to offer Ethel's mother? What did I ever have but a job and security? It's a hell of a thing when life gets down to that, when a man and a woman have no more for each other than habit and security. It makes you decide life is not worth living. And then you spend fourteen years living as I have, finding out that there's some reason, some plan behind the whole thing. To this day I don't know what it is. All I know is that a man can't fight it in this day and live happy."

Payson broke off suddenly, laughing.

"Let's forget this kind of talk," he said. "Let's get out of here and get a drink. That's what you need anyway. Hair of the dog. Ever try a whisky sour the next morning?"

Hank looked at his watch. "I guess I've time for one drink," he said. "I don't know anything about whisky sours. I don't drink that much. Besides, I don't think it was what I had to drink last night. I didn't have that much. And I was so sick it was all I could do to get home."

Payson looked at him as they started out of the office.

"Something upset you, eh?"

"Yeah. Something."

They walked out into the corridor. Payson pressed the down buzzer. He looked at Hank "Keep an even keel, son. You're a young guy and the whole world is in your hand—"

"Feels like it's on my shoulders this morning."

"Well, it isn't. A good job. Sales manager at Thompson's and only thirty-one. No reason to believe you won't go as far as you want to go. Or there is our scheme. You and I could make it work, Hank."

"I expect to," Hank said.

"You will. You've got the energy and the strength and the vision. But you need someone like Ethel to keep you level. Otherwise, I'd advise you now to break clean, and let's get started on that newspaper. But we've got to go slow. You must not end as I have. Just now is the most important part of your life."

Payson nodded. It was almost as if he were talking to himself, as he sometimes did. "And you're what's important, Hank. Why I could buy a two-bit job plant and make some money. But that isn't what I want. I want my printing to matter. And you'll make it worthwhile. That's why I want you to stay on here at Thompson's just as Ethel insists, until you have no debts. That way your mind will be at rest and we can really get to work."

They entered the bar on the ground floor. It wasn't crowded at this hour. They sat on stools and ordered. The bartender pushed their drinks before them. Hank paid.

Hank sat there just looking at his whisky sour.

"Drink up," Payson said. "You'll feel better."

"I don't know. This thing has got me." He was thinking about Ethel. Was Justin Payson right? Was the world so shot to hell that a man had a right to expect no more from life than a bloodless marriage and security? Where was the reason for living? Where was the purpose? Where was the urgency that was going to keep you wanting to wake up every morning?

Oh, God, please don't let Justin be right! Don't tell me finally that I've thirty more years at least of boredom and security. Of waking and sleeping.

"What's got you?" Justin was saying.

He couldn't tell Justin the truth. Whoever understood the terrible and incredible pull of desire in someone else? Nobody. A man could fall in love with a woman. But he couldn't believe that his neighbor could. With his neighbor it was always a quick itch, an urge to roll in the hay.

Besides, how could he tell Payson that he wanted another man's wife? Justin was Ethel's father. He was a pretty understanding guy. But Hank would bet his bottom dollar that was one thing Payson would never understand.

So Hank said, "Oh, there's some mess at the office. I've got to straighten it out, or a guy's going to lose his job."

"Is he worth saving?"

Hank frowned. Had he even thought about George Miller? Hadn't all his thoughts been about George Miller's wife? If he did try to save George, wasn't it going to be for Amy? Even if she never knew anything about it?

"I don't know. I guess so. It's just that it's such a rotten mess. It gives my ulcers ulcers."

Justin looked at him. "Don't let it get you, Son. Take it easy. Remember you will get out—"

"Will I? Or is this just the way you and I fool ourselves? Is this just something you and I smoke instead of an opium pipe?"

Payson looked as if Hank had hit him. "Don't talk like that. Please. For God's sake, don't talk like that! We'll make it. Hang on, Hank. Look. Four or five thousand dollars would take care of your half of the *Winona Star* for right now. Just get that much together. We'll make the down payment—and then we know damn well—"

"Then we know damn well that Ethel would walk out." Four or five thousand! He had part of it, but only a part of it. A guy could save just so much money these days no matter what kind of life he lived, no matter how hard he saved! Four or five thousand dollars. Why not four or five thousand stars pulled down out of the Milky Way? God, the thing was so close. The kind of job he wanted, a thing that would keep him busy, so he could get something for the hours of sweat he put into it. It seemed like such a little bit of money. Such an impossibly little bit! His voice was bitter. "This job and this house! That's what matters first. Okay, so it's not much longer. Three or four years? Five? All right, I'll pay off the house and we'll have what we want. Meantime, I've got to get back up there and tell George Miller he's got to take what's coming to him!"

CHAPTER FIVE
Hell of a Fellow

George Miller was waiting in Hank's office. Something had settled Hank's stomach by now and he felt better. Maybe it was the whisky sour. Maybe it was talking to Justin Payson. That always gave him a lift. Maybe it was the fact that it was now twelve hours since he had seen Amy Miller. That was the first time he had seen her and getting her out of his mind was still easy. Any woman could knock you for a loop if she threw it at you the way George Miller's wife had. She was a pretty hot number. A tramp. He tried to tell himself he was thankful he wasn't George Miller.

"Hi, George," Hank said. "Sorry I had to break it up so early last night. Got pretty sick. Something I ate, no doubt."

George was sitting in a chair at the side of Hank's desk. He was a very handsome blond man. He was at least six feet tall. His shoulders were wide, his hips narrow and his legs long. Hank looked at George and thought, there's a guy with everything.

Hank had envied George's free and easy life, his loud laughing friends and his sprees ever since Miller had come to Thompson's. Hank could remember when he had been a carefree guy. Well he could almost remember.

Why in hell had he ever thought George's wife would look at him?

Because she had looked.

George was smiling. "The babe outside said you wanted to see me."

Hank sat down behind his desk. He hated things like this. He hated it especially with George Miller. George had fun out of life no matter what else you said about him. Why in hell did Hank have to ride herd on him?

Here was Hank working like a slave, not because he liked to but because he hated his job and wanted to buy his way into a better one. He was always saving his money. He didn't even smoke and seldom drank. He and Ethel had a few friends and they visited them. But it was a quiet life they led and never did anything that cost very much money.

Hank liked the way George lived. George lived fast. Or maybe it just seemed fast when Hank compared it to the way he lived. George would gamble on anything. He lost so much money on the horses that he was borrowing money all over the office three days after payday. He was good looking and quite a salesman or he would never have lasted at all. He had certain customers from whom his orders were always big. Twice the size of the ones Hank had turned in when he was covering the same territory. There were some stores from which George never failed to get big orders.

George drank a lot. He had more flashy looking friends nailing on him at the office or riding with him in his car than Hank could count. He had plenty of women running after him, too. There was always some new woman nailing him on the phone or coming to see him.

George was one hell of a fellow with his tight blond hair and his straight profile. Except for being slightly too thin, he looked like a movie star. But the faintly gaunt look about him improved his looks. Women thought he looked more interesting.

Hank pawed at the papers on his desk. He hated this job and he hated George for putting him in a place where he had to show Miller that he had been caught robbing Thompson's as surely as though he'd held a gun at the cashier's head.

"Yeah," Hank said. He picked up the expense account sheet first and flipped it across the desk so that it landed in front of George.

Miller looked at it and didn't even touch it.

"My God, George," Hank said. "You must have known when you turned in an expense account like that, somebody was going to have to okay it."

George shrugged. "Okay it then."

"My God! Seventy-five dollars for lunch? How can I?"

"Why can't you? Why, Goddamn it. I'm working for this lousy outfit ain't I? When I take a client out to dinner, I pay for what he eats, don't I? You're the boy who said a lunch like that belonged on my expense account."

"I'm not questioning that, George. Hell, I don't care. But seventy-five bucks!"

"All right! It was old man Solomon and his partner from the West Coast. We had drinks, a couple of models. I had to pay their time and for what they ate and drank. Christ, I just put it down as lunch to save Solomon any embarrassment."

Hank looked at him. George's smile was insolent. His smile said, All right, I'm lying. Make something out of it.

"You got itemized statements?" Hank said.

"You ever get an itemized statement from a model who also lays?"

Hank sighed. He reached over and picked up the expense account. He stamped it, wrote okay across the face of it and initialed it.

"Okay," he said. His voice was tired. "That'll get filed. You ever try it again, George, God help you. I won't."

George just looked at him. The smile didn't waver from his face.

"She must have been a hell of a lot better than she ever was with me."

Hank felt his face flushing. His head jerked up.

"What are you talking about?"

"The kitchen. Hell, that drink of water you got last night. Amy says you're quite a wolf among the pots and pans."

Hank felt tight in his chest. He stared at the expense account. He wished with all his soul that he hadn't okayed it yet.

"I'm sorry," he said. "I was high."

George laughed. He threw back his head laughing, his even white teeth showing.

"Sure. You were high. My God, forget it. Amy has, I know. It's all right. Eskimos entertain that way all the time. Course I don't when I know anything about it. But what I don't know don't hurt you, does it?" He laughed again. His laugh really made something cheap and common out of it.

Hank's jaw tightened. He moved the pile of statements over to George.

"You better go over those again," he said. His voice was hard. "They're all out of balance."

George laughed. "No. They're not. They're okay. The cashier wouldn't pay that expense account voucher until it was okayed. But Fred's a friend of mine, so he kept it. He said he would pass it along until it was okayed. Now that it's okayed, I've got the cash to cover those shortages. That ought to make everything all right, huh?"

George picked up the expense voucher. Hank looked at him. "It ought to make everything all right now," he said. "But what about next month?"

George's grin was disarming and boyish.

"Hell, let's burn that bridge next month, kid."

The door opened and Lucile came in. She had three orders in her hands.

"Here are the Herviman orders you wanted, Mr. Ireland," she said. Hank was watching George's face. He saw Miller flush and squirm a little in his chair.

Hank looked up at Lucile. He took the papers. "Thanks," he said. She was standing behind George Miller's handsome head. She screwed up her mouth, making her lips form the words, "ten dollars!" She pointed down at George with her finger.

Hank nodded. Lucile smiled and started out of the room. She closed the door behind her.

"Herviman was in," Hank said.

George smiled. "How was the old boy?"

"Mad."

"At me? Why?"

"Making promises to him you couldn't fulfill."

"On what?"

Hank shoved the orders at him.

George looked at them. "I marked those things rush. Hell, the shipping clerk slipped up."

Hank took one of the papers back. "It isn't marked rush on here."

George looked at it. "Well, I'll be damned. It sure isn't. I guess I was rushed myself. You see, Herviman wanted that stuff, and I knew we had it—"

"Stop lying, George—"

George stopped, staring at him.

"Why, I'm not lying—"

"Look. We didn't even have that stuff when you took the order for it. You knew we didn't. But it boosted hell out of your accounts for the week and you got a bonus out of it bigger than your salary. I don't care what you tell Herviman. But you got to work with me. Stop acting like I'm a prize jerk. I know how to get up to this place mornings. That's all I got to know to see that this whole damned order was a phony, and you knew it when you took it."

George got up and went to the window.

"All right. So Herviman wanted something we didn't have just then. I quoted him a price, and he accepted it. I turned in the order and the purchasing department tried to get the merchandise. Hell, what's wrong with that? It just puts those birds in purchasing on their toes, that's all."

Hank exhaled. "If you don't know what's wrong with it, George, I'm not going to bother to tell you. Hell, you think somebody is going to straighten out every mess you make. You know damned well that Herviman is too big an account for us to lose by admitting that you lied to him. So I'm stamping this thing rush, and we'll mail it to him so he can see the stamp. That way Shipping will take the rap because they don't represent Thompson's at Herviman's Stores. You do. So we've got to protect you."

George shrugged. "So, okay. We both knew that's what would happen anyhow, so why the big stink? It's all right. Nobody is hurt."

"You're hurt," Hank snarled. "How long do you think Herviman will go on trusting you?"

"Too hell with old man Herviman. I'll ask Thompson for a new territory. And I'll get it. Who do you think has the best sales record in this office? I have. And by God, I resent it all to hell when you call me in here on the carpet about a few lousy dollars."

"That's fine, George. But now let me tell you something. You're going to have a hell of a time getting another voucher like that one okayed around here. What are you going to do then?"

George smiled. "I'll worry about it when it happens. Maybe I'll come in the kitchen and get you to okay it."

Hank flushed. "I've said I'm sorry. You can stop riding me about that."

"You better be glad I'm not a jealous husband, old buddy. I might shoot you."

Hank's voice was level. "You better be glad I'm not a better boss. I might fire you."

George laughed, "Okay. So there we are. Comes out even, huh? That's what I like about you, Hank. That's what I tell the fellows. Hank's regular. Even if you did get promoted. Even if there are guys older than you around here that got passed up. You're a regular guy and I'm happy as hell to have you as my friend."

Friend. Hank felt his teeth itch.

"Just don't count on it," he said. His voice went cold. "I don't know how much longer I'll be here. Even if I was here, I wouldn't go on okaying things like that last account."

George was leaning forward in his chair. "What you mean, you're leaving?"

Hank shrugged. "I don't know if I am," he said. "I don't even know when. Another job maybe."

"I heard talk there was something else you were saving for. Something you want to do, huh?"

"Yes."

"What is it?"

"On a newspaper. A country weekly. I've wanted to for a long time."

"Well, look. Say, that's swell. Let me tell you, Hank. I hope you make it."

Hank laughed. There was no mirth in it. Hell, there was nothing to laugh about George Miller's wife and George Miller's kitchen. He could see her now, lying beside George in their bed. Laughing. Telling George about the Casanova of the Dishpans. Well, he wouldn't see her again. That was sure. But not seeing her wasn't so wonderful.

That didn't leave him so much. Ethel. Her vacation at Lake Vital with her mother. Three or four weeks. Not that he would miss her. She might as well be at Lake Vital though she lay beside him in their bed.

What did he have here at Thompson's? George Miller making phony promises, and giving phony alibis for his lies, borrowing from everybody in the office. Padding his expense account until it was funny enough to make a bookkeeper laugh.

"I hope I make it, too," he answered George. "I'd like to get out of this. But I guess that newspaper is my own Shangri-La. Something I dream about to keep from blowing my top."

George laughed. "I didn't know you dreamed about newspaper plants. My little woman would be surprised to hear that, too. She says she bets you're a real devil with the women. I think you kind of impressed her."

Hank felt his face getting hot again. He wished there was some way they could forget that trivia about George Miller's kitchen.

"Look, George," he said. "There's just one more thing. Lucile thinks maybe you've forgotten you owe her ten bucks."

George threw back his head and laughed. "I did forget. By golly, Hank, thanks for reminding me!" He shoved his hand into his pocket and brought out a crumpled ten-dollar bill. He flipped it on the desk. "Give it to the babe for me, will you? You might tell her I'd have been willing to let her take it out in trade. But if she would rather have the money, what the hell."

Hank picked up the ten-dollar bill, straightening it between his fingers. "Thanks, George," he said. God, he hated playing such a holy role. He felt stodgy. He felt like a stuffed shirt.

George said, "Come on down to the bar and I'll buy you a drink, kid. We'll get this bad taste out of our mouths."

Hank looked at his wristwatch. He didn't really have the time. He sure as hell didn't want a drink. He looked at the smug grin on George's face. God, Hank was tired being a stuffed shirt boss.

He got up. "Sure. Come on."

As they went through the outer office, Hank made the okay sign at Lucile behind George's broad back.

George stopped at the cashier's office and Fred Vaught paid the expense voucher in cash. He looked up at Hank. Fred's knowing eyes narrowed. His mouth twisted a little.

Hank felt guilty. He felt like an accomplice in a holdup. He went out of the office and waited for George at the elevators....

"Hell, I was up to my can in debts when I took this job," George said. His eyes roved over the dimly lighted bar. They were across from each other in a booth at the rear. A jukebox whispered a new love song. George had said they would get the bad taste out of their mouths. But he hadn't talked about anything but his predicament since they sat down.

Hank sincerely wished he hadn't come.

"Amy is no manager," George was saying. "Hell, she don't know any more about handling money than a five-year-old kid. We'd stay in debt if it was left up to her. I got her a job a couple months ago. Cashier at Nesmith's Department Store. Got to know old man Nesmith when I called on him for Thompson's. He had an opening and I spoke to him about Amy. She's getting along pretty good. The money she makes helps a lot."

Hank didn't ask George what debts he had. He didn't care. He didn't want to hear about them. He was tired of George. He knew how much George gambled and how much he drank and how many debts he must have incurred for both. But if it pleased George to blame his wife for their indebtedness, it was none of Hank's business.

"Look, Hank," George said. "I want you and your wife to come out to our place for supper. Any night. Just say when—"

"I'm afraid—"

"Amy can cook a pretty good steak. But then, hell, anybody could cook the kind of steak I buy—"

"Ethel's going out of town for a while—"

"Well, come out before she goes! That way she won't have to cook anything. No messy dishes to wash before she takes off. Say! You're a pretty lucky guy to have your little woman go off on her vacation alone—"

"Yeah," Hank said. "Lucky."

"Well, how about tonight? At our place?"

"I thought you said your wife worked—"

"She does. So what? She gets off at five o'clock. What the hell? She's got nothing else to do—"

"I'll bet she'll love cooking for four people."

George's face was hard. "What difference does it make if she likes it or not? I'll tell her."

Hank shook his head. "Well, don't. We can't make it, George. We just can't make it."

He wasn't going to make it. He wasn't about to go out there. He had been to George Miller's house once. It had taken him twelve hours to get Amy out of his mind. It wasn't a big thing yet. It was nothing. He could forget all about her. Or else, he could keep fooling around with her. He'd be in so deep he'd never get out. Maybe so deep he'd never want to get out.

CHAPTER SIX
Invitation

Hank got home that night a little after five. He picked up the afternoon paper as he crossed the lawn and went in the front door.

Ethel was curled up in the wicker easy chair on the sun porch, painting her fingernails. Her hair was up in curlers again and she wasn't wearing any make-up at all on her face. But even so, in her green shorts and green halter she looked good enough to eat. But Hank knew better. He didn't like that taste she left in his mouth when he tried to love her.

He glanced in at the dining room table. It was bare except for the bowl of fruit on the knitted mat in the center of it.

"Going out somewhere?" Hank said.

"You're a detective, darling. How did you guess?"

"It was easy. Your hair was up last night. It's up again—"

"Oh. Did you notice my hair last night?"

"I looked at you."

"Oh, I know you did, darling. You were quite lecherous."

"Jesus Christ! Jesus H. Christ. I'm a guy who wanted to go to bed with his own wife. Is that lecherous?"

"Stop shouting. I was just teasing you. I even know why you were so excited last night."

He felt the chilling premonition of trouble. He stood there, waiting. He said, "What does that mean?"

She stopped painting her fingernails and looked up at him. "I had company this afternoon, darling. Guess who?"

"Gromyko. He came to take lessons on saying no—"

"Darling! You're really quite witty—"

"I know. And you'd die laughing, except you've got some putty on your face and it would crack if you smiled."

"—you're perfectly funny when you want to be. I don't see why you can't be funny when company comes. Usually you sit around as glum as an old man. I hope you'll do better tonight—"

"Where are we going tonight?"

"You haven't guessed yet who came to see me."

He flopped down in a chair and unfolded the newspaper.

"I don't know," he said. "Ed Gantner?"

"No. Silly. I haven't seen him in years."

"You two should get together. That's what your bloodless romance needs. A transfusion—"

"Oh. You're so awful! Ed wouldn't, anyway—"

He frowned. "Ed wouldn't what?"

"Oh, I know what you meant by transfusion—"

"Either I don't know how to talk or you've got a dirty mind—"

"Well, I certainly know the answer to that one. I didn't even know any dirty words until I met you."

He looked over the top of the newspaper. "Well, it comes out even, baby. I didn't know what some of them meant—until I met you."

She leaned forward on the easy chair. The wicker squeaked under her. "You awful thing!" she said. "Sometimes I wonder why I stay with you. The refinement of a jackass, the breeding of a bloodhound, the instincts of—"

"Who came to see you this afternoon?"

"George Miller."

He dropped the paper. "Who? George Miller? What in God's name did he want?"

She swung her legs off the easy chair. "Well, first he said he wanted to meet me. He said he wanted to know what I was like. He said he had such respect for you. So young in your job and all. He made me real proud of you—"

"Oh, he can charm the horns off a she-goat any day in the week."

"—and he said he was a good friend of yours. He said you were a friend of his and his wife's—"

"That friendship gag again," Hank muttered.

"What?"

"Nothing. What else did he say?"

"Oh. He said a lot. He was real nice. He stayed a long time. It was exciting. He's so good-looking. And I could see the old cat next door peeking through her window curtains when he left—"

"You've got him out of the house already and you haven't even told me what he came for."

"To invite us to supper."

"I'd already told him we wouldn't go."

"Well, George said that. He said you said you couldn't go. On account of me. You know, Hank, I never keep you from doing anything you want to do."

"His wife works. Why should she cook for us after she's worked all day?"

Ethel looked at him. "Well, you didn't think I should cook for us, did you?"

"No. I refused the invitation. I thought that ended it. Foolish clod that I am. I hope you told him we're not going."

"I didn't. I told him we would go."

"All right. You're going alone, then."

"I thought you'd want to go! My goodness, his pretty little wife and all. Oh, I heard about it. How you tried to kiss her in the kitchen—"

"I didn't try to kiss her. I kissed her. She wanted me to."

"Oh, sure, darling. All the women chase you. I know all about it."

"All the women don't chase me. No woman chases me. I got high. I kissed a dame. And that's all there is to it."

She laughed at him. "Not quite, darling. You got so excited you came home and practically raped me."

"Oh, Christ!"

"I suppose you told Miller all about it?"

"Well, he told me about what happened at his house. Why, he thought it was terribly funny. And he told me not to think a thing about it. His wife is like that with every man. It doesn't mean a thing."

"That's what I said! Not a damned thing!"

"Well, you don't have to yell at me about it."

"I am yelling. And I'm not going out to their place. Tonight. Tomorrow night. Or next year. Is that clear?"

"He told me about his wife working and all. So it ended with my inviting them to the Plaid Bar for supper. You owe me an evening out anyway—"

"Some other time—"

"You're going tonight, Hank. My goodness. What do you want me to think? That there really was something to that silly kiss in the kitchen—"

The newspaper was twisted in his fist.

"I want you to forget all about it!"

He got out of the chair. His mouth tasted like a dusty attic. He plodded into the kitchen and mixed a stiff drink. When it was mixed, he poured in another shot of bourbon.

He came back to the sun porch, drinking. Ethel was still sitting there, watching. Her mouth was tight.

"You must have had a pretty fine time with your little slut in the kitchen."

"Lovely. Now lay off."

"It must have been lovely. Or you wouldn't be afraid for me to meet her."

"I don't give a damn if you meet her. I hope you do. You've got a lot in common. You've both kissed me in the kitchen and neither one of you liked it—"

"So you did try to kiss her. She wouldn't let you—"

"She let me. If you've got to have a blow-by-blow account, she gave me everything there was to give, without undressing. Now. Will that do it? Will you let up?"

She sighed. "Poor George Miller. I can see what he meant. He envied everything here, Hank. A lovely home. Quiet. Refined. No wonder, with a bitch at home that throws herself at every man that comes along—"

"Maybe not every man."

Ethel shrugged. "Well, she's a married woman. If she'll do it with you, she'll do it with anybody."

"That doesn't speak too highly of you, does it?"

She stood up. "What does that mean?"

"You've been nice to me, too. Does that mean you'd do it with everybody?"

"It's different. Entirely. I'm married to you."

"I can see that all right. You *have* to be nice to me. Whether you find me revolting or not—"

"It isn't that. You're a perfectly nice-looking man. In a way I guess you're a lot better looking than George Miller. At least you look more like a man—"

"Well, thank you, Mrs. Ireland."

"That doesn't mean she has to throw herself at you—"

"She didn't throw herself. She just stood there and took it." He gulped down his drink. "Now, lay off. That's all I'm going to say about it."

Her voice was cold. "Except one thing. We're taking them out to supper. You might as well get up and get dressed. If she can get you this excited, I want to see her. She must really be something."

CHAPTER SEVEN
Strange Feast

She was really something all right.

George and Amy were already at the Plaid Bar when Hank and Ethel got there.

At first, Hank was a little shocked when he saw her get up from the red divan in the Plaid Bar reception room with George. He frowned. She didn't look like anything. What was all the furor about anyhow?

She was wearing an inexpensive dress with swirling dots and stripes effect. It was a little too long at the waist and not quite the chic length below her knees. Hank knew nothing about fashion, and cared less. But he knew that her dress was wrong. He could feel it instinctively.

He jerked his gaze up to her face, almost frantic looking for the suppressed excitement he had seen there last night.

God! How drunk could you get? She looked plain. And she looked tired. She looked like somebody's wife who had been working all day. A wife who was somewhere she didn't want to be and didn't give a damn who knew it.

She had on too much lipstick, too much rouge. It was as if she had been trying to hide how tired she was, and had been too tired to accomplish it.

But who was going to look at her with George around anyway? George looked immaculate. Handsome as a movie star, his gaunt cheeks making him look worldly and interesting. And people did twist their necks to look at George when they started into the lounge.

He took Ethel's hand. "I'm glad you came," he said. "I've been looking for you. I was afraid you wouldn't."

"But of course I would," Ethel said. "I said I would."

Amy stood uncomfortably in the background. Hank kept watching her. She hadn't even looked at him.

They started in to dinner. Ethel dropped back, putting her manicured hand on Hank's arm.

"Shoddy," Ethel whispered. "Why she looks shoddy."

As they went through the lounge, Hank watched Amy looking around. The walls were in Scotch plaid. The room was indirectly lighted. The bar gleamed dully. The lounge wasn't crowded but most of the tables were taken, and there were only a few empty stools at the bar.

"Hey," George said over his shoulder. "Let's tilt a couple before we eat."

He shrugged Amy's hand off his arm and led Ethel to the bar.

For a moment Hank and Amy stood looking at each other.

He offered her his arm. She smiled at him. It was a wan smile. Tired. She touched his arm. Her fingers closed on it. Just a little more pressure than was necessary.

He looked quickly at her again. She wasn't plain anymore. Like a chameleon she had changed with his own feelings toward her. Her head tilted back a little. She dampened her lips with the tip of her tongue. Hank felt his heart begin a steady, unnatural slugging.

"We can't sit with them," she said. "Here. Here are two places. Come on."

She sat with him at the bar. He looked at Ethel and George. Ethel was watching him. He nodded toward her.

He looked back at Amy.

"Hello," he said. "Imagine meeting you here."

"Imagine."

A bartender came to take their order. Amy ordered a scotch and soda. Hank said, "I'll take bourbon and ginger ale. And—a glass of ice water."

She looked at him and crinkled her nose. She laughed as though that were really funny. Now both George and Ethel were watching them. Amy looked down the bar at George and Ethel. Amy stopped laughing. There were tears in her eyes. She cried when she laughed. But now that she'd stopped laughing she sat there with her hands on the edge of the bar, staring at the bottle labels across it. She didn't speak. She didn't even look up when the bartender put a big glass of iced water beside Hank's bourbon.

She drank her scotch slowly. He waited for her to speak. But she said nothing.

"You want another drink, Amy?"

"Me? No thanks."

"I just asked to make conversation. I thought maybe you'd forgotten me."

"Me? No. I knew you were there. It's nice. I didn't expect this."

"You looked overjoyed. I'll bet if you were really glad to see me, you'd even smile. Hell, you might even go so far as to turn around and look at me."

"I thought we were doing all right."

"Sure. I made a joke. I asked for ice water. You laughed. We're getting along swell."

"I'm sorry. I'll do whatever you want. What do you want?"

"We couldn't do it in here."

"All right."

"My God. Did you even hear what I said?"

"Yes. You said we couldn't do it in here."

George and Ethel came down the bar then. They all went through the lounge to the dining room. A man was playing a small organ at the arched doorway between the lounge and the dining room. George was still walking with Ethel. Amy was at Hank's side, only she didn't touch him. She didn't try to avoid touching him but there was space between them and she kept it that way. His arm felt cold.

"You want to dance, Ethel?" George said.

"I love to dance. I'd dance all the time. Only Hank doesn't like it."

"The music interferes," Hank said.

Ethel got up. George put out his arms. They danced away from the table. Hank and Amy sat there watching them.

"George is a real smooth dancer," Hank said.

"Yes."

"If I'm keeping you up or anything," Hank said, "if I bore you, say so. I'll slit my wrists."

She was rolling bread crumbs on the table cloth.

"You don't bore me at all. I'm having a wonderful time. Really. I'm glad now that I came."

"What did you think when George said we were going out tonight?"

"That I was tired." She smiled. Now she looked at him, fully, for the first time. "I was glad though. I wanted to see you again."

"Why?"

"I don't know. I've been thinking about you all day."

"Yeah. I heard. Casanova of the Dishpans."

"I'm sorry. Really. I didn't know George would say anything to you. I didn't mean to hurt you."

He was banking parsley around the remains of his roll. "It doesn't matter."

"You're mad with me about it."

"No. I tell you. It doesn't matter."

"He told your wife, too."

"It still doesn't matter."

"But it does matter. It matters to me. I didn't want to hurt you. Why should I want to hurt you? Why you? But George saw us. That's why I was so scared, there at the end, when I finally did pour you the glass of water. He was in the hallway watching us. I saw him over your shoulder."

"Oh?" he said, sarcasm dripping like venom from his words. "What was there to be so scared about? Good old George expects that of you. Amy, the perfect hostess. Make your guests happy. Keep your hips high. Don't let their shirttails drag in the dust." He laughed. "Who are you trying to kid? Remember me? I'm the patsy who wasn't quite thirsty enough last night to go all the way to the well. And George knows you better than I do, poor slob, he's married to you. He knows you're ready to rattle the dishpans with any guy interested in your cups and saucers."

His voice was low and bitter. Suddenly he wanted to hurt her, to see her squirm under the whiplash of his words. He wanted to see tears streak her face, to make her bleed, inside and out. Suddenly he loaded all the frustrations of his own bloodless marriage, of the fight for dollars, of all the screaming, kicking, gut-tearing, ulcer-making crud of his life into his voice and aimed the whole stinking mess at the huddled figure seated next to him.

"George knows you're a round-heeled sow in heat who can't be trusted," he snarled. "Why should it matter to you what happens to me? You milked me last night, saw me for what I am. You know me as well as any woman ever knew me. You had your yaks with your bastard of a husband and now you're both here with me and Ethel trying to make me eat dirt. Why? What have you got against me? What did I ever do to you that makes you want to rip me apart? So I dirtied your hands last night. Does that make you want to dirty my whole life?"

"No—no, listen to me," she cried desperately, twisting a napkin in her hands. "I wouldn't have told him at all if he hadn't seen us. He made me tell him. Everything."

"Everything? What the hell kind of an everything was there? He made you," Hank sneered. "How did he make you?"

Her face was cold and drawn, a mask under its façade of cosmetics. "See all this goo on my face," she said. "All this cheap-looking, pancake junk? Do you think I like being made up like a three-dollar floozy? I don't like it. I hate it. Especially when I know I am going to see you. But I've got to wear it. To cover up the bruises where he hit me."

She ignored the sharp intake of Hank's breath, tumbling her words on the table before him, watching as they healed the wounds his words had made and opened new wounds of their own. "Don't look so shocked," she said. "You hardly even have a spitting acquaintance with good old George. Want to know him better? I'll pull down my dress and take off my brassiere. Will you be happier when you can see the black and blue marks on my breasts, when you can see the scratches his nails made, when you can see where that bastard twisted, to make me tell him all about you? How good you are, what kind of a man you are, how you measure up to him, whether you're as good as he is? We've got lots of time. I'll give you a blow-by-blow description. Would you like to see the welts on my back where he whipped me with his belt? Do you want to hear all the lies I had to tell him because he wouldn't believe the simple truth? Do you want to hear every lousy, humiliating detail I had to feed him, do I have to tell you of every stinking degrading thing he forced me to do, before you believe me?"

Hank was breathing hard and heavy.

"Put your eyes back into your head and stop staring at me that way. Being married to George doesn't show, and when he beats me he's smart enough not to mess up my face too much. He's real good at it. He can hurt me so it doesn't even show when I'm nude. I'll let you see some time."

Hank stared at her, drained. His anger was gone, transferred to the movie idol profile who was gaily steering Ethel around the dance floor. He reached across the table for Amy's hand, to touch her, as a gesture of belief, of understanding.

"Don't do that," she said, smiling her tired smile. "Let's look happy, but not too friendly. We're still on display." She reached under the tablecloth, so that the movement could not be seen, and patted him lovingly, to tell him she knew he understood and believed. He could feel his emotion respond, as if to reach for the compassion he knew was in the touch of her hand. He held himself rigid, afraid that with George and Ethel so close his desires would show.

"The son of a bitch," he said. "The dirty—"

She shrugged. "Don't let it bother you. I'm stuck with him. You only have to put up with that blonde iceberg he's trying to thaw out on the floor."

"How did you know?" he asked, his curiosity piqued by her rapid and uncanny appraisal of Ethel.

"A girl can tell," she said. "We're all sisters under the skin. All cats are alike in the dark, you know, and put a flag over our faces and all that. Really, it's easy, it's written all over her. Her mother was probably a raped virgin who hated her father and brought dear Ethel up to think that all men are dirty beasts. She's the kind of doll you'll find in Greenwich Village, the passive partner in a lesbian affair. But get her drunk some night, or come home wearing a mask, so she thinks you're someone else. You're liable to get a big surprise."

"I've had it," he said bitterly. "My big surprise. Once. One marriage, one surprise. But why did George have to tell her about you and me and the dishpans?"

She crushed some crumbs between her thumb and index finger. "George is a great little talker." Her voice was tense. "George will talk his guts out if he can find somebody to listen to him."

Hank didn't say anything. At last Amy spoke again. "It was a nice kiss, Hank. It scared me. That ought to build up your ego. It's the first time

I've ever been scared in my life."

"Why should I scare you?"

"It wasn't you. It was what your loss did to me. I didn't want to stop. I didn't want you to stop."

"Is that why you ran and told George all about it?"

"Let's not go into that again. Will you dance with me?"

"You heard Ethel. I can't dance."

"I don't care."

He shrugged and stood up. He put out his arms and she came in close to him. Too close. He could feel the slight shiver that went all the way through her slender body. He put his arms around her. He hadn't known she was so tiny. His hand closed over hers. Her fingers were as cold as ice.

And dancing with her, he knew the answer to the question that had puzzled him when he had first seen her tonight in the reception room. How could he have fallen last night for such a plain girl? A girl with too much rouge? And now he knew. It was inside her where Amy Miller was different. Inside she was charged the way an atom bomb is charged. She wanted what he wanted. She wanted anything he wanted. And that was in both their minds.

He didn't know how it had happened.

All he knew was that now, holding her in his arms, with the soft music around them, he really wanted her. He wanted her the way he had never wanted anything in his life. He knew. She could be anything he wanted her to be. A nun burning a candle in a church. A slut screaming drunk in the streets. She could be gentle. Candlelight shadows across her face in some cafe. She could be a hellcat, spitting and scratching. She had never been touched, not really. She was still complete, still waiting, inside where it mattered, for the guy who could make her know he mattered.

He knew he couldn't explain the way he felt about her. Any more than he could explain how he understood the truth about her. Just as he couldn't explain what was happening to them. It had to happen to you, or it was meaningless. If it never happened, you were blessed. If it happened to you, you inherited God's world, and everything in it, and the heaven and the hell beyond it. And that's what was happening to him.

"George says you may leave Thompson's."

"Yeah. Like I'm going to fly—without a plane. Hell, it's just something I dream about."

"A country newspaper?"

"Shangri-La."

"You're going to do it if you can though, aren't you?" She was looking at him. His answer seemed important to her.

"I'm saving my money," he told her, embarrassed. "Paying debts and saving money. That's all I do. Real exciting character."

"I think it's wonderful," she said. "Just being able to save money nowadays is wonderful."

"Well, I haven't saved enough. I need five thousand for a down payment. I don't have that much."

"But if you've got part of it!"

"That's what I've got. Part of it."

She burrowed closer against him. He could feel the warmth of her. He began to know what a guy would go through for something like this. It was like being on the edge of a precipice. The thought of the jagged rocks down below it had always scared you before. Now all of a sudden you were anxious to jump.

The music stopped. They started back to the table.

A man and a woman were coming toward them. Hank watched Amy's face light up for a moment. Obviously it was somebody she was really glad to see.

The man started to speak to her and she abruptly shook her head. It was a warning gesture! If Hank hadn't been watching so closely, he wouldn't even have seen her do it.

He glanced at the man. The fellow was frowning, baffled. But he didn't even speak to Amy. He took the woman's arm and moved by them.

Hank looked down at Amy. Why had she done that?

"Friend of yours?" he said.

"Oh, no. I don't even know him."

"Don't you? He thought you did."

"Oh, maybe I met him at the store or something. I don't know. I don't even know his name."

Why was she lying to him? What reason would she have for lying? He felt cold. She wouldn't have any reason. Except to keep in practice.

CHAPTER EIGHT
Friend George

A couple of nights later George asked Hank over for a steak dinner. Ethel was already at Lake Vital with her mother. Hank had spent one lonely evening. And he admitted it. He'd spent it thinking about Amy. Thinking about the things she'd said to him while they were dancing. Things that amounted to nothing, really. And yet he couldn't get them out of his mind. They added up to so much. He wanted to hold her again, too, just the way he had while they danced at the Plaid Bar.

George insisted on calling for him. George drove a late model green Chevrolet business coupe. He drove fast and carelessly, talking all the time with laughter and gestures.

When they parked in the driveway before George's house, Hank could see Amy standing in the doorway, awaiting them. He began to feel those hornets in his stomach and he no longer pretended to listen to George.

Amy came out on the front porch to meet them. Her smile for Hank made him feel he was really somebody. Her smile was special. Almost as good as the one she'd given the poor guy at the Plaid Bar. The guy she hadn't even known. He shrugged the thought out of his mind.

She was flushed from working in the kitchen. Her forehead was moist and she looked tireder than ever.

She was wearing a green dotted wraparound dress that tied together with a small bow at her waist.

She seemed hardly aware of George. She took Hank's hand and led him through the front room.

"Come on into the kitchen for a drink before supper," she said. "George will fix us one."

"Yeah," George said. "Only no ice water." He laughed.

Hank followed them into the kitchen. The dining table was set, and the food was waiting in the kitchen to be served. There were two fifths of whisky on the drainboard with ice cubes, glasses and chaser. Hank frowned. Wasn't he being paid a hell of a lot of attention?

George started mixing drinks. Amy stood in the middle of the room and looked at Hank. Nobody said anything. Hank leaned against the drainboard. He began to feel uncomfortable. For no reason at all, he felt like a lamb before a slaughter.

Amy smiled. "I'm just wearing this old dress," she said. "It's too hot to wear anything else."

"You look swell," Hank said. He couldn't decide why he felt they were both going to too much trouble to put him at ease. The dress that she was wearing, too much to drink on the drainboard, thick steaks broiled expertly.

"She's not wearing anything else, either." George was mixing the drinks and didn't look around. "Maybe she's got shoes on. You got shoes on, Amy?"

Amy didn't bother to answer George. She came closer to Hank. "You don't care what I've got on, do you?" she said. Her breath was hot with whisky. He noticed her eyes. They were dry, glazed. She must have been drinking ever since she got home. He wondered how she had cooked this meal so expertly.

George was shaking one of the bottles. It was almost empty. "Amy, what have you been doing, using this stuff for a shampoo?"

"I was hot," Amy answered him. Her voice was negligent "I needed something to cool me off."

She was pressed against Hank now. He was sweating.

"You still do," he said. He tried to move away. She hadn't lied. She wasn't wearing anything under that wraparound dress.

"Don't mind George," Amy said. "George don't care if you kiss me. Do you, George?"

"Hell no. He's my boss. How can I care?"

Amy put her arms around Hank's neck. Hank tried to disengage them without appearing ridiculous.

"Cut out that boss stuff," Hank said. He tried to laugh. "If you care, tell Amy."

George laughed. "Down, Amy. Down."

She laughed at that. "George has his little jokes," she said. "And I have mine." She mashed her parted lips against Hank's mouth.

He stepped back.

"We're not all as high as you are, baby," George said. He held out a highball.

"That's too bad," she said. "That's too bad for both of you."

George winked at Hank. "Oh, we'll catch up with you, baby. Won't we, Hank?"

Hank took a highball and drank it quickly. He'd never met people like these two before.

"I'm so far behind," he said. "I doubt if I'll ever catch up."

George laughed. "Oh, you'll catch up. Won't he, Amy?"

Amy wasn't even looking at George. Her glazed eyes were fixed on Hank's face.

"I hope so," she said. "I really hope so."

The telephone rang while they were in the middle of dinner.

They'd kept Hank's highball glass full all during the meal. The steak was thick and beautifully broiled. Amy said she'd learned how to French fry potatoes from the man who invented the idea. She laughed and said she couldn't remember what idea it was he had invented. There was a tossed salad, and garden peas. She had really taken a lot of pains to have this supper nice for him. But he hadn't eaten much. He wanted her too bad. It was hell even thinking about food.

The room was cool, a breeze tossed the curtains at them like white sails. But Hank was sweating. He was ill at ease with them. Maybe it was the way they kept watching him. Every time he would look up, one of them would be staring. He was beginning to be high again, too. It was the way it had been the first night here. Just being near Amy intoxicated him.

George got up and threw his napkin down on the table.

"Now who the hell can that be?" he said. "What can they want?"

He went over and picked up the receiver. Amy and Hank sat there waiting.

"George Miller speaking," George said. "Who? Oh. But can't it wait until tomorrow? I know I promised. But not tonight. I've a guest for dinner. I don't see how I can. Well. All right then. I will. In about thirty minutes."

He replaced the receiver and came back to the table.

"Otis Herviman," he said to Hank.

Hank shook his head. "Mr. Herviman? What does he want?"

"It's about an order. Like you said, he was afraid to trust me. I quoted him a price today. You know what he did? He called old man C. E. Thompson himself to check on me. Found out I was on the ball. Now he wants to see me at his office. In thirty minutes. I tried to get out of it—"

"Oh, hell no. I'll leave. I can come back any time."

"No, you won't leave!" Amy said that.

George laughed. "What can I say? Maybe you ought to go, Hank. But when Amy makes up her mind, we can't change it."

"I didn't cook this meal so I could sit around by myself all evening." She put her hand across the table and covered Hank's. "Please stay."

Hank couldn't look up at George.

"Stay with her," George said, as if they were humoring Amy because she was high. "I won't be gone more than a couple of hours at the most. We'll tie on a big one when I get back. What you say?"

Amy hadn't moved her hand from Hank's. "He'll stay."

When they were alone, they didn't say much at first. They both sat there, listening to George's car go out of the drive to the street. They didn't speak until they could no longer hear the car at all. Then Amy sighed.

"Well," she said.

For a moment they sat at the table, worrying their food with their forks. Amy pushed her plate away first.

"I'm not hungry now," she said. "I'm not that old."

"I'm not hungry either."

She got up. She was unsteady. She held on to the back of her chair.

"We'll leave the dishes," she said.

She went across the front room and flopped down on the couch. As she wanted it to, her dress fell open across her legs. They were very brown. She must have spent a lot of time sunbathing. She didn't close the dress.

Hank got up from the table. He looked at her. As she wanted him to. It wouldn't have mattered. He couldn't have stopped even if she had wanted him to.

She leaned forward. Like a perfect stage prop, the dress parted again, this time deep between her breasts.

"Am I pretty?" she said.

His voice was husky. "You're lovely," he said, "I've got to get out of here."

"Why?"

"Good God, I can't do this to George."

"If George had cared, he wouldn't have gone away."

He shook his head. "Don't talk like that."

She moved her hips on the divan. The pressure parted the dress so there was a wide space between the two halves.

He strode across the room and bent over her, resting one knee on the couch at her side. He thrust his arms under her back and lifted her. Her head flopped backward and she laughed up at him.

"Am I drunk?" She laughed at him. "Am I driving you crazy?"

"What are you trying to do?"

"I'm not trying to do anything. I'm doing it."

"Please, Amy. Tell me to get out of here. And tell me quick. I can't stand this."

She lifted her head a little, laughing at him. "Go ahead. If you want to."

All the color had seeped out of her face. Her arms went around him and she pulled herself upward toward him.

"If you're a fool, go on."

"I'm a fool all right. I want you."

"Then stop talking!"

With his left hand under her head he brought her face up under his. Her eyes were wide but they didn't look glazed. For a moment the terrible slugging of his heart slowed. She wasn't drunk at all! She was watching everything he did. And laughing like hell.

Let her laugh, damn her! he thought. *I'll give her something to laugh about. This time she'll really have something to tell her precious George.*

His face was close against hers. Her eyes were big. Big enough to die in. And all of a sudden he didn't give a damn if he did die. This was what he wanted. Exactly what he wanted. He was going to wipe that laughter off her damned gypsy face.

She held to him and he stood up, dragging her against him. He could feel her naked body against his clothes.

He was holding her as tightly as he could.

His breath was rattling in his throat like rocks in a can.

Her arms went around his neck and she kissed him hard. She may have started out faking it, but it ended no fake at all.

She pulled her head back, gasping for breath.

"My God," she said. In her eyes was that same alarm he'd seen the first time he kissed her. "My God," she said again.

His voice rasped. "What are we doing!"

"Don't care," she told him. "It's happened before, darling. A lot of times before. Only this in the first time I've wanted it to happen."

His voice was savage. "What about George?"

Her voice matched his. "What about George?" Her face contorted up close under his. "George would sell me for two dollars if he thought he could get it. You know that."

The smell of her and the hot throb of her body would have been too much for him even if he had been a good man. He wasn't. Hell, he was just Hank Ireland. Just a guy. Just nobody.

"Take it off! Take it off!" She spat the words at him without moving her head more than half an inch from his face.

He reached down, fumbled at the belt and had to rip it loose away from him. He had to pull it down. He saw it fall to the floor without even looking at it.

"Take me to the bedroom," she said. "Right now."

"Let me lock the doors."

"The hell with them!"

"Somebody will come!"

"I don't care. Why should you?"

He swung her up in his arms. She didn't weigh much more than a hundred. It wouldn't have mattered. He was as strong as a god. He was a god. He had asked for something and by some miracle he was going to have it. He'd move heaven and hell to have her. And he didn't care what happened to him after he had her.

He turned sideways and went through the small hallway.

"There," she whispered against his face. "The back room."

It was dark in there. Hank slammed the door behind them.

"Lock it," she whispered.

She was supporting herself with her arms locked around his neck. He reached behind him, turned the key in the lock.

He stretched her out on the bed and she lay there writhing. She was reaching up for him.

"Wait," he whispered in the darkness, watching her white body moving against the bed in the dark.

"Don't take any of your clothes off," she ordered. "You don't have to. I don't want to wait."

He fell on the bed beside her.

She thrust herself against him. His arms went around her.

He was holding her with every ounce of strength in his arms. She didn't even seem to breathe. There was never anything like it. Never before. Never would be again. She was wild. She was crazy. She sank her teeth into his chin and hung on to him. He could hear her moaning between her clenched teeth. He tried to pull away from her. He couldn't without losing his chin.

… They just lay there side by side without speaking. Her head was back and her hair was wild across the white spread. He started to speak. Or maybe he just wanted to sigh.

She clapped her hand over his mouth. She was covering it with all her strength. He heard something. A noise. Nothing really. The noise a mouse makes in your pantry.

She shoved him toward the edge of the bed. She sprang up and unlocked the screen at the window beside it.

"Get out of here," she whispered against his face. "Get out of here and don't come back. Don't ever come back."

CHAPTER NINE
Double Exposure

Hank was standing outside Amy's window when George and the fat man broke down the bedroom door.

He could feel his heart bumping in the hot darkness up close to the house. He was shaking all over. When Amy first told him to get out he had been too paralyzed to move right away. She had shoved him and he slid through the window. He was afraid he was making so much noise they'd hear him in the next county.

For a moment after he scrambled to his feet in the yard he didn't know what to do.

His common sense told him to get out of there. Just as Amy had said. Get out and never come back. But he had to know what that noise was. He wanted to know what was going on. Besides he was too scared to do anything but stand there.

He leaned against the house, hidden from the street by the shrubbery. His heart was beating like a chased rabbit's.

He heard them break the door down, saw them burst into the bedroom. George was first. Behind him came the little fat man in a derby and a dark suit. The fat man was carrying an old-fashioned flash camera.

Hank was sweating. All the blood seemed to have congealed in the pit of his belly.

He watched George thrust his way into the room like a man who knows just what he's going to find but is trying to pretend that he doesn't. George stopped, staring. When George saw that Amy was alone something happened to his face. His mouth twisted and his eyes were wide and wild. He ran his hand through his short blond hair.

"Where is he?" George said. His voice was rasping.

Amy sat up in bed. She was as naked as the day she was born. Only now her nakedness meant something, in spades.

They were all staring at her. She was gypsy dark with her black hair down around her shoulders.

From outside the window, Hank could see the fat man. He was gawking at Amy, his puffed lips wet. He looked like he'd never seen a woman before.

Amy glanced at the shamus and his camera. Her mouth twisted. She pulled the sheet up to the base of her throat.

"Where is he?" George yelled at her again.

She smiled. Bland. "Where is who, darling?"

"Cut it out!" George was breathless. "I was gone just long enough to pick up Desales. Just like I told you. Where is he?"

"I'm alone!" Amy said. "Look around. You'll see."

Hank drew back a little from the window. He knew he should get out of there. There were neighbors if there was no other reason. And there were plenty of other reasons. The main one being that the only Herviman call George Miller had gotten tonight was from the fat Desales in there. This was a sucker setup. For some reason they had planned to squeeze him in the middle of it!

Amy had given him the chance to get away. He had to give her that. His mouth curled. That was all he could give her. They had really played him for a sucker. Amy hadn't even been drunk at all. Whatever the stakes were, they were too important for her to risk being even slightly drunk! And what beat him was that he still couldn't figure why.

He couldn't force himself away from that window. Not yet. It was as though Amy were a magnet within that room with the sheet pulled up to her chin, and he was drawn to her by some force over which he had no control.

George bent over the bed.

"All right, Amy," he said. "What kind of business you givin' me?"

"Business?" Her voice was teasing.

"God damn you! Don't talk to me like that!"

He drove the back of his hand across her face so hard that it knocked her over against the headboard.

For a moment nobody in that room spoke. Hank's heart was slugging away under his ribs.

"Look around, Desales," George said over his shoulder to the fat man.

Desales nodded and poked around under the bed and in the closet. He walked over and stood by the window.

Hank drew back, holding his breath. But Desales only checked to see that the screen was locked.

"Look, Amy," George said. "This thing is important. How did you foul it? I told you I had to have that money. It was a chance to get that job. Now damn you, what are we going to do?" He grabbed her shoulder and shook her. "I'm asking you one more time, Amy. Where is he? You can tell me or I'm going to beat hell out of you."

Hank moved back to the edge of the window now.

Amy was sitting forward, looking up at George. She wasn't crying. Her eyes were cold and hard with hatred. The imprint of George's hand was still across her face. Red streaks stood out against the livid whiteness of her cheeks, against the whiteness of her hatred.

Her voice was level.

"He didn't fall for it," she said. "I told you he wouldn't and he didn't."

"Don't lie to me. He fell for it. He fell for it before I got out of the house. You know damned well he fell for it. Now what happened? Where is he?"

"If you know everything, tell me. I told you. He didn't fall for it. He thought you were a friend of his. He thought I was a bitch. He walked out."

Hank knew that's what he should have thought. That's what he should have done. But what he had done was a hell of a lot different. He'd wanted her. He'd ached, wanting her. It was like something that grabbed hold of his insides and shook until he was sick at his stomach with wanting her. He'd had to have her. No matter what happened.

He shook his head. And almost it had happened. The broken door. The squatty Desales with his flash camera.

George Miller had him pegged for a sucker. George Miller knew every trick for getting money. And that's what would have happened. Hank would have had to buy his way out of this mess! George had him pegged all right all the way around. And dumb Hank had fallen for it hook, line and sinker. The oldest game in the world.

"All right, Desales," George said. "You can get out of here now. It didn't come off."

"I want my twenty bucks," Desales said.

George wheeled around. "God damn it. I haven't got twenty bucks. I told you you'd get your money if you took the pictures. Have you taken any pictures? Get to hell out of here, or I'll throw you out,"

Desales laughed at him.

"Don't take your miff out on me because your gash crossed you!"

George's white face hardened.

Desales laughed again. "You and your big talk. What a smooth operator you are. Don't make me laugh. You can't pull any job unless you got a twist you can trust—and not even you can trust that screw!"

George leaped at him. He got his hands on the front of Desales' shirt, shaking him. Desales began sobbing and moaning. He was trying to hold on to his camera. George was cursing him.

Hank knew they wouldn't hear him. And he didn't care. He moved away from the window and crossed the yard to the street.

It was a beautiful night if you cared for a beautiful night. Stars hung clear and clean against the black sky. There was a slight wind and it was pleasant in the trees along the street.

Hank walked slowly, without direction.

He tried to tell himself that it didn't make sense. But he knew it did. Cold, sickening logic.

Amy was just what she seemed. Just that. They were two people who got along the best way they could. What they wanted they took, one way or another.

Hank shook his head. This wasn't the first time they had worked this trick. How many times before? Who else? Where else?

He began to walk faster. He kept remembering how high she had pretended to be when he first got there. She hadn't been drunk at all. She'd had maybe enough to color her breath. That was all.

He could see George planning the whole thing. Sure. Since the night at the Plaid Bar. This was an old trick, and they had worked it before and it didn't take much to set it up. Hank had told Amy how much money he had saved and Amy had run straight to George. Hell, Hank had bragged to her about it. She had made him think he was wonderful. He had begun to believe he was wonderful. He had talked his insides out. They knew how much he had. They knew how to get it away from him.

George had it figured closer than that, too. When Hank left Thompson's, somebody was going to get Hank's job. Thompson would be sure to give first consideration to Hank Ireland's recommendation. If George had gotten the pictures he had planned to take, Hank would have been allowed to make one recommendation. Just one. George

Miller.

He shivered. It wasn't cold. It was a mild night with a million stars strung clean and bright across the face of the sky. And he was cold all the way through.

God, he had wanted her all right. And it had been all a man could ever want in her bed with her arms around him. Why did it have to be like this?

Brother, this was life and he just didn't have sense enough to realize it. He was baffled and lonely and tormented. He had asked for it. And had gotten it. Good.

It was as if she had kicked him in the groin. In a way, he wished she had kicked him. It couldn't have hurt anymore. And that kind of hurt a man could understand and recover from, and forget.

CHAPTER TEN
Slow Burn

The next afternoon Hank was at Lake Vital.

He parked the Mercury out in front of the Lake Vital Hotel and told himself he was all right. The ache was gone. Amy was gone. Somehow he had lived through the night. It had been the longest night of his life. But from now on everything was going to be different.

Lake Vital was a swankier resort than he had imagined. The hotel was an old faded green frame building. But it had dignity. It was four stories with gables and scrolls. The grounds were kept manicured like a pet peke. Everything was freshly painted and there was an air of daintiness about the place that he didn't like right away.

It was a resort for women like Ethel's mother. Women with money and time on their hands. The men he saw lounging around looked like the sort these women liked to keep, too.

He lifted his suitcase off the back seat and started along the walk to the wide steps of the shaded Hotel veranda. He decided he would get a double room and then call Ethel. He wasn't crazy about walking in on her mother.

"Why, Hank!"

He looked up and there she was. She was coming down the steps, carrying a tennis racket and a vacuum can of tennis balls. There was a slender man behind her carrying a tennis racket. He sported a blond mustache and a printed scarf knotted at his throat.

Ethel ran down the steps to meet Hank. She was wearing brief white shorts and a halter that crammed her breasts up tight. He wondered what secured them when she played tennis, but this was her vacation. He said nothing about it.

She stood up on her toes and kissed him.

"Well, this certainly is a surprise! What in the world are you doing up here?"

"The Old Man gave me a few days off," he lied. "I missed you."

She smiled up at him. Twinkled in fact. He hated it. She wasn't doing it for him at all. He had been to bed with her and if she'd ever twinkled there just once, he had forgotten all about it. She was trying to impress the blond man behind her.

She reached her hand around and brought him forward.

"Bart Cavanaugh," she said, "this is my husband, Henry."

Cavanaugh put out his hand. "Say, it's fine to meet you, Chap. I'm frightfully pleased. Confidentially, there are darned few men around here."

"That's right," Hank said. They shook hands.

"Well, Hank," Ethel said again. "How are you feeling?"

"Swell."

"Come along for a set of tennis," Cavanaugh invited.

"You two go ahead," Hank said. "I'll get a room and take a shower. I'll be down later."

"Righto." Cavanaugh took Ethel's arm.

She shook her head. "I'll meet you at the court, Bart," Ethel said. Bart nodded and strode off.

She waited for Hank's wisecrack. But he said nothing. This astonished her. She said, "You are all right Hank? There's nothing wrong?"

"No. Everything's swell."

She smiled again. She looked at him nervously.

"I'll tell you, Hank," she said. "Get a room and then you come on down. There are some lovely people here. You'll like them all."

"All right."

Ethel smiled at him again and started off along the walk to the court. She seemed in a hurry to get away from him. Just as though he didn't belong here and she had nothing to say to him in these surroundings.

He didn't see her mother until dinner.

He stood around in the lobby, waiting for Ethel to come down in the elevator. She stepped out of it finally in a grey dinner dress that must have been a gift from her mother. He had never seen it before. The dress was exactly right for her, for her age, for her youthful look, for her full figure. It didn't stir him in the least to see her looking so lovely.

They walked toward the dining room together. There was a tinge of color in Ethel's cheeks. He knew her well enough to know what she was thinking. Ethel knew people were looking at them. She knew they looked well together.

"I've taken a double room," Hank said.

"How nice, Hank." She nodded to someone she knew. She looked back at him, biting her lip. "I'm—all settled and everything, Hank. With mother. You know she'd be awfully disappointed if I were to move out so abruptly. If you'd only let me know you were coming—"

"Sure," Hank said. It hadn't taken but a minute to settle that. She was going to stay with her mother. They didn't mention his room again.

Mrs. Payson was sitting at a table for four awaiting them. Silverware, glass and napkins gleamed on the white table cloth. Mrs. Payson had a spoiled, tight-lipped mouth. She didn't look any happier than Justin, Hank thought. But she showed her unhappiness in a different, self-centered way. She was a stout woman and her dress was off-white lace that was new. And that was all you could say for it. Her white hair had been rinsed stylishly purple.

"Well, mother, look who dropped in!" Ethel said as though she hadn't already told her mother up in their room.

"For heaven's sake," Mrs. Payson said. "Where did he come from?"

"The stork," Hank said. He smiled at her.

She turned up her rouged face and Hank pecked at it. He held Ethel's chair for her and then he sat down. For a moment they all looked at each other.

"We're having a wonderful time up here," Ethel said.

"Good."

"Lot of swimming. Tennis. Oh, there's Bart over there." Hank looked. The blond Cavanaugh was wearing a white dinner jacket. "I'm afraid I asked him to supper with us, Hank." She brushed at her forehead. "It was before I knew you were coming. I hope you don't mind."

"Of course he doesn't mind," Mrs. Payson said. "He can't expect to walk in here and find us all holding our hands just waiting for him."

"I didn't," Hank said. "Believe me, I didn't."

Hank walked aimlessly along the dark walk that made a half circle around the shoreline of Lake Vital.

The music from the string ensemble floated after him from the hotel ballroom. He looked back over his shoulder. He could see the dancers moving and their fantastic shadows on the glass doors. On the lighted veranda he could see Ethel and her mother playing bridge with Bart Cavanaugh and another pansy.

The music was faintly sad and for no good reason it started him thinking about Amy. It had been all right last night. Last night he had been tired from loving her. She took a lot of loving and it left you tired all over. Numbed. You felt like you were doped. Anesthetized even against pain.

But now the narcosis was wearing off. There was a stirring in his loins. There wasn't any use lying to himself. It was always going to be like that. He'd come alive inside and there was going to be need. All the whoring and the drink in the world wouldn't satisfy it. Need. Only one person could satisfy that need.

God help him. It hadn't done him any good to run. He wanted her more than ever.

He turned around and started taking long strides back toward the hotel. He was running when he reached the lower step; panting.

He stopped, craned his neck to breathe more deeply, and he looked down at his hands. They were shaking. He started up the steps.

He wandered along the veranda. Ethel looked up from her cards. She smiled, winked at him. But the plain truth was, he was in her way. She couldn't think about him and the cards before her.

He gave her a salute and walked past the card tables. Nearer the ballroom they were playing canasta and they were noisier. He looked them over. They didn't look as if they were having any better time though than the bridge players.

He leaned against the doorjamb watching the dancers.

A woman with purple hair came over. She was wearing a net evening gown. Her smile was professional.

"Won't you come in and join the dancing?" she said.

"Just looking," he said.

"We have an awfully nice crowd tonight. If there's anyone you'd like to meet—"

He smiled, nodding. "If I see anything, I'll call you."

She looked at him a moment and then moved away.

He decided it was time to do penance. There was a woman sitting alone across the room. She looked fifty-odd and miserable. He went over and asked her to dance.

She beamed at him. She jumped up so hurriedly she dropped her handkerchief and compact. He bent over and helped her pick them up. She couldn't even dance as well as he could. She kept stepping on his toes and apologizing.

And then he saw her....

She was standing near the bandstand. Her back was to him. She was talking to a man. Her dark hair was caught in a net. Her dress looked cool and blue and perfect. He kept his eyes on her. The music stopped. He almost shoved the little woman back to her chair. He thanked her without even looking at her.

He started across the room. He got halfway there. The music started. People streamed out on the floor. She turned around, starting out to dance with the man she had been talking to. He stopped. Of course it wasn't Amy. When you got this close to her, you saw she didn't even resemble Amy in the least.

At eleven the bridge games broke up. Hank sat out on the veranda bannisters and yawned. Ethel got up and came over to him. She was wearing some new perfume. Probably another gift from her mother. It was fine.

"Nice smell," he said. "You smell fine."

"It's new."

"Yeah." He yawned. "Gosh, I'm sleepy. Let's take a run up to bed, huh?"

She looked around to be sure no one had heard him.

"You know I can't," she whispered. "You know I promised to stay with mother. That was the first thing she asked me when we were alone after dinner. Was I going to move from her room to stay with you. Poor thing. She's so lonely. I promised I wouldn't. I'm sorry, honey. Really, I'm sorry."

"It's all right," he said. He shrugged. "I hoped you might come up for a visit."

She bit her lip. "I'd like to. But mother likes to go for a drive. What she really likes to do is eat. There's a little town about twenty miles away. It has a nice restaurant and lounge. We drive over every night. I've asked Bart to drive us. We didn't know you'd be here. But please come along—"

"I'm not hungry. Anyway, I don't want to eat."

"Don't be mad."

"I'm not."

"After all, I've some plans I've already made. You can't expect me to change everything on a moment's notice!"

"Welcome back!"

Hank smiled. "Thanks, Lucile."

He started past her desk to his office.

She followed him in. "I thought you were sick," she said.

"Amazing recuperative powers."

"You must have. I hope so. Herviman is on the warpath. Some George Miller trouble again. I hope you feel just fine. I told Mr. Herviman you wouldn't be back. I thought you were going to be gone two weeks."

"Now, whoever started a rumor like that?"

George barged in without knocking.

He put out his hand. His face was a wreath of welcome-back smiles.

"Well, keed!" he said. "It's good to have you back."

Hank stood up. For a moment he stared at George. How could George put on an act like this after what had happened at his place the other night?

And then Hank remembered. As far as George knew, Hank never got to that bedroom. That was one story Amy must have made stick.

He shook George's hand, dropping it as soon as he could.

"Have a nice trip, baby?"

"Okay."

"Ran up to see the little woman, eh?"

"Yeah. Little woman."

"Uh, look, I haven't got a minute. Got some calls to make. I heard you were back. I just wanted to apologize."

Hank's jaw hardened. "For what?"

George laughed. "Why the other night Amy says you walked out on her." He laughed again. "You know Amy. Can't hold her liquor any better than a five-year-old kid. She got pretty high the other night. Why, she admits it herself. Hope she didn't say anything to worry you."

"No. Not at all. I had a swell time."

The telephone rang. Hank picked it up. "Hello," he said. "Ireland speaking."

"Hank?"

He felt the abrupt quickening of his heart.

He kept his voice cold. "Speaking."

"Hank, this is Amy—"

Hank looked at George. Hell, he hadn't been back in town two hours. Were they already hatching a new sucker trap?

"No, I'm sorry," he said. His voice was level "We don't have a thing in that line."

He shoved the receiver back in its cradle. He held it down there tightly.

George said, "Well, it's good to have you back, baby. Tell you what, we'll get together sometime. What say?"

"I'm pretty damned busy."

"I hope to hell you're not upset about Amy. I have to watch her when she's high. Quite a fight keeping guys out of her pants."

"Yeah. Must be hell."

George laughed. "Don't forget now. We'll make it a date. Maybe we can go out on the town while Ethel is away. Just us. I got some snappy addresses."

Hank's hand was still on the telephone. It was wet with sweat. George started to leave. The telephone began to ring again. George waved from the door. Hank picked up the receiver.

"Hank?" It was Amy again.

His voice was tense. "Why the hell don't you leave me alone?"

"I want to talk to you."

"All right. Talk."

"Not on the phone. I'm going to lunch now. I'm taking two hours for lunch today. I want to talk to you. I'll meet you outside Nesmith's Main Street entrance. Can you make it in ten minutes?"

"Why should I?"

"Please."

"There isn't anything to say."

"Just this one time."

"All right. Just this one time. I'll be there in ten minutes."

He had to ring twice for the elevator. Somebody had blocked his car in on the parking lot. They had to find three men to push it out of the way. He hit three red lights. There was a no-parking zone before Nesmith's. He pulled into it, looking for her. It had taken him exactly nine minutes.

CHAPTER ELEVEN
The Shell Road

Amy was waiting just outside the doors. She came across the walk in the sunlight. She was smiling and yet not quite daring to smile, either. She wanted Hank to know she was glad to see him but didn't dare suggest that he had any reason for wanting to see her.

He didn't smile. "Right on time," he said. He reached over and opened the door for her.

She got in beside him and slammed the door. "I knew I had better be," she said. "I knew you wouldn't wait."

He didn't answer. He turned the wheel and moved the car out into the high noon traffic of Main Street.

"Where do you want to go?" he said.

"I don't care. Drive out of town somewhere. I've plenty of time. Two hours."

"Have you eaten?"

"No. But I'm not hungry." She touched his arm. He glanced at her. "Do you mind?" she said, "I—I'll lie down. There's no use having your friends see me riding with you—your wife out of town and all."

"Very considerate, aren't you?"

Her voice was cold. "Yes, I am. I didn't have to let you out of that bed the other night, Hank. Hate me if you want to. I don't expect you not to—but allow me that much anyway."

"All right." His voice was unrelenting. "Lie down if you want to."

She put her purse beside the door, pushed over in the seat and lay down with her head on his right leg. He hated her and he hated himself. But his heart was picking up speed.

There was a throb in his belly to match the throb in the motor. The place where her head touched his leg was hot. All the nerves in his body were concentrated there.

He looked down at her. Her hair was out across his leg. Gypsy black. As black as her heart, he thought.

She smiled solemnly up at him.

"What do you want?" he said. "What did you want to see me for?"

"Didn't you want to see me?"

"It's nothing I'm proud of."

"You haven't been out of my mind. You haven't been out of my thoughts. I called your house the next day, all day long. The phone rang and rang. Nobody answered. I called your office. They said you were sick."

"You're a real witch all right," he said. "When you make up your mind to take a sucker, you don't let up on him, do you?"

"Please, Hank. You don't really feel this way about me. You're hurt and you're angry. I understand that. I'm sorry. I don't want to hurt you."

"You've done a damned good job just the same."

"I know I have. Everything I've done has hurt you. I'm sorry."

"That's wonderful. All you've got to do is say you're sorry. That makes everything all right, doesn't it?"

She moved her head on his leg. She made a caress of it, the way she did it.

"I am sorry."

"That's a laugh."

"All right, laugh then. I sent you away because I didn't want you hurt. I knew, Hank, as well as you did, that what we have together isn't cheap and common—"

"How would you know? You're cheap and common. You're rotten all the way through and even you must know it."

"I do know."

"Then what else is there to say?"

"I love you."

"What do you know about love? Dollars and cents. That's all it means to you." He stopped at a red traffic signal. The air in the car was breathlessly hot. The light changed and he moved the car forward. "I'm no holy character. I've done plenty of things I'd be ashamed to have known. I'm not trying to tell you I'm any better than you are. It's just that the things you do, I wouldn't do, and I hate them."

"Are we almost out of town?" she said.

"Almost."

She sat up. She moved over near him and put her hand on his leg. In the same place her head had been. The same fiery place.

"Isn't there some place you can stop?" she said. "Some place we can talk?"

"What is there to say?"

"That you love me."

"God forgive me."

"And I love you."

"Rotten and no good."

"I'm no good but I love you."

A glance showed him the speedometer needle balancing between seventy and eighty. A marker warned of a side road. He slowed down, mashed the brake, and with the tires squealing, swung off the highway.

The side road was narrow black macadam. There were only a few houses, well-kept yards and trees in the parkways. The houses got scarcer with gardens and small groves between them.

"What the hell do you know about love?" he said. "I mean real love. Not sneaking a hug in the kitchen, or shacking up in motels with guys you meet in bars, or getting innocent jerks to climb into your bed so that George and his fat friend can get their pictures for blackmail? What do you know about love except that it's a dirty word that kids used to scrawl on the backs of barns? What do you know about love except that it makes a man sweat, and you enjoy the feeling it gives you to know that you've taken a man's strength. What the hell is love to you except something to flush down the toilet when you're finished?"

"Go on, Hank," she said, "keep it up. You'll feel better when you see me bleed."

"Did you ever love a man enough to be interested in him, not in yourself? Did you ever love a man longer than the time it took for him to put his pants back on?"

"Yes," she said bitterly, "I've loved a lot of men. Every goddamn man who ever gave me the eye, I loved and I climbed into the sack with. Old round heels Amy, that's me. Amy the Holland Tunnel, that's me. I worked my ever-loving horizontal way through the 44th Battalion. Now are you happy? Now do you know?"

"What makes you so damn hot? Why you? Why do the men give you the eye? What is it you've got that they recognize? You don't have even one-tenth as much as Ethel has."

"I know," she said, "Ethel has bigger bosoms. Her butt is rounder, her face is prettier, her hair is blonde. But if she's so goddamn good, what the hell are you sniffing around after me for? Men like me. Can I help that? How do I know why? I don't wave any catnip at them. All I know, they all want the same thing you want."

"How many men?"

"A dozen. A million. For God's sake, Hank, this isn't why I wanted us to have a couple of hours together, to argue!"

"What about that guy in the Plaid Bar? Is he one of the men who wants the same thing I do? He one of the guys who gets it?"

"I don't even know who you're talking about."

"Stop being cute and tell the truth for a change."

"I don't know him."

"Maybe you don't know his name, but I'll bet you've got more than a nodding acquaintance with his anatomy. By the look that was on his face, he knows you. He probably even knows the place George hurts you where it doesn't show...."

"Stop it, Hank! Stop it!"

"Who is he?"

"I never saw him before in my life."

"Who is he, Amy?"

"I don't know."

"Stop lying. I want the truth!"

"What are you, a jealous husband or something? What gives you the right to do this to me?"

"I thought you said you love me."

"I do. What's that got to do with it?"

"I want to know. I want to know about the others."

"Why? So when you know what a bitch I am you can say goodbye? I love you Hank. I love you. There have been other men, yes, but I never loved any of them. I've been to bed with other men, but none of them ever meant anything to me. Only you, Hank. You're the only one. The first man who ever really touched me. Not even George did. You're the only man I ever really loved."

"Then why won't you tell me who he is? What are you afraid of?"

She took her hand from his leg, opened her bag and found a cigarette. She fumbled for a few minutes, trying to light a match with shaking hands. All at once, Hank was contrite. He pushed in the car lighter, held it for her. The touch of her hands on his as she sucked in the flame sent tingles of desire running along his arm. He shook his head when she offered him a cigarette and settled back to his driving.

His anger was gone. Only passion was left. He glanced at her huddled figure on the opposite end of the seat as she pulled nervously at her cigarette. He let his eyes wander along her legs, up the sleek nylons to her crumpled skirt.

He was tired of talking. He wanted only to savor fulfillment of the sudden desire mounting in him. Seeing his eyes, Amy smiled, crushed out her cigarette and threw it out the window. Self-consciously, she raised her skirt a little higher and slid across the seat until her thigh pressed warm and soft against Hank's.

She took one of his hands from the steering wheel, toyed with it a moment, raised it to her mouth, and kissed it warm and wetly on the palm. She tasted each fingertip, nibbled it for a moment, then sucked it full into her mouth, gently pressuring the knuckle with her teeth. Five fingers of love. She held his hand away for a moment, looked at it lovingly and brought it back to her lips.

The pink tip of her tongue traced a path of acid along his wrist, along the lines of his palm and into the area between the fingers. With her tongue darting in and out, she looked at him from between his fingers, caught his eye and gave him a smile, a smile that held every promise of paradise. A smile that said, this is how much I love you. Only you. This is the love I have for you that no other man has ever seen or tasted. This is the virginity I have been saving, the virtue I have harbored. This is the precious jewel I have cherished only for you.

"Stop the car," she panted.

"Not here," he said, shaken.

"I love you," she said. "Touch me, so you'll know how I love you. So you'll know I'm alive and burning for you. Only for you." She moved his hand, guiding it, placing it. She rolled her head back on the car seat, rolled her head in slow ecstasy.

"Love me," she said. "I'm only alive for you."

Her words, her motion, something deep inside him, some unknown memory of his past, suddenly killed his rising desire. He took his hand away, dried it of saliva on his trouser leg and placed it back on the steering wheel.

"Who is he?" he said dully.

She shrugged. "It isn't important. But all right—I guess you've just got to know. He's a salesman, comes to Nesmith's. He's a friend of my boss."

"And what is he to you?"

She sighed. "It's not a pretty story, or even an interesting one."

"Tell it," he said, keeping his hands gripped tight on the wheel and his eyes fixed on the road ahead. "Tell it."

"Well," she said, resigned. "I'm Mr. Nesmith's secretary. He's got this big office with a bar in it, and a big overstuffed couch and some living room furniture and things. Mr. Nesmith's always making passes at me, because he likes me. I guess he likes any girl he gets close to, and as long as his passes don't become more than that. I let him get his cheap thrills because it's a good job and I don't want to lose it and there are plenty of other girls who'd go a lot further and give a lot more than I do to have my job.

"Anyway, I could always manage to keep him in line by being fast on my feet and telling him I'm a faithful wife and asking how he'd like it if other men were getting into his wife's pants, and asking him how he'd like it if some guy was doing to his teenage daughter what he was trying to do to me. I gave him enough of me and enough malarkey to keep him happy and everything was all right. He kept up the squeezes and the pinches, and I'd have to sit on his lap at times to take dictation, and he'd come rubbing up behind me at the filing cabinets, but what the hell— I work hard enough as it is, and I'm tired enough when I get home, without having to put out at the office too. And Nesmith is the kind of guy who wouldn't let pleasure interfere with business, so what did I have to gain? Besides, I'm a contrary sort anyway, and it became a sort of contest, and I didn't want to lose. I'm not the woman men think I am, Hank, not without love. Not the kind of woman I could be for you."

"Go on," Hank said grimly.

"Also, I figured once he found out that my promise was more fun than my performance, that the hunt was better than the quarry, he'd get tired of having me around and he'd start talent-scouting for a new secretary by pinching bottoms in the hardware department. So anyway, I just never let him have me—not all of me."

"Sure. But what about that guy in the Plaid Bar," Hank said. "What about him? Let's get to the point of the story."

"Well, one afternoon last summer, on one of those godawful hot days, the air-conditioning in the office conked out. We weren't too busy and Mr. Nesmith poured us each a gin and tonic so we could cool off. I guess it didn't work, all it did was make me sweat some more. It was one of those real sticky days and pretty soon my underwear and my dress were all damp and sticky and uncomfortable. We had another couple of drinks, and while they didn't affect me much, one way or the other, they heated up Mr. Nesmith."

"Go on," Hank said, glaring ahead at the road.

"Well, he locked the door so we wouldn't be disturbed and we kind of settled down on his couch for some quiet drinking. He got me into his lap and I swear it felt like he had nine hands. I never in my life had a harder time with any man. I guess though, the gin had me feeling pretty good, because when he kissed me, I guess I kissed back a couple of times."

"What else did you do?"

"Oh, I swear, I was still holding him off. But his hands were all over the place. I guess if I was cold sober I would have been able to stop him better. We were both all wet and sticky from perspiration, and I kept talking about how George wouldn't like it if I was really unfaithful to him, and why couldn't he respect me and treat me like a lady, and what about his wife and daughter? So we were at a stalemate, and I was getting more and more stubborn when the phone rang.

"It sounded like something important was up because he said into the phone that he'd be right there. So he left me, hopping out to take care of whatever had to be taken care of. I was so hot and sticky that I took off my clothes and went to wash up a little and cool off. Mr. Nesmith has this private bathroom inside his private office, and I thought the office door was locked. I'd had a lot to drink, but that only made me want more and I was tired of the tonic so I poured myself a real hooker of straight gin, then I went into the bathroom to clean up. That last drink must have gotten to me because I didn't close the bathroom door. Why bother? I figured the outside door is locked.

"Well, I was standing there, up against the sink, when this guy from the Plaid Bar walks right into the office. He saw me, and headed right for me."

"All right," Hank said, "I've heard enough."

"No, you haven't," she spat. "You wanted all the details of my love life, didn't you? You forced me to speak. Now, listen. Listen. Listen, dammit! He came right at me, and I guess that last drink had done me in. All the fight was out of me. I couldn't do a thing to stop him. I just didn't have the strength. So it happened. Right there."

"Some scene," Hank muttered. "So you were too drunk to fight. Were you too drunk to enjoy it?"

"We were still there," she continued, ignoring his bitterness, "when Mr. Nesmith came bouncing back into the office. I saw him over this guy's shoulder. I was so scared I was paralyzed, my boss catching me this way with a guy I hardly knew, after I'd been hard to get with him all afternoon. But there wasn't much I could do, the gin had got to my legs and while I could think pretty clear, I wasn't able to move much. And in a situation like that, what the hell could I say?

"Anyway, Mr. Nesmith started laughing like crazy and came running right at us. He pushed this other guy aside and was on me before I even knew what was happening."

"You knew what was happening, all right," Hank snarled, "and you loved it."

"I was so drunk and so tired. I couldn't feel anything, or care about anything. Besides it was so hot, and I kept thinking about my sweet husband, about George, waiting for me at home. I kept thinking about him and hating him and thinking that this was the nicest thing I could do to him, the best way I could get even with him for what he's been to me and done to me. I knew it wasn't right, what I was doing, but I was so drunk and so tired, and I hated George so much, and you hadn't come along, and before you there wasn't any reason for me to be anything but what I was. So I guess I didn't put up too much of a battle. You're correct in that. After all, nothing more could happen than had happened already, the cat was out of the bag. What did I have to lose? And I was so drunk …"

Viciously Hank asked, "You were laughing, right? It was fun, wasn't it?"

"It was horrible. It wasn't worth it, even to get even with George. It was a nightmare."

"I'll bet. Did you tell them both that you loved them too?"

"I only love you. I never loved anyone until I met you."

"I'll bet. If you didn't tell them you loved them, what did you talk about?"

"I was too drunk to do much talking."

"You were even too drunk to scream or something. Smash a window. Get to the telephone and holler for a cop—"

"Please believe me, Hank. Honest. I'd been fighting off Mr. Nesmith all afternoon."

"Yeah. That's why you were running around nude in his office, because you were trying to fight him off."

"But he wasn't there."

"But he could come back, couldn't he?"

"I didn't think of that."

"What about the other guy, didn't you think somebody else might walk in on you waltzing around in your skin?"

"I thought the office door was locked."

"Like hell, you thought it was locked. You knew Nesmith opened it to get out. And in any case, you knew he had a key. You knew he could get back in."

"I didn't think of that. I thought he'd be gone for the rest of the afternoon."

"Stop lying. You knew he was coming back. You wanted him to come back. You wanted him to have you. It was just too much trouble holding him off. You were just going to give up and let him have whatever he wanted."

"That's not true. I'd been fighting him all day. I was going to go on fighting him."

"That's why you were waiting for him with your clothes off?"

"I wasn't waiting for him. Stop making me out to be something I'm not."

"The only mistake you made, baby, you weren't expecting the other guy. So you got two for the price of one."

"No, Hank, no."

"How many other times has he loved you since then? How much do you charge him these days for a quick loving?"

"All right," she screamed. "I wanted it to happen. I'm everything you say. I left the door open on purpose. I took my clothes off because I wanted it to happen. I'm no good. I'm a slut. Any man can have me. I want every man I see. I'm a bitch in heat. I'm a nympho. After I've sucked you dry I'll find another patsy and take him to the cleaners. I'm no damn good. Give me three bucks and I'm yours."

"You whore," he spat. He lifted his hand from the wheel, and without looking at her, backhanded her viciously across the face.

She lifted hand to cheeks and suddenly the tears poured out. She twisted her fingers and her cries were little animal sounds deep in her throat.

"Stop it," he said. "You're breaking my heart."

"I can't," she sobbed. "I love you, and now I'll never have you."

"Stop it," he repeated. "There's always Nesmith, and the other guy. You won't be lonely."

"But I love you. Only you. Always you."

With a sudden movement she was up on the seat throwing her arms around him, grinding herself into his elbow. The car swerved and Hank grabbed for the wheel, fighting to keep the car under control, fighting with the other hand to keep her uninhibited passion from wrecking the car. She pressed her tear-wet face against the side of his head, her cries still wracking out from deep within her.

"Tell me you love me," she sobbed. "Tell me you love me and you don't care what I've been."

How can I, he thought. How can I love you when I know you for what you are? A cheap slut who can be had by any man with the time and the patience to back you into a corner. How can I love you when I know that even in the legitimate part of your life you're just part of a stinking two-bit blackmailing team?

"I love you," she sobbed. "I need you. Need me. Tell me you need me.

Tell me you love me."

"How can I love you," he said, more to himself than to her. "All you've ever been to me is degradation and trouble. I've never had you. I've never had peace with you, or a laugh with you. All we've meant to each other is a dirty, drunken kiss in the kitchen, and an incomplete one at that. All I've ever had from you is lies in a bar and a blackmail attempt in your house. All you've ever done for me is make me lose my self-respect in front of your husband and on my job. Why should I love you? You're a cheap, plain, dirty-mouthed, no-good, hot-pantsed dame. How can I love you?"

"Tell me," she repeated. "Stop lying to yourself. Tell me you love me."

"There's only one thing I ought to tell you," he grated, "and that's to get the hell out of my car and out of my life. You're trouble. You're bad. I was living a simple, uncomplicated life until I met you. I had a wife and a job and a dream. What have I got with you? An ache in the gut, a barefoot run through the city's streets to get away from your husband's cameraman? What do you offer me? A stinking animal existence of rutting with you in the mud on back roads, in motels when we can get away from your husband, and I can tell enough lies to my wife. What are you to me? Trouble. What do you bring me except a husband who's after my job and my money? How do I even know I can believe you, or trust you? You twist me all up inside. You cut my heart to ribbons with the small knives of your love. All I do for you is bleed."

"Oh, Hank. Need me, Hank."

"I haven't slept or eaten or laughed since I met you. I haven't done anything but hate you, and want you, and love you and need you. Yes, need you. I need you. Because I love you, you slut, you wanton, you bitch, you whore."

"I love you."

There was a shell road between two fields. Hank swung the car right into it and followed it to a tree-lined creek. He pulled off the road under the shade of an oak tree. He killed the engine.

For a moment they sat and looked at each other.

She put out her arms and slid toward him on the seat. She turned on her side, facing him.

He pulled her over against him.

He was holding her as tightly as he could.

Their mouths struck together. Her full lips were hot and parted.

He could feel her tears on his face.

She pulled her mouth away a little. "There was never anybody before you," she said. Her voice sounded like she had a sudden cold. "I never even knew what it was like. I never even cared."

"God help us," he said. "Please. God help us."

CHAPTER TWELVE
Hunger

The rest of that day he was dead tired. He was numb all over. He dragged through the afternoon. Even his mind felt sluggish. All he really wanted to do was to lie down somewhere and sleep. Maybe that was what God intended for a man and woman anyhow, before life and living got so complicated with wars and laws and convention. Hank sat at his desk and longed for a simpler age.

He even daydreamed. He was a caveman and he had found the woman he wanted, the one God meant for him to have. The one he would be happy with and contented with. The one woman who could carry him to heaven and carry him to hell. A caveman would take that woman, carry her off to his cave and build a fence between her and the world.

There they'd lie around. Loving and eating and sleeping.

He shook his head, laughing at himself. He was really tired. Only there was nothing to laugh about. At least there was one truth in his reverie. He knew now that he was never going to be free of Amy Miller. He was never going to want to be free of her.

He was yawning as he left the office at four o'clock.

He went down to the parking lot, backed out the Mercury and drove home. He decided to go to bed without supper. He wondered how in hell Amy had gotten through the afternoon at Nesmith's Department Store.

The telephone was ringing as he came in the front door. He answered it without even taking time to open the windows. The house had been closed all day and was like an oven inside.

"Hank?" It was Amy.

"Yes?"

"I haven't any reason to call. I just wanted to talk to you."

"I'm glad you called. I wanted to ask you something."

"Did you? What was it?"

"How in the hell did you get through the afternoon?"

She laughed. "Yawning. In fact I yawned so much that Mr. Nesmith gave me the afternoon off. I've been lying around home thinking about you."

"God I'd love to see you."

"Not tonight. I can't tonight."

"Tomorrow?"

"If you want to."

"If I want to! Of course I want to. All I want is to be with you. Did anybody tell you you're wonderful?"

"Not since noon."

She laughed again. "You heard the truth. I wish I were with you right now."

"I'm here. Waiting."

"Maybe.... If I can get away."

"You won't get away."

"How do you know?"

"I want you too badly. It'll never happen."

She was silent a moment. "I'll see you tomorrow anyway. At noon?"

"Yes."

"Will you take me back to the creek?"

The morning was the longest in Hank's memory. He left the office at ten minutes of twelve. At twelve he was in the No Parking zone before Nesmith's. He stayed there until a cop told him to move. He felt empty, worried about her, wondering if she were coming, wondering if maybe there had been some trouble with George since last night.

He found a parking place half a block down Main Street. He left the car and went back along the sidewalk. He walked past Nesmith's entrance. She wasn't there. He began to sweat.

When he started back, he saw her. She was hurrying through the swing door exit. She looked up and down the street, frowning. He was standing right beside her before she saw him.

"Oh you scared me," she said.

"I thought you were going to be out here at twelve."

"I would have been, but Nesmith kept me."

"I don't blame him."

She put her hand under his arm. They started down the street.

She looked at Hank. "He wanted me to go to lunch with him. I think he was mad because I wouldn't."

"How old is he, anyway?"

"Old. Forty."

"Oh, and still pretty strong?"

"Don't say it that way. He doesn't mean anything to me."

"You know it. And I know it. But does he?"

"He ought to."

"Why, when was the last time you and he ..."

"You're jealous!"

He jerked open the car door.

"You're damned right I'm jealous. If George can't trust you, how in hell can I?"

She waited until he went around the car, got in under the wheel.

"Because you're not George," she said. "Because I love you."

But something was wrong between them. She said he was silly even to think about Nesmith. But he knew better. There was a feeling in the car, tension. There was the worried way she looked at him. Nesmith meant something all right. Whether she wanted him to or not.

She lay her head in his lap. They drove out of the downtown business section without speaking. She pulled one of his hands off the wheel and began to kiss his palm. When he didn't look down at her, she began to nibble at the inside of his hand.

He smiled. She sighed.

He unbuttoned her dress and pushed it out of the way. He slid the straps of her bra down her arms and then pushed the bra off her breasts.

"How can I sit up now?" she said.

"Why do you have to?"

She smiled again and burrowed her head against him....

… She lay in his arms. Her tanned, bare body was moist. Her damp hair clung to her forehead. Her face looked pale and tired.

He was staring at the narrow little creek.

"What's the matter, Hank?"

"I don't know. I guess I'm getting what's coming to me all right."

"What does that mean?" Her voice was flat. "Don't you know I love you? Can't you tell I'm crazy about you? What do I have to do?"

"I don't know. It's knowing all I do know. About George. About you. About that guy with the flash camera. About Nesmith. About the guy in the Plaid Bar."

"I told you about them."

His voice was tired. "I know, Amy, but I can't help wondering. Whatever you do, I love you. More than I ever loved anybody. I know that. But don't hold back on me. This is a messy land of business, and we're not being honest. At least not with Ethel and George. So we've got to be honest with each other. *We've got to!*"

"I am."

"I worry about that guy at the Plaid Bar."

"Why is he important? What does he matter?"

"He doesn't matter. But what he knows about you does."

"So what can I do. Shoot him?"

"No. Maybe it'll be all right. Maybe someday—maybe I'll forget about you and me and George and Desales the private detective."

"I'm sorry, Hank. I didn't want to do it. I told George! But he said he was deep in debt. He had to have some money or get in trouble. More trouble. If you'd known the trouble we've had! He said you had all the money you'd been saving. You were going to quit your job. He went crazy with the thought that you had the money he needed and he couldn't get it from you. He was afraid that somebody else might get your job when you left Thompson's! He wouldn't listen to me. I did what I had to—"

His voice was sick. "Yeah. I know. What you had to. How many bruises did he give you this time?"

"Please, Hank, Don't torment yourself. I can't help it. People make mistakes. No matter what I did before I met you, it was because nothing mattered. Nothing ever mattered to me, one way or another, before you came along."

"I still don't like it!"

"And I don't! But maybe you've never been without money! Maybe you've never been so far in debt that you were scared and sick. All the time. Well, I have. All my life. Nothing was ever easy. Nothing was ever the way I wanted it.

"I've worked! Waitress in cheap restaurants and bars. Car hopping. Anything at all. I met George when I was a waitress. He was a salesman. He always had a big roll of money. I thought that with him I'd be all right.

"It wasn't until we were already married that I found out about him. The money wasn't his. The car wasn't his. Nothing belonged to him. He was just a guy who loved to gamble and drink. He always had big ideas. And before we got out of any of them we were always deeper than ever in trouble. Every time we were in trouble.

"When we came here and he started to work at Thompson's, I thought things were going to be different. They were. For a little while. We lived almost like other people. Until he got so far in debt again that he couldn't sleep nights for worrying about what they were going to do to him. He stayed drunk all the time so he wouldn't have to think about it.

"And then when he found out that you were attracted to me, he couldn't think fast enough. It had to pay off. There had to be some way you had to be made to pay for caring for me! That night you were there. That was going to be the payoff. He had met Desales and they had talked all kinds of trick deals for getting money from people. They were great friends by then and they worked it all out. Only I couldn't. I'd think about how clear and high you'd been the first night I saw you. Just such an ordinary guy, all muddled up with drink, and all mixed up inside. But trying to remember to be polite. It was the first time I'd ever loved anybody. Anybody.

"I knew there had never been anybody like you for me. I knew there never was going to be again. Not for me. You looked like the last chance in the world for me ever to be decent, ever to know anybody decent, to get away from sharp guys like Desales. So I couldn't go through with it."

"What are we going to do?" he said. "I want you."

"You've got me. Like nobody else ever had me."

"I don't want you like this. I want you to belong to me."

"I do. But I've caused so much trouble. I've hurt so many people. Don't let me ruin you, Hank. Please. We've got each other. Like this. This is good enough for me! I won't ask anything else. Don't let me hurt you anymore!"

CHAPTER THIRTEEN
Out of the Bag

Lucile looked up when Hank came in.

"Wow," she said. "What a day to take three hours for lunch. Old C. E. himself has been yowling for you since one o'clock."

"What's the matter now?"

She shook her taffy-colored head. "I don't know. It's really hush-hush. You better go on in to see him. I'll ring his secretary that you're on the way."

It was a long way down the corridor to C. E. Thompson's private office. It had never seemed so long before. There was time to review his whole life, Hank thought wryly, but he was too tired to make the effort. He was sweating by the time he reached the old man's inner sanctum.

Thompson's secretary was a lush blonde in a low-cut dress. She leaned forward and told Hank to go right in.

C. E. Thompson was fifty-six. He was a stout man with faded pink hair. The wholesale distributing business was his whole life. His whole soul was a matter of futures, volume buying and cash discounts. Sometimes he took two-week vacations from his office. But when he did, he left ten-page form letters of instructions for his hirelings' direction while he was away. His face was set in a hard and self-righteous mold when Hank closed the door behind him.

Thompson leaned across his polished desk and said, "Come in, Ireland."

Hank saw George Miller and the squatty little private detective, Pete Desales. He felt his throat tightening. He could feel the sweat breaking out across his shoulders.

"Three hours for lunch," C. E. Thompson said. "Doesn't sound like you have the best interests of Thompsons Distributing in your mind, Henry."

"I'm—I'm sorry. I had a call to make. A complaint came in," Hank said. His voice faltered.

Thompson's blue eyes hardened. "Did you?" he said. He swiveled around in his chair. He nodded toward the fat little detective. "Do you know Mr. Peter Desales?"

Hank shook his head. "No. I've seen him once, maybe."

"Mr. Desales, do you mind reading just a part of the report you have there? Just the part that concerns Mr. Ireland—"

Desales fumbled through his notebook. Hank was finding it difficult to breathe. Sweat was pouring down his forehead from his hair. He wanted to lean on Thompson's unlittered desk for support. But he managed to go on standing there.

"Well, this report ain't really about Mr. Ireland," Desales said. His voice was gritty. He must have been a carny barker at some time in his career.

"Just read the part where he enters it," Thompson said.

Desales nodded and began to read. Hank glanced at George Miller. George was looking down at his hands.

"—was waiting at the front entrance of Nesmith's Department Store. Time: Twelve noon. Uh, that was yesterday. A Mercury car pulled into the loading zone and she entered said car. This investigator jotted down the license number of the Mercury and later checked it with the county clerk. The Mercury car was shown to belong to Henry Ireland of 1382 Beecher Avenue, this city.

"This investigator followed the Mercury in a cab. The Mercury left the city at a fast rate of speed. For a time it appeared the driver was alone in the Mercury. However since this investigator had not seen subject leave the car, it was assumed she must still be in it.

"The Mercury was driven off the highway on Clemmons Lane. Since there is only one way out of this dead-end road, this investigator had the taxi wait at the mouth of it. This investigator waited two hours. The Mercury returned at the end of this time. This investigator again followed car and subject. Subject left Mercury across the street from Nesmith's Department store. The time was then 2:15 P.M.

"That's all about Mr. Ireland yesterday. Now today—"

"I think that will be enough," Thompson said. "I'm sure Mr. Ireland will accept the fact that you're a thorough investigator and that you have a complete report on his activities from noon forward today. Will you, Ireland?"

Hank was completely sweated. Completely defeated. He nodded.

"Yes," he said. "But why?"

Thompson's face was grim. "Mr. Miller hired Peter Desales to shadow his wife—isn't that the word, Mr. Desales?—because he didn't trust her."

"That's right, Mr. Thompson," George said. "That's certainly the truth. I can't tell you how shocked I was to find that she was meeting Mr. Ireland—"

Hank looked at George. His voice worked through his tight throat. "I'll bet to hell you were shocked! I'll bet it wasn't just like you planned it at all, was it?"

George stared at him. He jumped to his feet "Why, I don't know what you're talking about!"

Thompson held up his hand. "I'm afraid I do," he said. "Mr. Ireland is making loose accusations to cover his own guilt. Henry, I cannot say how astonished I was when George Miller came to me with this report. You have a good record with this company. Fine. Unblemished. I would have said you were a levelheaded honest young man with a splendid future—"

George Miller interrupted. "I never would have said anything, sir. I wouldn't do anything like that. But I thought maybe if you could talk to Mr. Ireland, it might be stopped. Before it goes too far. You see, sir, I'm pretty crazy about my little woman. Why—why our marriage is about all that means—means anything to me. If anything happened, why I just don't know what I'd do!"

"You were right," Thompson said. "You did just what you had to do. I'm afraid though, Ireland, that I'll have to do more than talk to you as Mr. Miller suggests. I've run this business like a family. Twenty-five years it's been under my personal supervision. I think of my employees as my children. Each one, my son or my daughter. A family. A happy family. A family that can work together. Pull together. Live together."

He stood up and leaned across the desk. His voice shook. "You've got to have harmony in a business like this, Ireland. Until today, I would have said you believed that as strongly as I do. But we can't quibble with the truth. We can't argue with facts. You were caught dead to rights. Not one day. But two days. How much longer it must have been going on, I'd rather not know. And so, I'm giving you warning, Henry. My first warning, my last.

"Do not see George Miller's wife again. You've got to give her up, or quit your job here. The issue is that clear. That simple. You have your choice."

Hank looked at George Miller. George sat back in his chair. He was looking straight at Hank. The expression on his face didn't alter. Hank's gaze moved to Pete Desales and the black notebook. Desales was fumbling through it. He didn't look up. Hank returned his eyes to the sweating man across the desk.

Hank was remembering the things Amy had said. The promises. The lies. He was remembering that flash camera and that broken bedroom door. He wiped the sweat off his forehead. His voice was level.

"I've made my choice, Mr. Thompson. The whole thing is a mistake. I won't argue that. But you have my word. I won't see George Miller's wife again. Ever."

He managed to walk out of the old man's office without bumping into anything. His legs felt too heavy to lift. He wanted a drink and knew he couldn't hold it on his stomach.

Lucile followed him into his office.

"Let me get you some aspirin," she said. "My God, you look awful."

"No. I'm all right."

"You look like a train hit you. Want to talk about it, Hank?"

"No. Good God, no."

"I was gabbing with the Old Man's secretary. She said she didn't know what it was all about. George Miller had blabbed something to C.E. I can look at your face and see that it was pretty terrible. My God, that George Miller is a sharp character. Always with the angles."

Hank stared at her. Her face was blurry before his eyes.

"No," he said. "He had a right to do what he did."

"Yeah. Sure. I don't know what it was. But it seems a pretty lovely way to repay the guy who okayed a robbery of an expense account, and kept him from getting fired for shortages and broken promises!"

"All right, Lucile. All right!"

"I know I'm talking too much. I'm sorry. I just don't like him."

Hank laughed mirthlessly. "I don't like him either," he said. "But it looks like it doesn't matter. This time he's really got me over a barrel."

He looked down at his trembling hands. There was work on his desk but he knew he couldn't get it done. He knew that he couldn't take the afternoon off, either. He had to sit there. Had to sit there knowing Amy had crossed him again. He thought of the way she'd lain naked in his arms out by the creek. His mouth tightened. My God, baby, he thought, you really made a sucker out of me this time.

And the hell of it was, he wasn't even really thinking about that. He was wondering how in God's name he was going to get along without her.

He was fumbling to get the keys to the Mercury out of his pocket as he crossed the rear lane of the parking lot. He started toward his car when he saw someone in it. It must be someone else's car, he thought. It was his usual parking place all right. It looked like his Mercury exactly. Then she turned around on the front seat, looking at him, and he saw that it was Amy.

His jaw tight, he strode around the car and slammed in under the wheel.

"Well. Not enough to kick me, huh, baby? Had to come around to gloat?"

She said nothing. His face, white with anger, he turned to look at her. She was crying. Her face was swollen with her crying. Her eyes were red and rimmed. Her lips were dry and puffed. She looked like she'd been crying for hours without stopping.

"I—I heard about it," she said. "I know what George did to you."

"I'll bet you do!"

"Oh God, Hank. I didn't know! I didn't know he was having Pete Desales follow me. I didn't know he'd want to! Sometimes I've even seen Desales two or three times a day without thinking anything about it—"

"Save your dirty rotten lies—"

"Please, Hank! Would I be here if I were lying? Why would I be here if I were lying?"

"That's easy, baby. Because I've got to see you again before George's little scheme really works. I've got one more chance. If I see you again, Thompson fires me. And so here you are. And somewhere around here is your buddy, Pete Desales. It won't work, sweetheart. Not this time. Either you get out of this car right now, or I'll kick you out. Stay in here and see if I don't mean it."

She sobbed. "I won't go. I love you. You've got to believe me!"

"Get out!"

"Hank, for God's sake, give me a chance. Listen to me."

"I've listened to you, baby, and look where it got me!"

"I'll do anything. Anything. Let me stay! Listen to me!"

She started toward him, tears streaming down her cheeks, her swollen lips trembling.

He snarled and struck her across the face with the back of his hand.

She moaned out loud and buried her face in her arms. She began to sob. The sobs shook her whole body. She caved in against him, her head still covered in her arms. He tried to lift her. She only burrowed deeper, sobbing.

It got him. It got inside him and twisted him dry. The ache in his chest was unbearable. He knew it didn't matter what she was. He was caught. He was all twisted up in her life no matter how hard he fought, no matter what he did. Her crying was his crying. Her tears burned his eyes. Her sobs shook him.

He touched her head. "Amy."

She didn't stop crying.

"Stop, Amy. It's all right. I don't give a damn. Let 'em fire me. Let 'em do what they will. I don't care. My God, Amy, stop crying."

Her hands moved from her face. She dug her fingers into his leg. She pressed her face against him.

"I'll leave him," she whispered. "I'll leave him. I won't go back. I'll get a divorce. I'll be just yours. All my life. You don't have to marry me. You don't have to do anything. Only please love me. Please love me."

He pulled her up close against him. She shoved her face hard between his shoulder and his throat. Her arms went around him. He could feel her hot breath against his neck, feel every time her sobs shook her.

"I'm going to have you," he said. His voice was cold. His eyes were hard. "You're going to be mine. I'll have you in my arms and you'll be mine. I don't give a damn what they do to me. I don't care what it costs. You're going to be completely mine!"

CHAPTER FOURTEEN
Spilled Milk

Hank prowled the lobby of the Lake Vital Hotel. The ornate furniture of the room cramped him. He was like a caged animal. A caged sick animal. He could feel the eyes of the old women of both sexes on him.

His anxiety was communicating itself to them. He should never have brought his tensions into this atmosphere of studied relaxation. Something was going to happen. The people in the room could feel it, and they didn't want anything to happen. They had paid money so nothing would happen.

All Hank could think of was that he was going to hurt Ethel. And she hadn't done anything to deserve being hurt. He didn't want to hurt her. He never had and he didn't now. But there were two sides to that: Would he hurt her more by breaking clean? Or by hanging on, sneaking to see Amy, wanting Amy all the time he was with Ethel?

Amy hadn't wanted him to come up here. She had moved into a hotel without even going back to tell George. Hank grimaced at that thought. Amy wasn't likely to make any move that George Miller didn't know about. Not as long as Pete Desales and his operatives were at work.

Amy had wanted to prove to him that she was breaking with George. She had told him it was final, but she didn't want him to doubt her anymore. She moved into the Hotel Senator, gave Hank a key to her room and said as far as she was concerned, she didn't even know anyone else in the city.

Amy had begged Hank not to hurt Ethel by asking her for a divorce. Amy said she had hurt enough people, more than enough. She insisted that she didn't ask Hank to marry her. If he would promise to see her when he wanted to, that was all she asked.

Amy said she had seen enough of married life. There was no more security, and no more peace of mind in marriage than in living together without marriage. She would never be a shrew, demanding anything. Inside her she felt more married to Hank than she ever had to George, no matter what the rest of the world thought about it. No matter how little of his time she had from now on.

But he was going to want to see her all the time, Hank had told her. He wasn't planning to stay away from her. None of them was ever going to be happy the way they were now. He wanted to be with Amy all the time. It was kinder to Ethel to tell the truth now than it would be to go on deceiving her, even if it were possible to do it.

He had arrived at the Lake Vital Hotel at ten P.M. It was now ten thirty. Ethel hadn't been in her room. By much telephoning, the clerk had located her at a card party across the lake. Ethel had promised to return to the hotel at once.

He circled the old-fashioned rug. He saw her coming in the front entrance. She was blondely beautiful, with a fragile scarf about her neck, a new evening dress that he'd never seen her wear before.

She saw him and smiled, putting out both her hands.

Hank went toward her. His steps were heavy like he was plodding through foot-deep snow.

"Hello, darling. Bart drove me over. I sent him back. I told him not to wait for me."

"Thanks, Ethel."

He led her to a divan near the double front windows. They sat down and she went on holding his hands. Her face was faintly flushed.

"Well, this is the funniest thing," she said. "You've never been up here before. This year, you've been up here twice already. I'm sorry I wasn't here. But you must understand. Every minute is pretty full. And we just don't know when you're coming."

"It's all right, Ethel."

She was studying his face. "What's the matter, Hank? You look ill."

He nodded, "I am ill, Ethel, I'm sick. I—I want a divorce."

For a moment she stared at him. She flinched slightly. And then she laughed.

"Goodness! For a minute I thought you were serious."

"I was never more serious, Ethel. I'm sorry. I don't want to hurt you. But I will hurt you more if I try to go on living with you."

"Is it because you want to quit your job and I object?"

"No."

"That's it. And it's all father's fault. He shouldn't fill your mind full of that country newspaper nonsense. That freedom he always talks about! It's the quickest way in the world to starve—"

"It isn't that, Ethel. It's that we're not happy—"

Her chin quivered. "Not happy? I'm happy. You—you're the best husband in the world, Hank. I—I wouldn't have anybody else."

"I don't want to hurt you, Ethel. But I can't go on the way we are—"

"The way we are? What way? Hank, we've the finest, cleanest life two people could live. A nice home, money to buy the things we want. A lovely future. Oh my lord, Hank, you get me so upset!

"Darling, look at father. He's the loneliest poor little man in the world. He left us for what he wanted. He wanted freedom. He left mother and me and was sure he was going to get it. Well, he got it! He got it! Look at him!"

Hank knotted his fists, released them, spreading his fingers wide.

"I can't help it, Ethel. You must let me go. I don't have what I want. If I go on like this, I may lose my chance—"

"Is it because I wouldn't have children, Hank? I would have. The doctor—"

"That doesn't matter. Thank God there aren't any. I'm hurting enough people—"

"It's another woman." She said it flatly. "Some slut who offers you excitement. Or says she does." Her face twisted. "I've been a good wife, Hank. I've been faithful, and I've made a good home for you. Please don't be a fool and throw that away for some whore who has made you think love ought to be higher than the clouds all the time! If that's what you want okay, but love isn't like that. I know it isn't. People are all the same, and after a while, there is no screaming excitement. It's routine, it's got to be—you can't stay up on the heights all the time. It isn't natural. It isn't human.

"We've got what's right. Companionship. Respect for each other. Understanding. Nobody but fools and whores think that love has to be drunkenness and excitement all the time—"

He got up and began to walk back and forth in front of her.

"What we've got is nothing," he said. "But you're right. There is another woman. And what you say is all true. I guess she's pretty low. God knows I can't pretend I'm blind. She isn't any of the things that you are. But I would be lying if I said I could get along without her. I don't see how I could. I would only be hurting you if I lied about—"

She began to cry soundlessly. The tears ran down her cheeks unchecked. She sat very straight on the divan. Her voice sounded as though she'd developed a sudden summer cold.

"Get me out of here," she said. "Don't let them see me like this. We—

we'll go out in your car. We'll talk about it there."

He drove along the dark highway. There were almost no other cars at this hour. He drove at twenty-five miles an hour, driving without direction, just keeping the car on the road and not caring where they went.

Ethel said, "I'm not going to give you a divorce, Hank. Go back home. Think. Use your brains. You've got sense. You're all mixed up. You'll come to your senses and you'll be glad I refused."

"No, Ethel. Either you give me a divorce or I'll leave you. I'm trying to be honest. Don't force me to go on when I tell you I'd be lying to you. It'll be a hell of a lot better for you if you file against me."

Ethel sat straight in the seat. Her face was set straight ahead. The tears were gone now. She dabbed at her eyes. Her voice was cold.

"Do you think I'll give you a divorce and leave you anything to take to your slut?"

His voice was sick. "I've got to be free."

Her voice raised slightly. "You'll be free. And you'll be broke. You've always been a fool, and I've thought about this. I've thought about what I would do if you ever did a thing like this to me. I hoped you never would. I'm content with you. I'm happy with you. I love you. There's nobody else for me.

"But I've known you might do this. Mother warned me about you. So I'm going to divorce you, Hank. Just as you want me to. Only in this state a woman is protected by the courts. I'm going to name your little slut, whoever she is, and I'm going to take everything in the world you've got, our home, our cars, the money you have in the bank. You're going to be stripped. We'll see how badly she wants you then."

"I'm sorry you hate me. I suppose I can't expect anything else."

"I don't hate you. It's just that you're a fool. And you—you're getting what a fool should get."

"All right, Ethel. All right. Just get the divorce. I won't fight. Just draw up the papers. I'll sign."

She sobbed. Once. "Hank, why must you be such a fool?"

He shook his head. "I've tried it the other way, Ethel, and I had nothing. Maybe—maybe I still won't have anything. But I've got to find out. I've got to try!"

"You're wrecking your whole life."

"I'm trying to get something out of it. It's all I know."

"You're breaking my heart, Hank. And I can't help it, it's you I cry for. I don't even hate you. I'm so sorry for you."

"Please don't cry."

"But I will. I'm sorry. But you're such a fool, you make me cry."

CHAPTER FIFTEEN
End and Beginning

"I'm sorry, Ireland. You're fired."

Hank stared at old C. E. Thompson. It was hot in the air-conditioned office. Even the old man was sweating and uncomfortable. He was walking back and forth behind his wide desk. He looked as miserable as Hank felt about this business.

"It's not the same situation as it was that first day in your office, Mr. Thompson," Hank said. This was nine years of his life that was being thrown away, a job he had worked like hell to get. A job he was losing the way you'd snap your fingers.

"So far as I can see, it is the same."

"No, sir. Then Amy was George's wife. And nothing more. Now she has left him. She is going to divorce him. As soon as we can, we're going to be married."

"That may be. But it is still an unpleasant matter. It leaves an unpleasant taste. It disrupts this office." Thompson stared at him. "Furthermore, I told you very clearly. I warned you that if you persisted in seeing Mrs. Miller that you would be fired."

Hank spread his hands. His voice was flat.

"It isn't quite that simple, sir. To tell a man to forget what's inside him is one thing. But for that man to be able to do it just because you ordered it done, that's something else again."

"It's a matter of discipline. If your job and your home had meant anything to you—"

"Well, there you are, sir. You're expressing my point. They did mean something to me. They do. But this other thing—the way I feel, the thing I want, is so much stronger—"

"So strong that you can throw over all that we decent people live by. You have broken up a home—"

"Perhaps I have, sir. I'm not arguing that. But it was broken up before I came along—"

"That's not my concern, Ireland. What happens here in this office does concern me. I'm interested only in the unity and harmony that exists among the men who work together in my employ. It does not make for unity when a man like you begins an undercover affair with another man's wife. It begins and ends there, Ireland. You had certain responsibilities in your position here. You chose to disregard them and throw them over. I'm sorry, there is no longer any place for you here."

Hank looked around the room. Ordinarily it seemed spacious. Now the walls were crowding in on him.

"I've been as honest as I could," he said. "I am being honest with you when I tell you that to deny what I feel so strongly would have been worse than admitting it."

"I can't see that."

Hank's mouth was hard. "You're very fortunate, sir. I hope that everything you want is always so easy for you to have. I hope that there are never any complications for you. But it isn't always like that, not for everybody. I'm fighting for the right to happiness. I feel that I've worked faithfully here and that because my personal life hasn't run smoothly, it's hardly a reason for being fired."

"You do have a good record here. Your work has been most satisfactory. If it hadn't been, you'd never have been promoted so rapidly. But now the harmony of this concern is threatened. There is no alternative for me. I'm not going to be harsh. I'm going to allow you to resign. I may be a stern parent, but I'm fair. You'll be furnished perfect references with no mention of the shattered unity in this office family which caused me reluctantly to let a valuable man leave my employ."

Hank's desk was cleared out, his personal belongings were removed from his office. With a sense of loss that he couldn't escape, Hank walked along the corridor and pressed the down button at the elevator.

He had been notified of Ethel's suit against him. He had signed the papers that made her owner of their joint property and bank account. For a few days, until some agreement was reached on the transfer of the property, he still had his car.

He had two-weeks pay in his pockets. In a room at a second-rate hotel he had his clothes and personal things from the house. A clerk from Ethel's lawyer had stood there checking everything he removed from the home.

And that was all there was left to him of the Henry Ireland who had married Ethel Payson, worked at Thompson's Distributing Company, and spent his days and many of his nights wondering what in the hell his life was all about. Well, he was finding out now.

He was finding out in spades.

The elevator stopped and he stepped into it. His jaw was tight. He told himself he didn't give a damn about his loss. He knew what he wanted. He wanted Amy. He wanted her to belong completely to him, to him alone. He didn't give a damn what it cost him.

The Senator Hotel where Amy lived was no better than Hank's. It was ten blocks away from the Commercial Hotel where Hank stayed.

They decided it was better like that. They had no way of knowing if

George was still having Amy shadowed. If he was, it wasn't going to help her divorce case to live openly with Hank while they were waiting for the final decree.

He stopped in the lobby and telephoned up to her room. Amy answered at once.

"Amy? Hank. May I come up?"

"Who do you think I'm sitting here waiting for?"

She kissed him through the telephone.

He crossed the musty narrow lobby to the elevators, feeling the tingling of anticipation. It was always a little hard to believe that she was going to be there waiting for him whenever he came.

She came out in the corridor on the fifth floor to meet him. She put out her hands to him. A thin woman curled her thin mouth at the sight of their happiness. Amy laughed and kissed Hank. She led him to her room and closed the door behind them.

He looked around. The room was small. A single bed, a bureau, a writing desk, a couple of chairs and lamps. A clothes closet and a narrow bath. It looked dingy. It looked dark.

"All right, so it isn't beautiful," she said, laughing at him. "We're going to get out of here. We're going to be all right."

She drew him down on the bed beside her. She tried to kiss him. He sat straight on the side of the bed, not responding.

"Hank?"

"Are we going to get out of here?" he said. "Are we going to be all right?" His voice was bitter.

She looked bewildered. "That's what you've been telling me, darling. You've told me that until I've stopped being frightened."

"Maybe it was different before. I had a job then. I don't have one now."

He heard her catch her breath. He looked at her. Her eyes were brimmed with tears.

"It's my fault," she whispered. "I'm no good. I'm no good for you. I'm a jinx. I always have been." She fell back on the bed, her arms above her head. Her mouth trembled.

"It's not your fault," he said. "I got fired, that's all."

"You were fired because of me."

He didn't bother to deny it. He shrugged. "All right, suppose I was. I told you, I want you. I didn't care what it cost me. I'm going to have you. Losing my job was part of the cost. Okay. I paid it. What the hell, I'm that much nearer to having you."

She shook her head, her hair loose on the white bed cover.

"No," she whispered. "You're that much farther away from what you want. A country newspaper—"

"I told you I'd never have that—"

"But I want you to. I want to make you happy, not miserable."

"You do make me happy."

"Yes. Sure. Right now. But what about when you're working at a job you hate. What about when you know that if it hadn't been for me, you'd have the things you want—"

He smiled. "I'll still come running home to you, every night. I'll never complain as long as you're there."

Her mouth twisted. "Will I be there? Or will I be out working?"

His voice hardened. "I'm going to take care of you. I told you that."

"Sure. George told me that too."

"I'm not George."

"I know. You're wonderful. You'll try. But maybe you don't know my luck. I've never had anything I wanted."

He looked at her. "I thought you wanted me."

"I do!"

"Do you? Do you still want me, or are you trying to talk your way out of something? I was a guy with a good job and some money in the bank when you wanted me. Now I've got what money is in my pocket and I don't have a job. Do you still want me?"

"You're all I want." She sat up. "There's something that we can do, Hank. There's a way I know. A way we can have each other, the newspaper you want, and the money we need—"

He looked at her. Her face was changed, lighted up. She was planning, he could see it. They needed money. She was like George. She knew how they could get money. All the money they would ever want.

He stood up. "Take it easy, Amy—"

She jumped up too, following him. "I'm telling you the truth, Hank. It's my fault that you're in this mess—without a job, and no chance to do what you've always wanted to do. And I can change that."

His voice rasped. "Now you sound like George."

"Please, Hank, listen to me—"

"I'm not going to listen. I don't mind working. I'll get a job. To hell with the rest of it. I'll have you—"

"You won't have me! I've been without money all my life. I don't want to go on like that—"

"All right! That's telling me. That's making it clear enough. Get yourself another boy—"

"I want you!" Her voice was tense. She grabbed his arms in her fingers.

"And I want you. But I don't want to hear any get-rich-quick scheme from you. It's been a pretty hot day and I don't want to listen to some plan that you and George Miller hatched up while you were still with him."

She sighed. "All right, we did talk about it. George and I talked about it. I don't care. It's a good idea. It's good because this time nothing depends on George. This time it was all up to me—"

"I'm warning you, Amy. So help me God. I'm no George Miller. You're not going to make me into one. I don't want to hear any rotten racket that you two figured. You're through with George, remember? You're mine."

She flared up. "There's no reason I can't be yours and still have the things I want. The things I've always wanted."

"Why didn't you just stay with George? You haven't changed! You're still with him in your mind. Get rich. Rackets. Dirty rotten crookedness. God help me, Amy, I'll beat it out of you. I want you. But I want you decent and honest, not a rotten little slut who thinks any crime is all right as long as she gets what she wants!"

"Is it a crime to want to be happy? I've hurt you. Oh, you can talk all you want to, but I've still ruined your life. There's one way I can make it up to you. And you're going to listen to me! Listen!"

He struck her across the eyes with the back of his hand. She toppled back away from him. The force of the blow drove her across the bed. He heard her head strike the wall.

He leaped to the bed and grabbed her up in his arms.

She was completely limp. The mark of his hand was red on her face. His hand searched her scalp frantically.

She opened one eye, laughing at him.

"Did I frighten you, darling?"

All the life deserted him. He could feel the strength seeping downward in his arms and his body. He sank to the bed. He couldn't even support her weight anymore. She toppled across his chest.

Amy lay there for a moment. She lifted her head a little, tickling his face with the ends of her hair.

"Nesmith's," she said. She whispered it just above his face.

"Stop," he said. "Please stop." His voice was lifeless.

"I was cashier there for months." Her voice was taut but it was no more than a whisper. A whisper of evil against his cheek.

"Damn you," he said.

"He was crazy about me—"

"God damn you—"

"I let him be crazy about me—"

"Damn you. Damn you. Damn you."

"It meant something. He didn't trust anybody. But he was crazy about me. I learned all about the night burglar alarm system. I know the combination of his office safe. I know how to get in the store at night without being seen."

"Go back to George, tramp."

"I'd never have done it with George. I'd never have taken the chance. But I'll take it for you. I'll do anything to make up for what I've cost you. Thousands, Hank. Thousands. Saturday night. The receipts. In the office safe until the armored car service calls for it on Monday morning. Just one time, Hank. Just one time. Never again. And we could buy the world."

He shoved her away and stood up.

"Thanks," he said. "I knew all the time what you were. I can't pretend I didn't. But all the time I told myself you'd change. You'll never change. You're rotten, baby. You were born rotten, and you'll die rotten. But there's just one thing about it. I don't have to stay around and watch it. I'm getting out of here. This time for keeps."

He thrust her arms down when she reached for him. He strode to the door. She ran after him. He opened it and slammed it after him. He didn't wait for the elevator. He knew he couldn't stop to think. If he did, he'd think nothing but loneliness and he'd go back to her. He walked down the stairs. He ran down them. All five flights.

He didn't slow down until he reached the parking lot.

He was breathing through his open mouth. Well, he had wanted her. He hadn't cared what it cost, but he wouldn't have her now. She was what she was, what she always had been, a cheap little tramp on the make. She wasn't going to change. What a jerk he had been to think she would!

Nobody changes. You take them as they are. Or leave them.

He was almost to the Mercury when a man stepped from between two cars and spoke to him.

"Hey, mister."

Hank was too sick to talk to anybody. Vaguely he could see the man was stocky, wearing a sweat shirt, khaki trousers and sneakers. His arms were short and heavy.

He reached out and grabbed Hank's shirt.

"I said hey, mister. I was talking to you."

Hank jerked himself free, pushing on the man's barrel chest. He took two backward steps. That was when the second man moved in and pinned Hank's arms behind him.

Hank reared, struggling to free himself. He twisted around, straining to see who was holding him.

It was squatty Pete Desales!

The thug struck Hank square in the face. Hank could feel his nose give. There was the sudden hot taste of blood. His head rocked back.

He tried to pull away. The man hit him again. This time high on the side of the face. The car lot reeled around Hank's head, all the parked cars spinning like the lighted buckets on a Ferris wheel.

He stretched tall to get away from those fists in his face. He was hit again, sharply on the other side of the face and for the moment, was blinded.

A blow in the stomach knocked him breathless and he doubled over. He was hit again. This time from all the way back. The fist exploded in his face and his head slumped.

He thought he heard a scream for help. But it was very faint and far away.

Hank's knees sagged, but Desales wouldn't let him fall. The thug kept hitting Hank until he couldn't feel the jabs anymore, until he couldn't feel anything.

He could hear the heavy man grunting now when he struck. The fun had gone out of it, it was work now. Hank could hear Desales' labored breathing behind him. But those were the only real sounds left in the noisy darkness.

Desales let him fall. He felt them going through his pockets. He knew his money was gone. He writhed on the ground. He forced his head up and tried to open his eyes. He got them open just in time to see the foot coming.

He went back when that foot landed in his face, all the way over on his back. His arms were sprawled out and he was helpless but not yet out. The world wheeled red before him.

He was aware of Desales bending over his head.

"I got a message for you," Desales said. "From George Miller. Stay away from his wife."

After that there was nothing but darkness.

CHAPTER SIXTEEN
The Chance

When Hank came out of it, Amy was bending over him. Beyond her he could see the worried face of the parking lot attendant.

"Are you all right, Hank?"

He spoke through the blood in his mouth. "Swell."

"I followed you, darling. I couldn't let you go away. I had to wait for the elevator. When I got downstairs, I saw you way ahead of me on the street. I ran. I got here while they were beating you. I screamed. The attendant came running. But he was too late. They got away between the cars and ran."

"Friends of yours," he said. He sat up.

"Desales?"

"Sure, Desales. It seems he and his friend disapproved of my seeing you. If they'd given me a chance, I'd have told them I wasn't going to see you anymore."

"But you are! You are."

He got up. The world wheeled around, skidding out from under him. He had to grab hold of Amy for support.

"Come back to the hotel," she said. "Let me take care of you."

"They also robbed me," he snarled. "I've even less money than I had before. You wouldn't want me at all now."

"I want you! You're all I want."

"I'm sorry. I'm going to my hotel."

"Then I'm going with you."

He staggered over to his car. The pain in his belly was bad. It was still too painful to stand up straight.

The attendant followed him. "Are you sure you're well enough to drive, Mr. Ireland?"

"Sure. I'm wonderful. I've been hurt a hell of a lot worse than this and nobody laid a hand on me."

Amy got in the car beside him.

He drove a block without speaking. The noises of traffic were abnormally loud. It seemed they were all inside his head. He kept shaking his head to clear his vision.

He looked at Amy from the corner of his eyes. His mouth was twisted and his voice bitter.

"We could keep driving," he told her. "We could drive as fast as we could go. We could sell this car wherever we were and start over, right there."

His eyes remained bitter as he waited for her answer, knowing she was going to refuse.

"This car isn't yours anymore, remember?"

"I think even Ethel would allow me the money for it if she knew the fix I'm in."

"You know better."

"All right! I'll steal it from her."

"You're the one who is too holy to steal."

Nobody could possibly be blowing horns as loud as the sounds wailing around inside his head. For a minute he was sure he was going to blank out. He gripped the steering wheel until his knuckles turned white.

"Listen to me, Hank. You must know by now. We've got to have money, you and I. That's the only way two people like us can stay together. We've got two strikes against us. But if we've got money we can buy what we want and people will let us alone. If you've got money enough you can do anything you want to. But without money you and I haven't a chance in the world."

He shook his head. And even that hurt now!

"There's no use to start that routine about Nesmith's. I'm not even listening. I want you, Amy. More than anything in the world. But I'll let you go before I'll rob anybody. I don't want to sit in a jail cell. I want to be free. I want to have you. I don't want to be caged up where I can't get to you. To me that's the most horrible thing that could happen to a human being. I want you. I need you. I'd go crazy inside a jail. And that's all you're asking for when you start thinking about robbing anybody."

"People do get away with robbery. Sure, some of them are caught. But a lot of them aren't. It's worth a gamble—"

"You sound like George! You've lived with him so long you think like him. You better go back to him."

"If you won't help me, I will go back to him."

"Then, baby, you're on your way. And pleasant dreams in the state pen!"

"I'm going to get that money. If you won't help me, George will."

"The needle's stuck, baby. You said that once."

"I've got to have it. I've robbed you. I've ruined you. I'm going to get money to give you the things you would have had if I hadn't messed you up."

"Stop talking like that. You've gone crazy."

"I haven't gone crazy. I tell you, I know how easy it would be. How perfect. We could get that money and we could get away. Nobody would ever suspect—"

"What kind of fool are you? You've been listening to George so long that you can't even think anymore. You're the first one they'd suspect!"

"Why?"

"Because you were gone. The minute you ran, every cop in this country would be on your trail."

"No, they wouldn't. I've told Nesmith before that I might quit without notice. He begged me not to—"

"And I don't give a damn about your rotten love life, either—"

"But I told him if I quit it would be one night and I just wouldn't be back again."

"That's swell. He might not think anything about it if you quit and there was nothing missing when you were gone. But, baby, when a man loses thousands of dollars—he suspects everybody, even the little tramp he's been laying in the back room—"

"He never touched me!"

He parked the car in the Commercial Hotel garage. He looked at her. "I'm beat up, baby. I'm sick all the way through. I don't want to hear any more of your funny jokes."

"You can't get rid of me. I won't let you."

"You're mixed up. I don't want to get rid of you. You I want. It's that damned screwy robbery idea that I'm sick and tired of. I'm going to have you, but not until you come to your senses."

"Come to my senses! That means back to a hash house waiting tables—"

"I told you I'd take care of you—"

"How? What have you got? How can you take care of yourself?"

"Give me a chance. Let me try to get a job. Let me find out."

He got out of the car, leaned against it for support.

"Look, Amy. Let's put it like this. I'm paid up until Monday in this hotel. That's day after tomorrow. After that, I'm getting out. I don't know where I'm going. I want you with me. But not until you're through thinking like George. Not until you're through talking like George.

"I'm too sick to talk anymore. I don't want to talk. I might hurt you. I might try to beat some sense into your head. You got the rest of the day and tomorrow to think, Amy. If you want me, just like I am, you better come running before Monday."

"You're bluffing."

"Am I? Or are you thinking about George Miller? Don't get us mixed up in your mind. I'm a kid with a broken heart, baby, as well as a broken face. I'm praying that between now and Monday, you'll see that we can either go to heaven or straight to hell. I'm praying to God that you'll see it my way because I don't see how I can live without you—but I won't have you like you are."

Amy got out of the car. She stood there with her hands on her hips, her chin tilted defiantly. Her eyes mocked him.

She laughed.

"All right, Hank. I'll go back to my hotel. You know my number. When you want me, I'll be there. The rest of the afternoon, I'll be there. I think you'll miss me. I think you'll be willing to see it my way. You gave me two days. I'm surer of myself than that. I'm giving you until seven o'clock tonight. If you don't call by then, I'm going back to George."

He stared at her. She seemed to be spinning out in front of him. All he could see for sure was the defiance in her face. Her arrogant will set against his. The noises from the street filtered into the garage and went screeching around through his brain. For a moment she was enveloped in fog, and then it was smoke, and then she was clear again.

"You can't, Amy!"

She laughed again. "Oh, I'm not worried, darling. You're going to see it my way. You'll call. Before seven."

CHAPTER SEVENTEEN
They Get You

People stared at Hank as he crossed the Commercial Hotel lobby.

Nobody said anything to him and they stepped back out of his way to pass. He knew what he looked like. There was blood on his rumpled clothes and he was aware that his face resembled a chopped steak. He wouldn't have been surprised if somebody had called a cop.

But none of that worried him, the people, the cops, his bloody appearance. He was afraid that every step was going to be his last one. The room spun before his eyes, and the whirring traffic noises pursued him across the lobby.

In the elevator, he leaned against the wall and shut his eyes. That was better. The operator had to tell him twice that they'd reached the eighth floor. Hank left the elevator, thinking that once he got in his room he was going to be all right, perfectly all right.

Ethel's father was waiting for Hank in his room. Shabby, disreputable as ever, and either still needing a haircut or needing one again, Payson jumped up smiling when Hank unlocked his door.

Hank groaned. He didn't know how he could talk to Payson. If he had had the strength to talk, he'd have run after Amy. He would have caught her before she got out of the hotel garage and brought her here with him and here he would have beat her until she came to her senses. Somehow he would have knocked that senseless idea of robbery out of her head. But he didn't have the strength. All he could think was to lie in a tub of hot water until the coagulated blood soaked off him and some of the pain in his body subsided.

Justin Payson stopped in the middle of the small room, staring. He caught his breath.

"My God, Hank! You've been in an accident."

"Yeah. I ran smack into the tail end of a romance."

Payson paced the room. "I've been hearing, Hank," he said. "They told me at Thompson's that you're no longer employed there. Ethel says you've asked her for a divorce."

Hank toppled across his bed.

"I'm sick," he said. "If it's a lecture, save it."

"I have no lecture. I came up here hoping that since you and Ethel have parted that perhaps out of the tragedy, you might be saved. We might go ahead and buy the *Winona Star*—"

Hank began to laugh. Once he started laughing, he didn't think he would ever stop.

Payson stood there in the middle of the room, a tired little man, watching him.

Hank managed to sit up.

"There's no newspaper, either," he said. "I'm broke. I haven't a dime for a cup of coffee. I couldn't even use that telephone if there was a toll charge."

"Hank, for God's sake, why have you thrown your life away?"

Hank laughed. A sour sound. "Because I fell in love with a two-bit tramp. Does that answer your question? I wanted her. Any man could have her for nothing. But I had to do it the hard way."

"You're not even the same person I knew—"

"Love does that for you. Or haven't you ever tried it? You ought to try it sometime. It beats whisky all to hell. It's quicker. You can go to hell in half the time and there's not the danger of cirrhosis of the liver!"

"Hank, get your balance back. Save yourself. What are you trying to do?"

"Find happiness. Find out why in hell I get up every morning. What's the reason? And I thought I had it."

"A man doesn't buy happiness with another man's misery, son. You can't rob another man and find happiness. You can't take his wife and—"

"They had nothing together. At least that's what I thought," Hank said.

"That doesn't matter. If they part, let them part of their own volition. If they're really unhappy together, they'll part. You won't need to part them.

"But as long as they are married, their happiness or unhappiness is their problem. What you're trying to do is wreck something that doesn't suit you just because it doesn't seem right to you."

"All right. All right. It's over now."

Payson looked at him. "Society has made laws to protect itself. I told you I don't know what's right about bloodless marriages or evil marriages or unhappy marriages. But they are sanctioned. They are protected by law. You go against the people that made those laws and they'll get you. They'll always get you—sooner or later, one way or another.

"I'm not saying that's right, either. I'm only begging you to stop fighting. You haven't a chance to win, and all you'll do is hurt yourself."

Hank's bloody mouth tightened. "That's where you're wrong. All wrong. I'll have her. I'll have this one. God meant for me to have her. I know it as sure as I'm sitting here. And I'll win. I don't care what it costs me, or who I have to fight. I'll have her. I'm going to have her, I tell you. She'll be mine!"

It seemed twenty hours later, but Hank was alone, finally. He was glad Payson had come. There was nothing left of their plans now. Shangri-La was rubble. Payson hadn't pretended to like the way Hank had treated his daughter. But for Hank, the visit had paid off in an odd way. Ethel's father had made one thing clear.

Everybody felt he was wrong because he wanted Amy with all his heart.

All right. He was wrong. But he was going to have her. Nothing else offered him very much and he loved Amy. It burned like a furnace, roared like a hurricane. It was no petty damned thing like trying to be something your neighbor might approve of.

He was going to have her. They wouldn't let him have her his way.

He had been as honest as he knew how with everybody he knew. But they fired him from the job that would have supported her.

They barred him from having her any way that was honest.

There was just one more way. There was George Miller's way. Take what you wanted whether it was honest or not.

There was the thing Amy wanted to do. The robbery. Just this one. This one time. He'd have her then.

They'd run. God knew he didn't try to fool himself about that. They'd have to run. But he'd have her, even if they spent the rest of their lives running.

He was just so tired. He ached all over. And yet he had strength enough to laugh. He was giving in to her. He could still see the way she'd looked at him in the garage. She had told him he would miss her. She'd told him he'd call before seven. Well, he was going to call. He was going to call right now.

If only it wasn't so damned far across that room to the telephone. He pulled himself up, sitting on the edge of the bed. The room went out of kilter. Everything got blurry. He was in worse shape now than he had been at the moment when Desales kicked him in the face.

He stood up. Hell, it was only three steps across to that telephone. What a kick Amy was going to get out of hearing his voice when he told her he was ready to see it her way.

He took the first step. But they must have moved the flooring. There was no place to put his feet and he went sprawling out on his face. But he didn't even know it when he struck the floor.

He had been lying there a half minute when the telephone rang.

Hank didn't hear it. It rang twenty times and he didn't hear it. All afternoon it rang. At twenty minutes after seven it stopped ringing.

By that time Hank was snoring. He'd rolled over on his back. It was a wonderful place to sleep. He slept there all night. The telephone didn't ring again. Nothing disturbed his sleep. The floor made such a lovely bed. He'd never slept so well before in all his life.

CHAPTER EIGHTEEN
Countermarch

Somebody was pounding on top of his head.

Hank opened his eyes. It was broad daylight in his room. Amy! She was going back to George. He was to call before seven o'clock last night! It was now morning. He had fallen on the floor and slept all night. And while he slept, Amy had gone back to George.

He sat up. There was the pounding again. It was at his door. He got up. He was stiff, scarcely able to walk. He was afire with pain all the way through.

He opened the door.

Amy brushed past him into the room.

Her face was taut and white. Her eyes were distended. She turned around and stared at him.

"Hank!" she whispered. Her voice was distracted. "Where have you been? What have you been doing?"

"I passed out," he said. He closed the door.

She ran to him, pressed in close against him. She touched the bruises on his face from which he hadn't even washed the blood.

"I called. All afternoon. I waited until after seven. When you wouldn't answer your telephone, I went crazy. I hated you. I went back to George—"

He looked at her, holding his breath. "The robbery? Nesmith's? Last night?"

She shook her head. "We were going to. George and I talked about it. That's why I went back to George, so we could rob the store. We had talked about it before and I never would go through with it. But when I thought you didn't want me anymore, I didn't care. I didn't care what

I did and I didn't care what happened to me. Always before, I've hated the things George made me do for money. But we were always in debt and always in trouble. We had to do the things he wanted to get money. Only they never worked out. We always ended up in deeper than ever.

"Last night, I went back to George and told him I was willing to go through with the Nesmith robbery.

"We might have done it, too. But George was drunk when I got there. I know what he's like when he is drinking. I was afraid to trust him.

"Besides he was raving about you, about what he was going to do to you for taking me from him.

"I told him that nobody had taken me from him. I told him that I had never really loved him and that he always had known it.

"He went wild. He was going to kill me. So I began talking fast to him. I calmed him down. I told him I was sure that he and I could get away with the money from Nesmith's store.

"I kept getting him drunker. As fast as he'd empty his glass, I'd fill it up again. He began to plan what we'd do when we robbed the store. He even decided that after the robbery, I would go on working there, and playing up to Nesmith. Even drunk as he was, he made it sound good. George was always wonderful with plans. He could make anything sound good.

"Only I kept thinking about you. I kept thinking about what you had said about afterwards. I knew certainly they'd keep after me until I went crazy if I stayed at Nesmith's. I began to see they'd chase me if I ran. And I knew what you meant when you said George and I could never get away.

"I knew you were right. I knew then what had always been wrong with George's fine plans. He never figured beyond the thing he wanted to do. He never figured how he was going to get away with anything. Maybe he never figured because he always knew that the plan wouldn't sound so good when he talked about it afterwards. So that's why he played up the easy part. He always made it sound good—he had never really been trying to fool anybody more than himself.

"So I knew you were right. You couldn't get away with things like that robbery.

"I sat there watching George get drunker and drunker. I sat there while his eyes blurred and his voice got thick. I began to see myself in a prison dress, in a prison cell. I saw what you meant about being caged away from the person you needed. With me, it was you I'd need and I kept seeing that I was going to be barred away from you.

"I knew I had been a fool for ever listening to George. And I knew that I wasn't going to be able to get what you and I wanted by being dishonest anymore.

"Pretty soon, George forgot what he was planning. He began to talk about you. How he hated you. What a stuffed shirt you were. What a fool. He was going to kill you if he ever saw you near me again.

"I kept pouring the whisky and saying yes to him. I never saw anybody who could drink so much without passing out.

"He told me how he had hired Desales and some man named Tony to wait for you and beat you in the car lot. I didn't say anything.

"At two o'clock this morning we had to go out of town to buy him a new bottle. There wasn't anything left to drink in the house. I pretended to be drunk with him. But I was in better shape than he was, he knew, and so he let me drive. We rode out to a package store beyond city limits and George bought three more fifths.

"He began to rave about how he was going to get your job at Thompson's. It was all fixed. He was in like Flynn with old man C. E. He was going to have a good salary and a good job.

"And all I could think was that I was so thankful I hadn't gone through with it, that I hadn't been able to force you to do it.

"George didn't even get to open one of the new bottles. The car or something lulled him to sleep. He passed out.

"When we got home, I tried to get him out of the car. But he had passed out. I went into the house, got my purse and called a taxi.

"I went to my hotel and packed my things. This morning I checked out. I came here. I knew one thing. You were right yesterday. There is only one thing for us to do. We've got to get away from here."

He sat on the bed and pulled her down beside him.

"That was yesterday," he said. "How can we now? I'm broke."

"You have Ethel's car. There hasn't been any settlement agreed on yet. It's still yours to use. We could drive. As far as we could drive. I've money for gas and for food. When we find a town we like we can stop there. I don't want a lot of money anymore, Hank. Not anymore. I don't want anything but you."

She shook her head. "I never have had money. Maybe I thought I could get it some way. But now I don't care. All I want is you. Maybe God never meant for me to have money. Maybe He meant for me to have you."

"Look. We know this town, Amy. I can get a job here. I haven't even tried yet. We'll be all right."

"Hank, haven't you even listened to me? Don't you know what I'm saying? George has gone crazy where you're concerned. He's threatened to kill you. Maybe if he was sober, he wouldn't. But he drinks all the time. He goes crazy when he drinks.

"Do you think he's going to stop thinking about robbing Nesmith's store? You must know how he's always treated me. Like I was something that belonged to him. Like a servant. He always expects me to do just what he says, whenever he says it.

"Hank, he doesn't even believe I'll divorce him. He said so. He doesn't think I've got the nerve.

"He's not going to let us get away, Hank. He wants me to help him rob Nesmith's. He hates you because you've taken me away. We've got to run, Hank. We've got to find some place where people don't know us. That way we can get along without money. We'll be all right. We'll be happy. Get ready, Hank. Let's get away while we can.

"When George wakes up, he'll begin looking for me. He'll start looking for you. He'll get Desales and some other goon to help him. Please, give us a chance."

"We can't run away. We've got to face it, whatever George does."

"We could, Hank, if he were sane. If he were sober. But he'll stay drunk until this is settled. I know. I know him. When he is drinking, he really is insane."

"I don't want to run away—"

"You wanted to yesterday. Now, I'm begging you to take me away. I've given up everything else, Hank, just to be with you. I don't care about anything else, just so we're together. Only I don't want trouble. That's what there will be unless we can get away. Maybe just for a little while. Just until George sees I'm not coming back and he gets settled down again. Maybe when he gets the job he wants at Thompson's, it'll help. Then we'll be all right. Then we can begin to live the way we want to."

In less than an hour they checked out of the hotel.

Hank drove to a filling station, bought gas and they headed south out of the city. Amy moved over on the seat and laid her head against Hank's shoulder.

"Gosh," she said. "It's so peaceful. It's like something I've always dreamed about. And never had. Did you ever dream about something, Hank? Just a simple something that was always out of your reach? I've always wanted to be like this. With somebody I loved. Not on the run. Not on the make. Not worried about money—"

He laughed. "You mean you're not running, you're not worried about money?"

"No. I'm not. Not now. Not anymore.

"It was like I had a fever yesterday. Like I had a burning fever. Like I was going through a crisis. You know like when you're sick? The fever has to get so hot, it has to burn itself out, you either die or get well. That's what happened, Hank.

"All afternoon while I was calling you and you didn't answer, and then when I first went back to George, it was the fever. That awful need for money that was almost as strong as my need for you.

"And then sometime while George was talking, I began to get well. I knew I needed you. And I knew all the money in the world would never take your place. And I knew I had to get back to you, even if we never had a dime again.

"I'm so glad you didn't answer the phone, Hank. Thank God, you didn't answer it. We might have done something awful. We might have lost this chance to be happy and good and decent."

He remembered the way he'd gotten off the bed in the hotel room last night and started toward the telephone. He'd almost called her. What would have happened if he had called her? Where would they be right now?

He shivered.

CHAPTER NINETEEN
Honeymoon

Hank was driving with his arm around Amy. She was asleep with her head on his shoulder. It was now late Sunday afternoon. The sky was a burned-out orange. It was almost dinner time and traffic was lighter.

He began to see signs advertising tires and soft drinks and beer and hotels. The signs that meant they were coming into a town.

He removed his hand from under the soft upper part of Amy's arm. He straightened a little on the seat, his hand on the wheel taking a firmer grip.

He glanced at the City Limits sign: "Winona. Twenty-five hundred population, 1940 Census. County Seat, Winona County. Welcome."

He laughed.

The sound of his laughter wakened Amy. She sat up blinking at him. She straightened her bra and began to rebutton her shirt waist.

"What is it darling? What's the matter?"

"Winona," he said.

"What's that?"

"It's a town. It's a county seat. They have a weekly newspaper here. Old Man Payson wanted to buy it. How would you like to live here?"

"With you?"

"That's why we came this far."

"I'd love it. What'll we do? Where will we stay?"

"Let's drive around. We'll find a cottage to rent. You can always rent a house on Sunday. We'll start out respectable as hell."

The cottage was furnished. The rent was sixty dollars a month. Hank wrote out a check on his funds in the bank. The money that he had already signed over to Ethel. If Ethel stopped payment it would take time. And time was all he needed.

Tomorrow a job. Tonight it was nothing but Hank and Amy. She wandered around through the little house, opening windows, patting up the pillows on the front room divan.

She laughed. "I've lived in a lot of houses, Hank, but this is the first one that seemed right. Really we have no right to it at all. A bad check. Unmarried. I'll bet that we'll be the happiest unmarried couple in this town."

He took her in his arms. "Maybe we'll make the headlines in the *Winona Star*."

The owner of the Winona Wholesale Company practically drooled over the references from the Thompson Distributing Company. There wasn't an immediate opening, no territory available at the moment, but if Hank wanted to come into the shipping clerk's office until there was an opening....

It was Monday morning and Hank had a job.

Amy had dinner ready when he got home at five o'clock. But she looked too good to him. They didn't get to the dinner table until after seven.

That night they lay in bed side by side without talking. The street light made shadows on the ceiling and Hank watched them dance up there.

"Hank?"

"Hmmm?"

"If we had a baby, what would it be, a boy or a girl?"

"Sometimes it's hard to tell. What would you want?"

"I'd want a boy. I'd want him to look just like you. I'd want him to grow up to be just like you."

"Girls are nice. You're nice."

"No. Being a girl is hell. I wouldn't want a girl. If we had a girl baby, I would be sorry. A little boy, it doesn't matter. They don't get hurt so easy."

"Well, maybe you won't have any."

"Yes, I will." She snuggled closer to him. "I want to. Even if it's a girl, I want to. I want to feel it inside me. I want to know I've got part of you inside me. It'll be wonderful. You and me. Making a baby together, and me feeling it growing inside me."

The grocery store owner leaned across the counter and grinned at them. "You're the new folks, eh?"

"Yes."

"Just moved in the Sutter place on Lynne Street, huh?"

"Yes, that's right."

"Working for old John Meffert at the Wholesale house?"

"Yes."

"Well, you folks will be needing a lot to eat. Young people in love need a lot to eat. I don't care what the poets say. I seen 'em. Fellow works hard all day and comes home nights, he needs a lot to eat. I went ahead and opened up a charge account here for you folks. Just look around and pick out what you want. I already got your name writ down on a charge book. Been looking for you. Most everybody in town charges with me."

Somebody at the Wholesale House told Hank about Winona Springs and Wednesday night after dinner, Hank and Amy drove out the eight miles to go swimming.

It was dark by the time they got there. The springs were almost deserted. The water was so clear they could see the white sand bottom. It was icy cold. They swam out together and let the current move them downstream away from the dimly lighted pavilion.

Somebody shouted to them. "The current is mighty swift. Be careful it don't take you too far!"

Hank shouted back that they were all right. They swam in close to the far shore. They stood up on the white sand. Amy put her arm about his neck and locked her legs about him.

She kept kissing him and refused to let go. Finally he could feel her mouth begin to shake with the cold.

"Come on," he told her. "We're going back. We can do better than this in bed. Besides, it's warmer."

They started swimming back against the current. He could hear her panting in the dark and hear her teeth chattering.

The current was stronger than he remembered it. She wasn't beside him. He stopped, treading water in the darkness.

"Amy!"

She swam up beside him. She caught on to his shoulder with her fingers. There was frantic strength in her fingers.

"It's the silliest thing," she said. "I can't do it. The current is too strong. I think I've got a cramp."

Panic made him weak. His voice was a snarl. "It's not far, Amy. Just hang on to me. Don't move. Don't try to help me swim. Just hang on. I can get us there, easy."

He began to swim, using a breast stroke so he could be sure he kept her head out of the water. Her teeth went on chattering. He could hear her rapid breathing. The pavilion lights seemed a mile away.

When they got out into the middle of the springs, the current suddenly released them, and it was as if it was no longer any effort to swim at all. Hank began to feel good. He wanted to laugh. Hell, if you just kept fighting long enough!

He staggered up on the pavilion, scooped her up in his arms and ran with her all the way to the car. He put his shirt on her over her clothes and wrapped her in a blanket. She lay with her head in his lap. He closed the car windows. He drove toward town at sixty miles an hour.

Her teeth stopped chattering. She lay there massaging the cramp in her leg until it let up. She sighed and burrowed her head against him.

"I wonder if God wouldn't let me stay this happy," she said, "and let me keep things just like this, if I promised to be good all the rest of my life?"

It was Friday night. Hank was lying on the divan. Amy came in the front room from the kitchen. Her hands were pink from the hot dish water.

He held out his arms to her.

She lay down on top of him.

"I started to call you to dry the dishes," Amy said. "But I thought I'd wait until after the honeymoon was over."

"By that time I'll be too old to dry dishes."

"Then I'll never complain."

"Besides, I started to come in to help you. But you beat me down before supper. I was too tired to get up."

"I'm already complaining."

"Don't worry," he said. "I'll never be too tired for what you want."

"How do you know what I want?"

"A guy doesn't have to know you very long to know what you want."

"You'd be amazed to find out how much I never wanted before I met you."

"That's what every woman tells every guy."

"Then a lot of women are telling the truth. I don't pretend to understand it. I just know that for every woman there's a certain one right guy. He can do anything to her—anything with her. She has no defenses against him, because she doesn't want any. That's how it is with you and me."

"What a lovely speech."

"It wasn't so good. You're still lying there. You're not on your way carrying me to the bedroom."

"Baby! It seems to me we just came from there."

"Already tired of me!"

"I am not. I'm just tired. I'll tell you what. I'll go to the bedroom with you—if you'll carry me!"

She laughed and burrowed her face against his throat, biting him. He fought her but she held on. He could feel her teeth sinking into his flesh. He thrust her away. She pulled, her arms around his neck. They fell off the couch, landing hard on the floor.

The sound of their falling almost obscured the sound of the doorbell the first time it rang.

For a moment, Hank and Amy lay there on the floor and stared at each other, frowning.

"Who now?" Hank said. "You suppose they've stopped payment on that check?"

She got up, straightening her dress. Hank pulled himself up and went across the small front room to the door.

The doorbell rang again. It had a sharp impatient sound.

"All right," Hank said. "I'm coming."

Amy followed him. She was standing at his side when he opened the door.

He heard her gasp, felt her hands clutch his arm. It was as if she were pulling him away from that open doorway. Outside it stood George. His grin was smug.

CHAPTER TWENTY
Full Stop

"May I come in?" George said.

"No," said Amy.

George came in. He looked around. His face was hard. He was unsteady. He reeked of whisky.

"Quite a charming little nest," he said.

"How did you find us?" Amy said.

"Desales moves in mysterious ways his wonders to perform." George said. "Hell, I knew where you were this morning. I waited until tonight because I wanted to see lover boy here when I came to get you."

"Came to get me!" Amy laughed at him. "I told you, George. I'm through. I'm getting a divorce. Hank and I are going to be married."

"Now ain't that cozy. Ain't that as cozy as all hell? You and Hank are going to get married. It so happens, baby, you're married to me. I'm not letting you go for any lily-livered punk who don't know the time of day."

"We're here," Hank said. His voice shook. "We're going to stay, George. Say what you've got to say and get out."

"Keep your mouth shut. I'll talk to you when I'm ready." George lunged across the room. "Get your things, Amy. I'm taking you back home."

"Get out, George. There's no use in all this. No sense. I've left you. I've filed for divorce."

"You're out fifty bucks, baby. I don't want no divorce. I want you. My sweet little tramp."

"Get out, George," Hank said. "Whether we're married yet or not, we're going to be."

George wheeled around. His face was livid. "I told you to keep out of this."

"Whether you like it or not, I'm in it. We live here, we're going to stay here."

"Are you, sonny boy? Well, ain't that sweet? How long do you think you'd last in this town if I told the truth about you?" George laughed. "A guy fired from his last job, and not even married to the woman he lives with. How long you think you'll last so happy in this pretty little town?"

Hank looked at George. He felt tired all over. What had Justin Payson said about fighting for something that didn't belong to you? Sooner or later, one way or another, they get you. Anyway you lose.

"Why, George?" Amy cried. "You and I were never happy together. You don't want me. Hank and I are happy together. You can let us be happy. If you've got your new job at Thompson's, you'll make more money, you can pay your debts, you can find what you want—"

"Job?" George snarled. He looked at Amy. "What job? You think I work for that lousy Thompson outfit anymore? A bunch of lily-livered jerks like Ireland there!"

She stared at him. Her voice was a whisper. "They fired you."

"All right! So what? There are plenty more jobs. Lover boy there got another job. I can get another one!"

"—for drinking!"

"What difference it make? I don't need that job. I'll get along. I didn't come here to talk about that. I came here for you, baby. You're going back—"

"I'm not going back, George—"

"Don't scare you if I tell people you and Ireland ain't even married, huh?"

"No, George. Hank and I are going to stay together. If we have to leave this town, we'll find another one. As long as we're together—"

"How pretty!" George railed at her. "Does he know what you are? Does he know the things you've done? Did you tell him about the time we took the sucker in Macon—just like Ireland, the same kind of dumb honest jerk—"

"Stop it!" Amy said. "Whatever I did, I did to try to keep you out of trouble. Whatever rotten things I did, I did because of you."

"Because of me! That's for laughs! For money. That's the only reason you ever did anything! That's why you're coming back with me. Because this time we're really going to get money. A real stake."

"I've got what I want, George. You might as well make up your mind to that."

George ran at her. He drew back his hand to strike her.

Hank caught his arm and shoved him. George toppled back against the side of the divan. He kept his balance, sat there staring at Hank. George's mouth pulled down.

"You're going to hear the truth about her. You won't want her. You're too nice. Too holy. You won't want her when I'm through."

Hank took a step toward him. His hands were trembling. He knotted them, feeling the sweat boil up in his clench palms.

"I don't want to hear it. I want you to get out—"

George laughed. "Don't you want to hear about the Air Force Major she met on a train. He got hot for her so we—"

Hank leaped at him. George sprang back out of his way, his feet apart waiting.

"Hank!" Amy screamed. She ran to him, grabbed his arms. "Don't. Don't fight him. I'll make him go."

George laughed. "Sure you will. You'll make me go. You'll go with me. Get your things." His voice rasped, he was shouting. "I got debts, I'm in plenty deep. Some of them you made. I ain't got no job, and I got to have some way to pay that money back. There ain't but one way to pay it, baby. You're going back with me. You told me you'd let the sucker here in on the Nesmith deal, so I'm making no secret of it. You got Nesmith hot for you so you could take him, and that's just what we're going to do—"

"I'm never going back, George."

"You're going back. You know the way to get in that store at night. You know about the night burglar alarm. You know the safe combination. I ain't losing this chance for the kind of take I've always wanted. You're coming back. You're still my wife and you still do what I tell you."

"Not anymore, George."

Hank pushed her aside. "There's no use talking to him, Amy. There's only one thing he can understand. He's getting out of here because I'm going to put him out. He's going to stay out because he'll know I mean it when I'm through—"

"That's fine!" George railed at him. "That's what I want you to do. Start something, sucker. You dirty wife-thieving jerk. This is what I been waitin' for. You brought my little woman up here, and I've come for her. Just take one step, sucker. Just one."

He shoved his hand into his coat pocket and brought out an automatic. It took both hands to push off the safety. He steadied the gun without taking his eyes off Hank.

George laughed. "You're one guy that's set up like a pigeon in a shootin' gallery, sucker. A wife stealer. If you don't think I can kill you and get away with it—before any court anywhere—just try to take one step toward me—"

"Hank!" Amy cried.

"He's bluffing," Hank said. "You ought to know him well enough to know that. He's drunk and he's bluffing. He's a fake and that's why he's where he is right now. If he had the guts to do anything he wouldn't be where he is."

Hank had taken one step toward George while he was talking. He took another.

George licked his tongue across his mouth and backed up. He waved the gun.

"Stay there, sucker. Don't try to touch me."

"I'm going to touch you," Hank said. "I'm going to throw you out."

Hank started forward. George yelled at him. The sound was almost fright. The gun came up.

Amy screamed and Hank felt her strike hard against his shoulder. He went off balance as the gun roared in the small front room.

For an eternal minute there was only silence after the sound of the gun died away. The smoke rose in a gray cloud toward the ceiling.

Hank leaped toward Amy. He was staring at her face. He growled out the agony that welled up from his belly. Her face was a mass of blood. The bullet must have struck her right between the eyes.

She was crumpling. Hank grabbed her up in his arms. All he could think was he had to get her to the doctor. Then he looked at George. George still had the gun in his hand.

George was staring at Amy. Her head was back, hair trailing toward the floor. Her arms and legs hung loosely.

George's mouth worked. It took a long time for him to believe what had happened, what he had done. "She's dead!" The words spilled from his trembling mouth.

He looked down at the gun in horror. He opened his hand and let the automatic fall to the floor. He looked again at Amy and then turned and ran out through the door into the darkness.

Hank started again toward the front door and a doctor. His steps slowed. He knew it was no use. He knew that she was dead. He stopped in the middle of the room with her in his arms and looked around him.

They stopped him. One way or another. Sooner or later. He'd had happiness in his hand, but he had to break laws to keep it, and nobody ever got happiness like that.

He looked down at her and suddenly knew that he *had* got what he wanted. The terrible irony of it twisted his belly and made him ill. He had vowed to have her. She was going to be in his arms. She was going to be completely his. That was what he had wanted and that was what he had got.

He stumbled across the room and sat down in a chair, holding her body in his arms.

THE END

Harry Whittington Bibliography
(1915-1989)

NOVELS

Vengeance Valley (1946)
Her Sin (1947)
Slay Ride for a Lady (1950)
The Brass Monkey (1951)
Call Me Killer (1951)
Fires That Destroy (1951)
The Lady Was a Tramp (1951)
Satan's Widow (1951)
Forever Evil (1952)
Married to Murder (1951; reprinted 1959)
Murder is My Mistress (1951)
Drawn to Evil (1952)
Mourn the Hangman (1952)
Prime Sucker (1952)
Cracker Girl (1953)
So Dead My Love! (1953; reprinted in Australia as *Let's Count Our Dead*, 1954)
Vengeful Sinner (1953; reprinted as *Nightclub Sinner*, 1954; abridged as *Die, Lover*, 1960)
Saddle the Storm (1954)
Wild Oats (1954)
The Woman is Mine (1954)
You'll Die Next! (1954)
The Naked Jungle (1955)
One Got Away (1955)
Across That River (1956)
Desire in the Dust (1956)
Brute in Brass (1956; reprinted as *Forgive Me, Killer*, 1987)
The Humming Box (1956)
Saturday Night Town (1956)
Sinner's Club (1956; reprint as by Hallam Whitney, 1953; reprinted as *Teenage Jungle*, 1958)
A Woman on the Place (1956)
Man in the Shadow (1957; screenplay novelization)
T'as des Visions! (1957, France; rewritten as *Passion Hangover*, 1965, as by J. X. Williams)
One Deadly Dawn (1957)
Play for Keeps (1957)

Temptations of Valerie (1957; screenplay novelization)
Trouble Rides Tall (1958)
Web of Murder (1958)
Backwoods Tramp (1959; reprinted as *A Moment to Prey*, 1987)
Halfway to Hell (1959)
Lust for Love (1959)
Native Girl (1959; reprint of *Savage Love*, 1952, as by Whit Harrison)
Strictly for the Boys (1959)
Strange Bargain (1959)
Strangers on Friday (1959)
A Ticket to Hell (1959)
Connolly's Woman (1960)
The Devil Wears Wings (1960)
Heat of Night (1960)
Hell Can Wait (1960)
A Night for Screaming (1960)
Nita's Place (1960)
Rebel Woman (1960)
Vengeance is the Spur (1960)
Desert Stake-Out (1961; reprinted in UK as by Hondo Wells, 1976)
God's Back Was Turned (1961)
Guerilla Girls (1961)
Journey Into Violence (1961)
The Searching Rider (1961)
A Trap for Sam Dodge (1961)
The Young Nurses (1961)
A Haven for the Damned (1962)
Hot as Fire Cold as Ice (1962)
69 Babylon Park (1962)
Wild Sky (1962)
Cora is a Nympho (1963)
Don't Speak to Strange Girls (1963)
Drygulch Town (1963)
Prairie Raiders (1963; reprinted in UK as by Hondo Wells, 1977)
Cross the Red Creek (1964)
The Fall of the Roman Empire (1964; screenplay novelization)
High Fury (1964)
Hangrope Town (1964)
The Man from U.N.C.L.E #2: The Doomsday Affair (1965)
Valley of Savage Men (1965)

Wild Lonesome (1965)
Doomsday Mission (1967)
Bonanza: Treachery Trail (1968; pub
 in Germany as *Ponderosa in
 Gefahr*)
Burden's Mission (1968)
Charro! (1969)
Rampage (1978)
Sicilian Woman (1979)

As Ashley Carter

Master of Blackoaks (1976)
Sword of the Golden Stud (1977)
Panama (1978)
Secret of Blackoaks (1978)
Taproots of Falconhurst (1978)
Scandal of Falconhurst (1980)
Heritage of Blackoaks (1981)
Rogue of Falconhurst (1983)
Against All Gods (1983, UK)
Road to Falconhurst (1984, UK)
A Darkling Moon (1985, UK)
Embrace the Wind (1985, UK; pub in
 the US as by Blaine Stevens)
A Farewell to Blackoaks (1986, UK)
Miz Lucretia of Falconhurst (1986)
Mandingo Mansa (1986, UK; pub in
 the US as *Mandingo Master*)
Strange Harvest (1986, UK)
Falconhurst Fugitive (1988)

As Curt Colman

Flesh Mother (1965)
Flamingo Terrace (1965)
Hell Bait (1966)
Sinsurance (1966)
The Taste of Desire (1966; revised &
 reprinted as *Winter Girl*, 2012, as
 by Harry Whittington)
Sin Deep (1966)
The Latent Lovers (1966)
Sinners After Six (1966)
Balcony of Shame (1967)
Mask of Lust (1967)
The Grim Peeper (1967)

As John Dexter

Saddle Sinners (1964)
Lust Dupe (1964)
Pushover (1964)
Sin Psycho (1964)
Flesh Curse (1964)
Sharing Sharon (1965)
Shame Union (1965)
The Wedding Affair (1965)
Baptism in Shame (1965)
Passion Burned (1965)
Remembered Sin (1965)
The Sin Fishers (1966)
The Sinning Room (1966)
Blood Lust Orgy (1966)
The Abortionists (1966)

As Tabor Evans

Longarm on the Humboldt (1981)
Longarm and the Golden Lady
 (1981)
Longarm and the Blue Norther
 (1981)
Longarm in Silver City (1982)
Longarm in Boulder Canyon (1982)
Longarm in the Big Thicket (1982)

As Whit Harrison

Body and Passion (1952)
Girl on Parole (1952; reprinted as
 Man Crazy, 1960)
Sailor's Weekend (1952)
Savage Love (1952; reprinted as by
 Harry Whittington as *Native Girl*,
 1956)
Swamp Kill (1952)
Violent Night (1952)
Army Girl (1953)
Rapture Alley (1953)
Shanty Road (1956)
Man Crazy (1960; originally
 published as *Girl on Parole*)
Strip the Town Naked (1960)
Any Woman He Wanted (1961)
A Woman Possessed (1961)

As Kel Holland

The Strange Young Wife (1963)
The Tempted (1964)

As Lance Horner

Golden Stud (1975)

As Harriet Kathryn Meyers

Small Town Nurse (1962)
Prodigal Nurse (1963)

As Blaine Stevens

The Outlanders (1979)
Embrace the Wind (1982)
Island of Kings (1988)

As Clay Stuart

His Brother's Wife (1964)

As Harry White

Shadow at Noon (1955; reprinted in
    UK as by Hondo Wells, 1977)

As Hallam Whitney

Backwoods Hussy (1952; reprinted
    as *Lisa*, 1965)
Shack Road (1953)
Sinner's Club (1953; reprinted as by
    Harry Whittington, 1956)
Backwoods Shack (1954)
City Girl (1954)
The Wild Seed (1956)
Lisa (1965; originally published as
    Backwoods Hussy, 1952)

As Henry Whittier/Henri Whittier

Nightmare Alibi (1972)
Another Man's Claim (1973)

As J. X. Williams

Lust Farm (1964)
Flesh Avenger (1964)
The Shame Hiders (1964)
Lust Buyer (1965)
Passion Flayed (1965)
Man Hater (1965)
Passion Hangover (1965; revised &
    reprinted as *Like Mink, Like
    Murder*, 2009, as by Harry
    Whittington)
Passion Cache (1965)
Baby Face (1966)
Flesh Snare (1966)

As Howard Winslow

The Mexican Connection (1972)

SHORT WORKS

The Man from U.N.C.L.E. novelettes
    as by Robert Hart Davis

The Beauty and the Beast Affair
    (March 1966, V1 #2)
The Ghost Riders Affair (July 1966,
    V1#6)
The Brainwash Affair (September
    1966, V2#2)
The Light-Kill Affair (January 1967,
    V2 #6)